stop at nothing

LUCY MARTIN

WELB

Published in 2021 by Welbeck Fiction Limited,
part of Welbeck Publishing Group
20 Mortimer Street London W1T 3JW

A CIP catalogue record for this book is available from the
British Library.

Paperback ISBN: 978-1-78739-637-1
E-book ISBN: 978-1-787-39-638-8

Printed and bound by CPI Group (UK) Ltd., Croydon, CR0 4YY

10 9 8 7 6 5 4 3 2

PROLOGUE

It's a feeling you wouldn't know unless you'd been there.

Something between triumph and revulsion, heart-stopping excitement and raw terror, as she bumps down the stairs. The rush of adrenaline to every part of your body as she lands on the cellar floor.

There's a moan with the shock of the impact, a plaintive call for help, then blackout silence.

You go down a few steps to get a closer look, but it's dark except for a thin sliver of streetlight. All you can see is her hair, darkly matted with blood.

There isn't as much blood as you'd imagine. It's not spurting out of an artery or the pink river gurgling and bubbling out of parted lips that you see in films, just a dark pool spreading across the concrete floor.

The twitching is unnerving. You've heard of rigor mortis but you can't remember what it is. Has the moment of death passed, is it in progress, or is it imminent?

Anyone else might feel for a pulse now, kneel by her face and listen for breathing sounds.

But what if she opens her eyes?

A tiny noise outside, wind in the trees. Then more silence.

Think.

The murmur of traffic brings the world closer.

The thrill fades. Stifling reality descends on you, making you sweat.

The sudden squawk of a crow and the flap of wings against leaves.

You need to get out of here.

Before they find you.

CHAPTER 1

Maeve Slade was standing at the kitchen island, guarded by shafts of morning sun that slanted either side, throwing her into shadow. Her lips were tight and her brow furrowed with concentration as the knife hammered on the chopping board like a prisoner beating on a locked door.

Sensing something, she looked up. A smile surfaced, then disappeared as suddenly as it had arrived.

'Can I help?' Amie offered.

Maeve straightened up and wiped her brow with her sleeve, brushing aside a wayward lock of hair; then, taking a pineapple by its spiky crown, she positioned the knife and beheaded it with one neat stroke. Pale juice trickled off the board and formed a pool on the worktop. Inside the prickly armour, soft yellow flesh glistened. She reached quickly for the kitchen roll to clean up the mess.

'Mum?'

'No need,' she said, curtly, then, 'You can go and get ready. Wear something nice.'

Upstairs, the intermittent murmur of football commentary floated out from under Andrew's closed door. An exclamation, a protest, a whoop of triumph. Amie could

1

picture the scene – darkness, blinds drawn, a single console controlling avatars who performed tackles and scored goals to his order.

The commentary reached a crescendo, then, 'Yesssss . . . Four-one . . .'

She opened her wardrobe. *Wear something nice.* But the array of clothes to choose from filled her with dread. Clothes were like human wrapping paper, the cover by which you judged the book. She picked a floaty dress Nana had bought her for her birthday, and the gladiator sandals Dad used to comment on. *Ready for battle, are we?* She liked the way the straps wound right up the ankles, as if they were holding everything together. That was her job – always holding everything together, always ready for battle.

She made a nest in her pillows, pulled up the duvet around her and scrolled through social media feeds. Snapchat and Instagram. Follow and be followed. Post and count the likes. You could be who you wanted to be on here, edit your photos beyond recognition, make yourself better. It was a new you, facing the rest of the world. You could click on the Search icon and make new friends, create another link in the chain. You could dig right into the heart of somebody, see who they followed, and then who *they* followed. Skinny girls in bikinis followed other skinny girls in bikinis. Then there were the ones who went further, posted photos and videos of themselves doing things that made Amie's eyes widen in disbelief.

Her finger hovered over the screen. There was one story she wanted to see, one person she wanted to be connected to, but she couldn't do it. She only wanted to know what he'd been doing over the summer holidays. Nothing wrong with that. But then again there was everything wrong with that.

It was a minute before twelve-thirty when she looked at the time and leapt off the bed, straightening out the duvet as she did so. Mum liked it tidy. She tapped on Andrew's door on the way past but there was no response.

Maeve had changed into a beige tunic dress with a tiny cardigan, a small string of pearls around her neck, hair sprayed into a sculpted chignon. Amie had once called it a bun, but Maeve had corrected her and she never thought of it that way again. She watched Amie come down the stairs, raised her eyebrows at the shoes and looked at her watch with a barely audible sigh. There was a tired look on her face, as if she was running out of batteries. She nodded towards the kitchen and Amie went to collect the fruit salad.

Andrew slouched down the stairs in his socks; the frayed hems of his jeans sagging around his ankles; long hair plastered diagonally across his forehead. Amie watched him force his feet into trainers that were still done up and pull a hoodie off the banister. His stuff was always cluttering up the hallway, while Amie's was tidied away upstairs. He'd be eighteen in three months, but you'd never know it. He seemed to be going backwards in time.

The white Mercedes turned into the drive just as they opened the front door, indicator winking, radiator grille smiling a metallic smile. The driver's door opened and there was a pause, that pause where you gather the energy

3

for what's coming next, and then Stuart Slade swung himself out and clunked it shut.

He stood there, silhouetted against the brightness, and smiled at his family, who looked back, expectant, hesitant.

'You're late.' Maeve used the nothing voice, the one that jarred with its lack of expression.

'I know. Sorry.'

It was an automatic sorry. Too quick. Defensive. His hands went up as he said it. He clicked the lock with his key and orange lights blinked in response. He looked from Maeve to Amie to Andrew, seeing who might smile back. Andrew stared at his feet, chewing something. Amie gave a double grin for both of them, a triple one for all three of them. Time to reconcile, to undo the damage, placate, resolve.

'How was Nana? Did she like my card?' she asked, regretting it as he only half responded, his eyes on Maeve, worried. She had spoken too soon. The words weren't warm enough to cut through the ice. She held her breath in case it might disturb the air, reverse the beginnings of a thaw.

'Nana . . . was fine.'

He had a habit of pausing mid-sentence, which made Amie's mind race to explore all the possible endings: that Nana was sad, that she was dying, that she was dead.

'She sends her love.' He regained his concentration. 'And there's a new carer there she's not too keen on, who keeps sighing when people ask her to repeat things. Nana said they shouldn't work there if they're that impatient.' He was looking at Amie now, the only person listening. 'I mean, it's an old people's home. What does she expect?'

Amie let her breath out, slowly, carefully. Detail was good. It meant you were telling the truth. If someone asked you what you were doing last night when the crime took place and you said, *I was watching TV,* they would think, Hmmm, that's a bit vague, because if you were innocent, you'd give them more information, like, *The cat was sitting on my lap and the doorbell rang at eight-thirty with the Asda shopping delivery, and I had to change channels at nine because I can't stand that woman on* I'm a Celebrity . . . Then they'd believe you, because nobody could make that up on the spot.

Maeve muttered something under her breath, then, cleared her throat and said, 'I don't know what she thinks she has to complain about, the amount that place is costing.'

And with that she turned and stepped neatly across the front garden on tiptoe, so her heels wouldn't sink into the grass. In a few delicate seconds, she was at the gap in the pine trees which divided the garden from the neighbours like a row of soldiers. Amie picked her way across the lawn in her wake, until a hand on her shoulder made her turn around.

'You OK, Monamie?'

Dad used that name when he wanted her to feel safe. *My friend.* But in French, in code, so nobody knew their secret. Mum had wanted to call her *Amy,* with the normal spelling, but he had campaigned for this one, because *Why not be different? Why not actually* mean *something?* Mum said people would think they didn't know how to spell a simple name like *Amy,* but he didn't mind taking the risk.

That day was probably the last time he'd got what he wanted.

'Hello, neigh*bours*!' Colin Morrison had a habit of putting the stress on his words in the wrong places, like a spy with a fatal flaw, or a game show host with a quirky catchphrase. He threw the door open wide and kissed Maeve loudly on the cheek, while she floated past, barely acknowledging him. 'And Andrew, good to see you – finally a man in the house that Max and Jake might actually listen to.' He shook Andrew's hand, clapping his other hand on top as if in a double greeting to make up for Maeve's just walking on past, then held his hands out again in exaggerated delight. 'Stuart, looking more handsome than ever. What's your secret? Midlife crisis? L'Oréal?'

Then it was Amie's turn. He leant down and brushed her cheeks with the faintest kiss and the whiff of something soapy, gave her shoulders a squeeze, and reached out to take the bowl she was holding. 'My goodness, that looks *ab*solutely divine.'

Mary, stout and rosy as a peach, ushered Amie and Andrew into the vast games room that stretched from the front of the house to the back in the place of the original garage. A giant screen filled the wall at one end and in front of it, on an enormous sofa, sprawled two teenagers, entranced, too taken up with destroying an alien universe to notice the new arrivals.

'Right, you two, make yourselves comfortable in here and I'll get you some drinks,' Mary twittered. She was another one who had to do double and triple politeness to make up for other people. She was open and kind in a world of closedness. While the other neighbours kept themselves to themselves, Mary had tried to start up a residents' association, but nobody wanted to come to the meetings. It was no wonder the Morrisons were leaving.

Andrew lost no time in taking charge of the boys, who handed the controls to him dumbly. On the screen, soldiers leapt over buildings and blew up cities. A timer raced in the corner as unexpected villains descended in their path, each one dismissed with the flick of a joystick.

Amie slipped out of the door and was passing the kitchen when Maeve called her in. 'You can take something to the table outside,' she said, handing her a huge glass bowl full of salad. Mary reached out to intervene, but in vain. 'Let her make herself useful for once,' Maeve muttered.

The dish was heavier than it looked. Amie carried it into the living room, where the brightness of the garden rendered her momentarily sightless. She stopped to let her eyes adjust.

On the terrace a few feet away, a gleaming black barbecue spat and sparked as the coals whitened. Colin and Dad were standing on one side of it, laughing about something. On the other side was Mum's friend Celia, slim and tanned in her white sundress, sunglasses perched on her head, her neat bob even blonder in the harsh light. Her little boy, Alfie, was pushing a truck around their feet. Celia was talking to Jeremy from across the road and watching him pour pink fizz into a forest of glasses. There was a shriek as the first and second ones both overflowed, sending white foam cascading on to the silver tray.

Then Celia reached out to touch Dad's arm and pointed at Amie and suddenly they were all watching her with anticipation. She looked back down at the bowl. *Concentrate.*

Mary was behind her with more plates, and Amie was the drummer at the front of the procession, the leader of the banquet conga. She walked onwards, dodging armchairs and sofas, guided by light and voices towards the outside. As she approached, wordless chatter ballooned into exclamations and whoops of delight at the sight of the food. Colin exclaimed an overenthusiastic, 'Look *at* this!' and Dad slapped him on the back and replaced the steel drum lid, making the fire inside hiss and thick smoke pour out of the vent.

It was just at that moment, as the lid clicked shut, when she had almost reached the open door to the garden, that the shiny surface caught the sun and a searing shaft of light bounced back right into Amie's eyes. She took another step forward blindly and hit something hard.

There was a bang, a crack of glass on glass and a collective, staggered gasp as the bowl fell and smashed on the stone floor.

Amie backed away in shock and sank to the floor. Mary was at her side in a flash. 'Oh, my goodness, you poor darling. Are you OK? I knew Colin shouldn't have cleaned the windows this morning.'

The boys were in the doorway, staring at Amie with a mixture of horror and amusement. Someone had handed

Andrew a shoebox and he was picking up the broken glass, smirking. 'Did you seriously walk straight into the window?'

Stuart pushed past them and squatted down next to her. 'It's all right, I'm a doctor,' he grinned. Then, to the boys, 'Nothing to see here. As you were, chaps!'

Mary bent down and scooped the salad off the floor with a dustpan as if it was fun, rather than as if she'd spent all morning making it. Then she went off for a cloth, Stuart was summoned back for barbecue duty, and Amie was alone.

It was a moment or two before Maeve appeared, framed in the doorway like a portrait of someone who didn't want to be painted, her mouth downturned, her gaze somewhere far away outside, where the other guests talked quietly, pretending nothing had happened and nobody had just walked straight into a glass door and spoilt everything.

'I don't understand why you're so clumsy, Amie. You certainly don't get it from me.'

She only moved when Mary needed to get past her, which gave Amie the chance to escape. All she could think of was getting away and going back home where there was no one to humiliate her. She made a whispered apology to Mary, who hugged her tightly, then looked her in the eyes, arms outstretched to her shoulders.

'I am so sorry about what happened, Amie. I feel completely responsible.'

'It was my fault. I'm sorry I broke the lovely bowl. But I just need to go home, calm down a bit.'

'It wasn't your fault, but if you're dead set on going home, I won't stand in your way.'

Amie smiled and reached for the shoebox of broken glass. 'Thanks, and let me take this out to the recycling. It's the least I can do.'

Back next door, Amie realised she had never seen the house so empty. She drifted from room to room, taking in the things she never usually noticed, seeing it all with a stranger's eyes. The neat row of toothbrushes in the bathroom, air freshener pumping out intermittent wafts of sandalwood. She pushed open the door of her parents' room – the smell of clean laundry, bedspread folded back at the corner, cushions stacked neatly like columns of square soldiers backing into each other in retreat. The fitted wardrobe was Maeve's. Stuart's chest of drawers stood hidden in the corner behind the door like a naughty schoolboy. Today it caught her eye because on top of it was the only thing in the room that was out of place.

An envelope.

Amie recognised her own handwriting on the front and frowned. He must have forgotten to give Nana the card. Perhaps he was too embarrassed to say so before, didn't want to let her down, didn't want to make things worse than they already were.

Or perhaps he hadn't gone there at all.

Perhaps she should find out.

CHAPTER 2

Lakeview Care Home smelt of something between a hospital and school dinners. Amie signed the visitors' book and hung the lanyard around her neck. 'Can't have anyone just walking in,' said the carer, as Amie followed her down a brown carpet to Nana's room. 'I'm Marina, by the way.' She smiled at Amie. 'Your gran talks about you a lot, you know.'

Marina tapped at the door and pushed it open. In front of them, a frail old lady sat upright in an armchair. Her head lolled, and one arm hung over the side of the chair. Amie's stomach lurched in horror. Was it too late to say goodbye?

Marina read her mind. 'It's OK. She's asleep.' She pointed at the rise and fall of the blanket.

Then the eyes flickered open and lit up. 'Amie Rose, what a wonderful surprise! And *what* a pretty dress.'

Marina went to pull back the brown curtains and the sun streamed in.

'Hello, Nana.' Amie held out her card. 'Dad forgot this when he came this morning.'

'This morning?' She frowned. 'I don't think he came this morning, did he? Maybe I was asleep.'

She mustn't assume anything yet. Maybe Nana had forgotten. She was always saying her memory wasn't what it used to be.

Nana opened the envelope with shaky fingers. 'Oh, Amie Rose, that is a very lovely card indeed. Now, tell me everything you've been up to. How have the holidays been? And are you excited about your new term?'

And Amie sat down in the armchair opposite and made things up. About the summer break, about meeting up with friends she didn't have and doing things she never did, going shopping, to the cinema, parties, day trips to the seaside. She pretended she was looking forward to meeting the new form teacher, keen to start filling the piles of smooth crisp exercise books, relishing and embellishing every detail until she ran out of words.

'And you're going into your GCSE year? Ready for the hard work?'

'Yes, of course.' She wasn't sure if she was, but the gladiator sandals said otherwise.

'Well, I think you deserve top marks in everything. And, even if you don't get them, life has a way of working itself out. You can charm your way through most of it, like your father . . .' She laughed.

Amie frowned, half in doubt that she would ever manage to do that, half wondering what Nana meant.

'What was Dad like when he was younger?'

Edith Slade looked at Amie then, as if she was deciding something. 'Well, he certainly had an eye for the ladies, shall we say.'

'Did he have lots of girlfriends, then?' She didn't really want to think about it, but she'd asked the question now.

'They were never in short supply, let me tell you, and I think he broke a few hearts along the way, but that was before he fell in love with your mother and had two gorgeous children . . .'

They laughed and for a wonderful moment the world was a safe place again as Amie's worries lifted from her shoulders. Then Marina returned with a tray of food. Metal lids were removed and steam rose, clouding the air in front of them. It was time to leave, and Amie got up, but hovered in the doorway.

'There's just one thing I wanted to ask . . .' It came out all wrong, but, now she had started, she had to go on. Her words came straight out before she could think. 'Are you new here, Marina?'

Marina looked confused. 'New? I've been here five years, even longer than Edith! I don't think we've had any-one new here for months. Why do you ask?'

'Oh, it's nothing,' she said. But it was everything.

Back in the house, Amie curled up on the sofa and switched on the television.

After a few minutes, there was the sound of the key in the lock, and a voice. His voice. He strode into the room and stood looking at her for clues, but she gave nothing away.

'I was going to send out a search party. You weren't here when I popped in earlier.'

Amie said nothing, just stared at the TV screen.

'Where did you go?'

'To see Nana.'

He flinched the way you did if someone clapped right in front of your eyes.

'I took her my get-well card. You must have forgotten to give it to her when you went there this morning.'

Stuart looked straight ahead at the television screen, footage of Syrian hospital corridors filled with trolleys, sobbing, dying children crammed three to a bed, nurses and doctors looking desperate and exhausted. Then the face of a journalist, the latest to be kidnapped and murdered. 'How about trying something cheerier?' He reached for the remote.

'Like what?'

He flicked through the channels. Golf. A black and white film. Racing. Cricket. He settled on the black and white film and leant back on the cushions, lacing his fingers behind his head. An open-top car was driving fast along a mountain road. The driver reached across the woman in the passenger seat as if he was going to open the door and push her out.

'Hitchcock. The best.'

Amie frowned. 'Didn't he just try to kill her?'

'Ah, that's the thing you *see*. You don't know for sure that that's what it was. Is she imagining it? Maybe he's trying to save her – stop her from jumping out and killing herself.'

'I suppose. So which is it?'

'The whole film's like that. You're never completely sure what the truth is. That's why it's called *Suspicion*.'

They watched in silence for a while, then he reached for her hand and squeezed it. 'You sure you won't come back over? It's not the same without you there.'

'I'd rather stay here, if you don't mind.'

He tipped her chin upwards with his finger. 'Friends?'

Did he mean proper friends, or did he mean *Are you my ally or are you going to give me away?*

'Friends,' she replied, but she wasn't sure she had decided yet.

She must have fallen asleep, because when she opened her eyes, the light had changed: the sky was bluer and the sun was lower. The trees in the garden reached their twiggy finger shadows into the lounge and waved them in her face. From upstairs, the muffled bass of Andrew's music measured the passing seconds. The lounge door was ajar and from the kitchen there were angry voices and the *glug glug* of wine into a glass. They were arguing because of her.

'Has Amie finished sulking yet?' Maeve said, loudly so everyone could hear.

'She's not sulking. She had a shock.'

The thump of a bottle on the table. 'Why do you always have to stand up for her? She can't just run away every time something goes slightly wrong. How's she ever going to manage real life? The rest of us have to keep going. We don't have that luxury of ducking out when things get difficult.'

'You know, I worry about you, Maeve.' Amie had to strain to hear him. It became a dialogue of intonation that she interpreted by the ups and downs, the urgency, the momentum. Stuart muttered things, while Maeve hurled insults back at him: what did he know about parenting, because he was never around to do any? She wanted Amie to hear all of that, and there was more.

'I can't believe you left me with Colin all that time. Do you honestly think I have any interest in anything he has to say? Talks about cars and sport non-stop. I don't know how Mary puts up with him.' Then, 'Where do you think you're going? Stuart?'

Dad must have been trying to leave. He said something about needing to pop back to see Nana. Amie strained to hear, willing Andrew to turn the music down upstairs.

'Twice in one day? Or were you somewhere else this morning?'

No reply.

'Couldn't you choose a more convenient time to go?'

Still no answer, or none that was audible, whereas *she* wanted the whole neighbourhood to hear what she thought of him.

'Does she even realise you're there when you go on these visits?'

His voice finally went up then, as his anger took control of the volume. He only shouted when everything else had failed. 'Jesus Christ, Maeve! She only had a fall, for God's sake; she's not senile.'

Why doesn't she know when to say sorry and retreat? thought Amie. Her head pounded with frustration. She closed her eyes and pictured them on the edge of a cliff,

Maeve holding her hostage, challenging him to come to the rescue.

But he didn't. The front door slammed, and Amie crept upstairs. Later, Maeve appeared in the bedroom doorway, larger than life against the light behind her and casting a long and crooked shadow. Amie inched away to give her room to sit on the bed and leant up on one elbow. She wanted to hear that it was all going to be OK, but Maeve just bent down and brushed a hair off Amie's face.

When she left, Amie dreamt about a marching band that marched right off the edge of a cliff. She woke up in a sweat, the way you do just before you hit the ground. The rest of the night she tossed and turned.

Then it was Monday.

CHAPTER 3

Detective Sergeant Ronnie Delmar was ready to go home. A long Monday of chasing the CPS and finalising a less than compelling case against a shoplifter had left her in need of a challenge, or at least a gin and tonic and a dose of Netflix.

A face appeared around the partition. Since CID had gone open-plan she was lucky to have even a trace of privacy, but it still made her feel like a triage patient waiting for the nurse to bandage up her wounds. Playing the role of nurse today was DC Baz Munro, with his trademark twinkling eyes and Slavic smile.

'Sarge?' He used her rank instead of her name, but DI Lydia Burnett had reminded them at that morning's briefing to *keep things professional* and not to let a few cutbacks send standards plummeting at Halesworth. Within Lydia's earshot, Ronnie dutifully adopted a tone of formality and made sure she spoke loudly enough for the boss to hear.

'Ah, DC Munro. Last job of the day, promise. I know you have a home to go to.'

'Before we go, your mother's on line one.' He looked apologetic.

'Line one? Not like her to clutter up the CID hotline.'

'She said your mobile was switched off.'

'Ah, OK. It might be on *do not disturb* . . .' She pulled open a drawer and checked the screen. Four missed calls. Guilt flooded her for a second. But there was always *line one*, as her mother had just made clear. The discomfort subsided.

'Shall I put her through?'

'Just a minute. I need to see what we've got.' She flipped open the file on her desk and scanned the notes on the first page. The colour drained from her face. She should be careful what she wished for, because it certainly wasn't this. This was what she had been dreading.

'What shall I tell her? She sounded a bit anxious . . .' Munro trailed off and his smile evaporated.

For a moment, she was no longer DS Ronnie Delmar, but just another mother of teenagers whose whereabouts and pastimes were too often unknown, their minds a mystery that she would never fathom. It was the thought of the twins that decided it. 'Put her through. Thanks. I'll be quick.'

She sat back down and spun her chair round to face the window. Clouds were gathering, making it clear that summer was well and truly on the way out. On the street below, a woman was ushering two small children in school uniform down the crowded pavement, looking over her shoulder, apologising to a young man who had been hit by one of the swinging school bags.

When her own children were that age, she had always thought it must be the hardest part of parenting. But the challenges had never let up, only changed in their nature. The more you let your children go, the more dangers they faced in the real world – sometimes even in the safest places.

The phone on her desk buzzed, and she pressed the speaker button. 'Hello?'

'Hello? Darling, is that you?' The delicate tone betrayed nothing of a woman Ronnie knew to be strong beyond measure. It was a deceptive fragility that hid the wisdom of generations. Ronnie picked up the handset and gestured to Munro to leave. He nodded, performed a brief driving mime and headed for the door.

'Hi, Mum, what's happened? Are you OK? Are the twins OK?'

'Yes, we're all fine, sorry, I didn't mean to worry you by ringing you at work . . . it was just about the arrangements for the memorial, and I couldn't get through on your mobile.'

Ronnie sighed with more relief than she expected. Eddie and Tilly were fine, then, or not missing, at least. 'I'll be there. You don't need to worry. Everything's organised for afterwards: the buffet at the pub, cash behind the bar, all sorted.'

This should have been a simple text exchange, but Alice Delmar wasn't inclined to use technology if she could possibly avoid it. 'We managed perfectly well in the old days,' she said.

It wasn't a battle worth fighting. 'Was that all, Mum? I need to get going.'

'It's just . . . well, I wondered if you could drive me. I'm not quite myself at the moment. I mean, I'm fine with the twins, of course. Eddie brought home some sort of contraption he'd made in DT today. I can't believe how clever he is. Apparently, it actually plays music—'

'Of course I'll drive you,' interrupted Ronnie, aware that her mother could probably go on for a good half-hour if left unchecked.

'Perfect. And we can pick up Serena on the way.'

'Sure, but now I really do have to go. There's been an incident out at Millhurst and I've got to get over there.' The file was still open on the desk, making her blood run cold.

'Oh, darling, of course. I mustn't keep you. Bye for now.'

Putting the phone down, Ronnie half stood, then hesitated, making a mental note to call Serena on the day to make sure she'd taken her meds. Their father's memorial was going to be a huge anxiety trigger, that much was certain.

But she was needed elsewhere now.

Munro was waiting in the car and started the engine as she climbed into the passenger seat. 'Where to, boss?'

Ronnie looked at her notes. 'Millhurst village, 16 Pine Walk. It's the private estate with the big white gates, if I remember right.' She tapped the postcode into the GPS and a map flashed on to the screen, telling them it would take eighteen minutes. 'Last place you'd expect an incident like this.'

Munro glanced at her as he reversed out of the parking spot. 'Do we need to be there? Uniform are with them now, taking statements. Not that I'm complaining, just thinking about resources, as we're constantly reminded to . . .'

He was right, it was a uniform job and there was no reason for CID to be involved first off, but that didn't mean they *shouldn't* get involved. As long as she was still prioritising the right cases, Ronnie had no qualms about taking on extra work where her gut said she was needed. It wasn't as if it happened often these days, and she missed being first at the scene of a crime. It was there that hearts were laid bare and lies couldn't hide.

Munro was right about resources being an issue. She just had to hope he might come round to her way of thinking. It was only his second month in CID and he was more concerned with making an impression, which to give him his due was working very well so far. He was always ready with a chirpy greeting and a coffee for the DI, and his child-free existence would no doubt clear the way for a smooth path to the top. Ronnie tried not to notice, but noticing things was ingrained in her. She decided to play it carefully, but firmly enough to make her point.

'I get what you're saying, Baz, and I know it's the end of your shift. I'll take the flak if need be.'

'If you say so, boss. I know you don't like to miss out.' He looked at her with a grin. 'It's not as if we're asking for overtime.'

'I just want to be there, get a feel for the case before it all gets retold in some official narrative. Sometimes things get missed off a witness statement because they don't seem relevant, and I like to make sure I have the whole picture when I'm interviewing a suspect, not working off a PC's notepad. Sometimes there's more to what people say than what we choose to hear.'

Baz nodded. 'I get that. And you're right. You get a feel for people that doesn't come through on paper.'

'Thanks, Baz, I appreciate it.'

'Was everything OK with your mum, by the way? No dramas?'

'Perfectly OK, as it turns out,' Ronnie said, looking ahead. 'When my mother rings, I just assume something's happened to the kids. But they're fine. In the grand scheme of things they're *more* than fine. I mean, we live here in this middle-class bubble; they go to a great school. Their family is only partially dysfunctional; their dad is out of the picture, where he belongs.' Seeing a look of shock on Munro's face, she added, 'Not dead, just divorced. So far . . .'

'Bad news, was he?'

'Simon? Not to start with, but it takes time for people to reveal their true colours.'

He glanced at her while they waited at a red light. 'We're all a bit like that. Try to keep the bad stuff under wraps, but *it all comes out in the washing*, as my mother would say.' His voice took on a full Slavic lilt as he said the words.

Ronnie laughed. 'Maybe we are.'

He had a point, but when it came to her own marriage there had been plenty of disagreement on what the *bad stuff* was. She had put her heart and soul into her work, going back to finish her police training when the twins were only five months old, and Simon had never been comfortable with that. His mother had never worked after her own children were born, and he had had the same unspoken expectation for his own family. But by the time the damage was done to their relationship, it was too late to go back and change the past.

'I'm not saying I got everything right. The whole work-life balance thing was a constant challenge. You can't win as a mum when it comes to going back to work; you're damned if you do and damned if you don't.'

Baz nodded. 'I can imagine it's not an easy choice. Was there a turning point?'

'I was pretty much in denial about how bad things were until one Monday morning when my daughter said, *Bye, Mummy, see you at the weekend.* That kind of brought me down to earth with a jolt.'

'Back after bedtime, off to work again before breakfast. That old routine.'

'Yes, exactly that. Makes you re-evaluate things.'

'Then what happened? Why leave the Met?'

'It was a sideways move: a DC job came up at Halesworth and I took it. We found lovely schools, lots more living space. Never looked back.'

It was a practised narrative with a happy ending, but the truth was that, despite the move, Ronnie's passion for her work had never abated, and Simon hadn't been slow to point out that her hours hadn't changed much either.

She had maintained that she was just doing her job, as he was, and he had argued they were all suffering because of it, and that if she wanted a family, she'd have to make a choice.

Remembering the conversation now sent a familiar pang of anguish through her heart, but she pushed it aside. When all was said and done, her family was actually a pretty happy one. She should remember that.

'Well, it seems you're a legend at Halesworth.'

Ronnie smiled. 'Not always for the right reasons. Take a left here. It's all blocked up ahead.'

Munro glanced in the mirror and indicated.

'So, DC Munro, your turn. What's your story?'

'Oh, nothing of any interest, sarge. No dependants that I know of.'

Ronnie laughed. 'Yet. You wait till it's time to cough up for university fees. Then they'll all come out of the woodwork.'

Baz grinned. 'I very much hope your prediction is wrong. So your mum has the kids when you're at work?'

'Yes, if I'm working late. And Simon has them every other weekend now, and most Thursday nights.'

'Ah, so Thursday's party night?'

Ronnie smiled at the idea. She couldn't remember when she'd last been to a party. 'Actually it's my father's memorial this Thursday, so not exactly a party, but in a manner of speaking, I suppose, if you like Scotch eggs and muted conversation with strangers.'

'Memorial?'

'Ten years. Since he died.' She took a deep breath. It had been a long wait without resolution, and she hadn't found any solace in the time that had elapsed.

'I'm sorry. Was it expected?'

'You mean how did he die?'

'Well, yes. I mean, you don't need to say. I was just . . .'

Ronnie recognised the tactic. I do this, she thought, I get the kids in the car and ask them lots of questions because they can't escape and we're facing forward, so somehow it's less intimidating.

'Bit of a mystery, to be honest. It was years ago now. We had a place down at the seaside in Sussex. Dad had a boat. One day he went out fishing and never came back. The boat was found empty, drifting.'

She had distilled the shock of a lifetime to a few choice words, as if reducing the narrative would alleviate the pain.

'Did they ever find his body?'

'No. Not surprising, though, given the circumstances. Coastguard drew the line at dredging the entire English Channel for us.'

He gave her an apologetic look, or it could have been a pitying one. 'Must be tough, without the closure . . .'

'It's even harder to accept that sort of thing when you work in CID. We need things to be resolved, don't we? So it was a proper test in that respect. But time passes and you get used to accepting what you can't fix.'

'What do *you* think happened?'

'Do you mean was it murder or suicide?'

'Or an accident?' He sounded genuinely concerned. Perhaps he was more of a softie than she gave him credit for.

'*Or* an extra-large fish dragging him overboard?' She forced a grin. 'It's OK. He would probably appreciate the light-hearted approach, to be honest. But I don't really know what I think. It was probably just an accident. He had no real reason to commit suicide. He and Mum were good, or as good as you can be after forty years. He had his fingers in a few pies, though: played a lot of poker, owed people money all the time . . .'

'Money trouble is the biggest cause of suicide, they say.'

'And owing people money is a pretty direct route to being taken out, if you watch enough gangster movies, or work in the Met. The weather wasn't great, either, so it could even have been a freak storm. We just don't know.'

'Even worse for your mother, I'm sure.'

'Yes, I suppose, but right now she's stressing out about a memorial service that she's barely taking part in, and a few sausage rolls in the pub after. She hasn't had to do any of the organising, but she does nothing but fret that we've forgotten something.'

He laughed. 'Well, try having a Russian mother. She's a non-stop worrier. Thinks I'm risking my life every second I'm at work, has no idea how boring it is out here in suburbia.'

'Ah, yes, how could I forget your Russian connection, *Vasily*?'

'Yeah, I like to forget that name too. Stick to Baz, if that's all right.'

'As long as you stick to Ronnie.'

'I'm stuck to your side, like superglue.'

'Put your foot down, *Vasily*.'

'Yes, *Veronica*.' They were back on the dual carriageway and the traffic was flowing again. Baz found the accelerator and pulled into the fast lane.

Pine Walk was clearly not accustomed to police cars, and curtains twitched as they crawled over the humps looking for No. 16. They pulled up behind the patrol car and a white Mercedes in the drive, and Ronnie took in the scene before them. The house, which might have recently been called a new-build, was a red-brick mock-Georgian mansion. The neat lawn was guarded by a row of leylandii. It wasn't often that they were called to homes as plush as this, apart from for the odd burglary.

The front door was opened by a long-haired, gum-chewing teenager. There was a dull look in his eyes that gave Ronnie a twinge of sadness. She thought about Eddie, who was a similar age to this boy. A misfit adolescent trying to make sense of the world.

'I'm DS Ronnie Delmar and this is DC Baz Munro.' Ronnie smiled and held out her badge, which the boy ignored. 'We're here to see Amie Slade.'

'They're in there.' He pointed to the kitchen, where two uniformed officers sat around an island with the girl and her parents. The place was spotless. Gleaming. There was a faint smell of bleach, and not a thing out of place.

The uniforms departed, grateful to be relieved, and Baz saw them out.

Ronnie shook hands with the family and pulled out two vacated stools at the island. 'DS Delmar. And this is my colleague DC Munro.' Baz was on his way back into the room and nodded solemnly at the assembled group.

The man who she presumed to be Amie's father stood slightly apart. He was strikingly handsome, tall, broad-shouldered, and had a charm about him that was almost tangible. Ronnie hadn't noticed a man in that way since the break-up.

It might have been her imagination, but she felt his eyes rest on her a fraction longer than necessary. He held out his hand and gestured to the others with a tilt of his head. 'Stuart Slade. This is my wife Maeve, and Amie, our daughter.'

He looked from Ronnie to Baz and back to Ronnie again, as if wondering who was in charge. Ronnie drew a line under his confusion by pulling out her notebook and addressing the wide-eyed teenage girl in front of her. In those eyes she saw her own sister twenty years earlier. A frightened animal caught in a trap. She met Ronnie's gaze with a look that said, *Can I trust you?* And Ronnie did her best to look back at her with eyes that said, *Yes*.

She flipped the notebook open. 'Amie, I need you to tell me what happened. Right from the beginning. Take your time.'

CHAPTER 4

Monday 3 September had felt like a new beginning, and the first Monday of the first term of the school year should have meant a clean slate and a spring in her step. But, for Amie, September mornings had a double edge to them. While the world was marvelling at the crispness in the air and the russet leaves, nature was preparing to turn a corner. And around the corner was winter.

It was with a strange sense of trepidation that she had climbed into the back seat of the car that morning. A feeling of inevitability, like when you sit down and push yourself off the edge of the helter-skelter and there's no turning back. When she thought about it later, when the police came, it was as if she'd known how that day would unfold, as if she'd already lived it and could do nothing to stop it. It made her wonder whether life was like that, whether free will was an illusion and humans were programmed to behave in a certain way from the start.

The route to school took them down the new Grayshott Road, with its smooth tarmac and bright white lines. It ran parallel to its previous incarnation, where a row of derelict houses stood waiting for the wrecking ball, all boarded up and sprayed with graffiti. Amie dared herself to look at them, brick faces with eyes gouged out and patched up, mouths taped over, lined up like prisoners in front of a firing squad. She wondered who used to live there, where they were now, and how it must feel to be one of those houses, like waiting for your own death.

Andrew didn't wonder any of this. He got out on the corner just outside his school, slammed the door, didn't look back.

A few more minutes in traffic and then it was Amie's turn. They pulled into the bus stop outside Millhurst High and she got out of the back, dragging her rucksack behind her. 'Thanks for the lift, Dad.' She tried to smile but no smile came.

And from there it plays on in slow motion, on repeat, for the rest of her life. Later that day, when the police are coaxing her to tell the whole story, she will miss this part out, because she desperately doesn't want it to be true.

Dad surprises her by getting out of the car and for a minute she thinks he's going to hug her goodbye, but he just takes off his jacket and hangs it on a hook in the back. Then he's standing up again, patting his pockets, looking for something. His phone, he says. They open all the doors and rummage around for it. Amie tries ringing it, but he says it's on silent. He stands up again and feels around in his pockets, but it's still not there. He's frowning, his eyes flicking this way and that as he pats his other pockets and thinks about where he might have left it. Then suddenly Amie sees it sticking out between the driver's seat and the gearstick and she reaches down and pulls it out.

There's a message on it from an unsaved number. Just a few words on the screen, but it's enough to make her stomach somersault and send pain slicing through her body like an electric shock.

Dad takes the phone off her roughly. Then he regrets doing that because he smiles and says, 'Thank you, Monamie, what would I do without you?' and suddenly she feels stupidly better. They are a team again. She is valued, indispensable even.

He puts in his passcode and reads the whole message. The next minute he's back in the car, pressing buttons, holding the phone to his ear.

It's nearly time for registration so she turns and walks away to face the day, and then suddenly her heart is racing.

Because the first person she sees is Daniel Foster.

CHAPTER 5

Daniel Foster was acting site manager at Millhurst High, following the death of his father the previous winter from a sudden and aggressive brain tumour. Since the school seemed in no hurry to find a permanent replacement for Mr Foster senior, he had carried on in the position for another two terms, and it looked as though he would be there for at least one more.

Today he was fixing a sign to the gates asking parents not to park on the zigzags. Stepping back to look at his handiwork, he pushed a flop of blond hair out of his eyes and gave Amie a wave. She smiled back, blood pumping in her ears as she willed herself to stay calm.

'Good holiday?' His voice was all cheeriness.

'Yes,' she managed. 'How about you? What did you get up to?'

He put down his drill, leant on the gate and glanced back at the school as if to check for observers. 'I went travelling, saw a bit of the world. After Dad died, I needed to get away. Life's too short and all that.'

Amie nodded, desperate to think of something kind, something he'd remember, but all that came out was, 'Must have been a very sad time for you.'

Sad time? She imagined her own father leaving, dying, abandoning her in a world of strangers, and felt repulsed by her own words. She was just opening her mouth to say something better when they were interrupted by a herd of late arrivals, a flurry of hair-tossing, bag-swinging Year Elevens racing to avoid being last in class. From the safety of a crowd, they would giggle and nudge each other whenever Daniel was around, checking their reflections in their phones and fluttering cloggy black eyelashes under long fringes. They were doing it again now. He was pretending to ignore them, but Amie saw him struggling to suppress a smile at all the licking of lips and flicking of blonde hair.

Katie Green did all that better than anyone. Every break time, she would pore over her phone with all the other pretty girls in the class, showing them a picture of this or that boy who apparently fancied her. That morning they had just found Daniel Foster on Instagram and were admiring his latest posts. It was their strength as a pack, the power of the hunters over their prey, that transfixed and disgusted Amie at the same time.

The first day of term was always intense, as they zipped around from lesson to lesson and were bombarded with new books and new rules. Teachers gave stern warnings about the importance of this stage in the education process, about balancing work and play, iPads in the bedroom, keeping boyfriends at bay in the interests of GCSE results.

This couldn't be aimed at Amie. More of a message for the likes of Katie Green.

In maths, she sat at the back with her bag on the desk in front of her until she was told to take it off. She tried to say it stopped the sun getting in her eyes, but Mrs Hargreaves just pulled down the blind, leaving her in shadow. Just below the blind, she could still see the spot where Dad had dropped her off, where she'd read the message on his phone, and her stomach churned. She put her head in her hands, making another barrier between her eyes and the window, looked down and counted the lines in the grain on the desk in front of her.

'Amie?'

Mrs Hargreaves was leaning on her desk, arms straight, knuckles white, frowning eyes looking straight into hers. 'Did we lose you there for a minute?'

'No.' She looked right back at her.

'Well, perhaps you could tell the class what a convergent sequence is.'

'It's a sequence with a limit that's a real number, so if the sequence is—'

Mrs Hargreaves nodded and lifted her hand as if to say 'enough'.

It was at lunch break that it happened. The bell rang, and Amie was washed out of the classroom in a sea of chatter and giggles. It was safer to head for the library until the queue went down in the canteen, and she had a whole holiday's worth of books to return. A group brushed past her in the corridor and she waited for the rest of them to pass, standing against the wall to avoid contact until they had gone ahead, like when Maeve drove in the slow lane and got overtaken by everyone. *We're not in a hurry*, she would say, when Amie worried about the hooting and flashing of headlights behind them.

Amie wasn't in a hurry now, but everyone else was. Perhaps she hadn't stood out of the way enough, but suddenly she was dragged sideways, overbalancing, sending an armful of books skimming down the slippery corridor, and as her legs went from under her, she went down after them, a crumpled mess.

Some stragglers behind the main group ran past, skipping over her spilt load like hopscotch, casting amused glances over their shoulders as she scrambled to collect the debris. Katie Green was one of them, but instead of going through the swing doors at the end of the corridor she leant against the wall, smiling, holding up her phone – and it wasn't for a selfie, because she wasn't pouting or rearranging her hair.

Amie tried to say something, ask her to stop, but no sound came.

Then a blonde tousled head appeared round the swing doors, an arm reached out for Katie, beckoning. 'Leave her. Come with us.'

It was unusual for someone to tell Katie what to do.

Then another voice cut through the agony of Amie's humiliation. 'Oi, what do you think you're doing?'

The phone went down. Katie was running her hand through her hair, apologising.

Amie felt herself redden all over. She didn't want Daniel to see her like this and wished hard that he would just move on, but here he was, offering her his hand. Hers was bleeding. She must have cut it on a staple in the wall as she slid downwards, in a fruitless attempt to save herself. She ignored it and tried to get up by herself, but there must have been another book just under her foot because she slipped again and reached out wildly, finding Daniel's arm.

'Ouch, Amie, Jesus!'

'Oh, my God, I'm so sorry.' In her head, she saw her mother's face full of disgust, Katie Green's pitying look over her shoulder, the shattered bowl on Mary Morrison's floor, bemused faces looking down at her, heads shaking. The images flashed past in succession, making her head dizzy with the collage of shame. When people talked about wanting the earth to swallow them up, this must be what it felt like. Panic pounded in her chest; her breath came in gasps.

'Amie, you need to calm down. Breathe slowly.' Daniel's voice came through the fog, but the scream in her head drowned it out.

A chill swept through her body, her knees gave way and all was dark.

Seconds had passed, maybe minutes. A hand was on her arm. Everything was the same, just a scuffle of footsteps and voices beyond the door. Bright lights. As her eyes regained focus, she could make out a figure deterring curious onlookers. 'Move away from the door, ladies . . .'

'Drink.' It was Daniel again, holding a plastic cup of water. She took it, sipped, handed it back, unable to meet his eyes. 'A bit more, if you can.'

She shook her head.

'You've had a panic attack. Has this ever happened before?'

'No,' she said, too quickly.

'You want to get that cut on your hand seen to. Let's get you upstairs to the Sanctuary where you can have a bit of a calm down. Come on. I'll sort this lot out.' He nodded towards the faces trying to peer through the swing doors.

'What about the mess?' She was looking at the books scattered down the corridor, but he was already collecting them, loading them on to the trolley he'd been pushing. Then his hand was on her shoulder, directing her up the stairs, while at the other end of the corridor, the swing doors swung, and Katie Green was telling everyone everything.

Millhurst High School had not achieved Ofsted commendations for its pastoral care for nothing. Any girl could come to the Sanctuary at any time to talk to a member of the team or just to sit and escape the stresses of school life, which were not inconsiderable. Once the doors opened, the new unit was awash with teenage tears on a daily basis, as everything from unrequited love to self-harm was poured out and worked through. The Sanctuary was held up as a shining example to other schools. *Mental health should be at the centre of education policy*, insisted the local MP in a newspaper interview, and applications for places rocketed.

'Right, I just need to fill in this thing . . .' Daniel was sitting next to her, completing a form on a clipboard. 'Paperwork . . .' he mumbled, scribbling something in the box with one eye on his phone. There was a message open that Amie couldn't quite read from where she was sitting, but then he clicked on it, replied two words, no more, and signed the form with a flourish. 'I'll just go and talk to the nurse, and she'll be out to see you in a sec.'

'There's no need, honestly, I'm fine,' she protested.

'I have no choice, Amie: you see it, you report it, or you're in trouble with the boss.' By that he meant Miss O'Shea, the new head teacher who had declared it her mission to rid the school of bullying at every level, staff included. There were zero tolerance posters all over the walls in the corridors. The only trouble was, as she had discovered in her few months in the job, bullying seeped like water through the smallest of cracks. Girls would protest their innocence to a chorus of 'she started it' and 'now *you're* bullying *me*, miss'. It had become the latest bandwagon.

Amie watched Daniel leave and looked at the table in front of her where his phone lay, still illuminated from a second ago when he had put it down. The home screen showed a picture of him with his arm round a woman, both of them in sunglasses, golden skin, sitting on a white beach. It was weird to think of people who worked in her school having a life outside. She couldn't imagine Miss O'Shea in Sainsbury's or watching TV in her pyjamas.

Through the glass door, she could see Daniel talking to Trish, the head of pastoral care. She was nodding and looking at him sadly. He was leaning on her desk with one hand, while the other gesticulated. Trish shuffled the papers together and looked past him, catching Amie's eye and smiling. Amie looked away. They talked for a while more, then the door opened and Daniel was telling her to come on in.

Trish was kind and understanding. Amie reassured her that it was a one-off, there was no need for follow-up, but she had to explain the whole episode again, promise to report any more incidents as soon as they happened. *We have a zero-tolerance policy*, she was reminded.

'Please don't do anything. I mean don't bring Katie in for questioning or anything.'

'Oh, Amie, this isn't a police station. The Sanctuary is a place where we talk things through, find resolution. We don't interrogate.'

'Whatever. I just don't want you to do anything. I don't want to press charges.'

'Amie, it's not that kind of situation . . .'

'I'm joking.'

There was an awkward pause, then they let her go and Daniel spoke to Trish alone for a minute before escorting Amie back to class. She was about to go in when he asked how she was getting home that afternoon.

'Mum's picking me up later. I've got to wait for her in the spinney so she can pull into the bus stop at the bottom of the hill. Saves time going round the one-way system – and of course she can't stop on those new zigzags . . .' Words came tumbling out, unfiltered.

'Ah, yes, my morning's handiwork. Well, I might see you later when I'm doing the grounds after school, if you manage to stay out of trouble till then . . .' He smiled and she reddened, because trouble was all around her.

She tried to keep a low profile in the afternoon despite the whispering and pointing. They made no effort to pretend they weren't doing it. At the end of the day, she hung back and watched from the window as they made their way outside in pairs and clusters, then in smaller splinter groups, followed by the odd straggler. As the place emptied, quiet fell and her spirits lifted.

She should check what time Maeve was coming to get her. She picked up her phone, then suddenly remembered the message she'd seen in the morning and her heart went crashing back down to the fires of hell.

The spinney was nothing more than a cluster of overgrown bushes and a bench behind the sports hall. She would see the car from there and it wouldn't take her a minute to get down the hill. She flopped down on the bench and closed her eyes, feeling the afternoon sunshine warm her face. On the road below, the occasional car swung round the bend, heading onwards with that purpose that adults always had in the world, always going somewhere, looking for something.

Her phone pinged. Maeve would be in the usual place by half past.

Amie squeezed her eyes tight and focused on the sun, imagined it pouring energy through her body, keeping her safe. *It'll all be the same in a hundred years*, Nana used to

41

say. Amie never really understood what she meant by it, but she knew it was supposed to stop you worrying about things.

'Hey.' A familiar voice broke her reverie, making her jump. 'How'd the rest of your day go?'

'Fine. I mean, nothing exciting. All good.' She spoke in staccato offerings, as if she had hiccups and couldn't risk longer sentences. Her thumping heartbeat filled every space. She hadn't expected company.

'Pleased to hear it.' He stood silhouetted in front of her, the sun behind him. His closeness made her nervous. She looked at her phone to see the time, avoiding looking Daniel in the eye.

'Mum's on her way. Bad traffic.'

'I'll wait with you if you like.'

She didn't have a choice. He was already next to her. 'OK.' She moved to the side, making room for him to sit.

He stretched out his legs, put his hands behind his head and let out a sigh of contentment. 'Not quite Bali, but not so bad.'

'You still living with your mum?' asked Amie. She didn't want to think about sunny places she'd never go to.

'Yeah, she's working in the school office. And I can't afford anywhere else, so it's pretty perfect.'

They sat in silence for a few seconds, then she said out of nowhere, surprising herself, 'Do you enjoy your job?'

He turned to look at her with a smile. 'Well, it's great to have everyone back in. Bit lonely working on site in an empty building. There are always a few teachers around,

42

but it's not the same as having all you lot shrieking away in the playground.'

She didn't shriek. So it couldn't have been her he'd been missing. Couldn't be her that he was glad to have back.

'You should be a teacher if you like it so much.' Stupid thing to say. It sounded sarcastic.

'Funny you should say that. I'm just about to start training to be a special needs teaching assistant. College one day a week, and in the classroom the rest of the time, so who knows what the future will bring.'

She imagined him standing over her, helping with handwriting, counting the blue Smarties and setting them out in rows of ten. 'Why special needs?' she asked.

'I think because they're so misunderstood.'

Amie thought, I know how that feels. She shifted her position slightly, aware that he had chosen to sit nearer her than he needed to. The scent of his skin close to hers reminded her of Dad, reminded her of what she could lose, if someone took him away. There was a pause that seemed to last forever, and then adrenaline surged through her body the way it did when something was about to happen. The sun slid behind a cloud and a chill settled in the air. She jammed her knees together to stop them shaking.

'You OK, Amie?'

His hand reached out. His face was too near hers. She could feel his breath; she could almost see her reflection in his eyes. She tried to speak, but no words came. When she looked back at this moment, all she would remember would be that she had no power to stop what happened next, or what followed, but that it changed the course of both their lives.

Time stands still when the unthinkable happens. It may have been seconds or minutes later that Amie was tearing herself away from Daniel Foster, hurtling down the hill to the road, running for her life, school bag slamming into her side. Below, careful drivers concentrated on the bend, obeying the 'School' warning sign, and nobody took their eyes off the road, so nobody saw what happened to Amie Rose Slade.

When she sank into the passenger seat of the car, she couldn't get her words out through breathless tears. Maeve just drove on in stony silence. At home, Dad demanded to know *what on earth* had happened. Maeve said she had *no idea*, that Amie was hysterical. When Dad asked, 'Did someone hurt you?' and Amie finally nodded, he called the police.

Two uniformed officers arrived within minutes, but it was only when some detectives came to take over from them that she was able to say, in gasps and whispers at first, what Daniel Foster had done to her.

Once she started talking, the words flowed and she couldn't stop. Maeve had her head in her hands, and when the story was over, she stared at Amie, then at a point behind her head, as if she had seen a ghost.

After the uniformed officers left, the detectives wanted to know everything she remembered, because soon her mind might blank it out. DS Delmar was kind and serious at the same time, as if she were talking to her own daughter, and Amie wondered what it would be like to have this detective for a mother, looking at you and listening to you as if you mattered.

She told them what they needed to know. Then they wanted to take samples of DNA, fingerprints, scrapings from under her nails; they wanted her clothes, they wanted to check for bruising on her arms. But they were so kind, she let them take everything they wanted, gave herself up for inspection. They left, saying they'd be in touch soon, and the house was silent again. Dad told her to go and have a lie-down, that he'd bring her up some supper on a tray.

'I should have been there to protect her,' Amie heard him say through the closed doors of the kitchen afterwards. Maeve didn't reply, as if to say he'd failed them all again.

CHAPTER 6

'Mum, have you heard a word I've said?' There was a clatter of spoon in bowl and the scrape of a chair on the floor.

'Every single one, Tilly darling. Just because I'm not interrupting you, it doesn't mean I'm not listening.' Ronnie knew that for her daughter a conversation was something more like a game of Chinese chequers, a fast-moving, turn-by-turn race to get the point across, jumping over each other to reach the finish line.

'So, what do you think? Can I stay at school instead of going to Grandpa's memorial? I don't want to have to catch up on work and stuff. It'll be a nightmare. Last time I was ill, I failed the physics test after missing just one day. Please?'

Ronnie suppressed a smile. The twins went to extraordinary lengths to persuade her of their point of view sometimes, especially when there was no need.

'That's fine with me. I'll explain to Grandma and I'm sure she'll understand. How about you, Eddie?'

'Same.' He had none of his sister's verbosity. They were the perfect team in that way. Tilly was his advocate, while he would nod in approval or shake his head, as if his words on earth were limited and once used up would leave him mute for the rest of his life.

'Just come straight home after school. Together. No sloping off to the chippy. I'll be back in time for dinner.'

Eddie looked at her knowingly, but Tilly narrowed her eyes. 'Why do we suddenly need to stick together?'

'I just don't want you thinking that because Grandma's not in charge you can go off and paint the town red.'

'Paint what?' Eddie looked mystified.

'Has something happened?' asked Tilly. 'You're being weird. Like you do when there's something at work you can't tell us about.'

'No. Nothing's happened. I just want you home straight after school. Is that understood?'

'Yes, Mum,' they chorused in gloomy unison, gathering their bags.

Ronnie watched them from the window of the flat as they came out of the main entrance and then stood collecting her thoughts on the Slade case. Sexual assault was an uncommon occurrence in these leafy suburbs. Or the allegations were, at least. The few that had landed on Ronnie's desk were swiftly retracted, witnesses baulking at the prospect of giving evidence in court, identifying their attacker, even signing a statement. Charges had been few and far between, which was unlikely to reflect reality, if you looked at the statistics across the country. Whether these crimes were continuing unabated behind the neat façades of the private estates was anyone's guess.

Ronnie was pleased she and Munro had made the journey to Millhurst on Monday evening, and if Lydia wanted something to justify the visit, she could show her the notes. There was certainly a great deal more detail in hers than had been given to the uniformed officers they had taken over from. Perhaps, after letting the first drips of truth out to those two, Amie had felt more able to share the rest.

The allegations were disturbing enough as they were, but Ronnie found herself having to push away the memories they brought back. Rage was too dangerous an emotion to let loose if you wanted to make a difference, and the past was the past.

The memorial service was going to cut short her day, but there was enough time to get to the station for a couple of hours, and she needed to start by concentrating on witness evidence.

Munro had been thorough, she had to admit. The previous two days' investigations had revealed no record of abusive behaviour on Foster's part, but the head teacher had admitted to having had words with Mr Foster senior on more than one occasion for being *a bit over-friendly with some of the older girls*. The allegation was vague, unrecorded and unsubstantiated. Mrs Foster had no knowledge of it, but when questioned had broken down in tears, saying that her husband had only ever wanted the best for the kids, and that if he had been out of line, it would have been just him being his lovely friendly self. *You can't do anything these days, if you're a man. Everyone thinks you're a pervert; you only have to look at a girl nowadays to end up in prison.*

Daniel Foster hadn't given anything away. He had looked scared and confused, which could indicate guilt as much as innocence, and wouldn't be drawn on the allegations against him. His face went white when they read out a summary of Amie's statement. *That did not happen,* he had repeated over and over, until they 'd terminated the interview to gather more evidence.

As for Miss O'Shea, she had assured them during her interview that she had made it her mission to make Millhurst High School a beacon of good practice, and she was at pains to prove that it was through no fault or oversight of hers, or her staff, that this shocking incident had taken place. Munro had assured her that they would deal with the matter as quickly and cleanly as possible, and Ronnie had given him a few words of caution afterwards.

'Don't promise a quick resolution unless you can guarantee it. They think quick means tomorrow.'

Baz had looked at her quizzically. 'Tomorrow it is, then.'

She had barely had time to open her emails that Thursday morning before he walked in and slid the file on to her desk. Ronnie pushed her chair back and looked up at him expectantly. 'You seem pretty confident?'

'I say we're just about ready to go to the CPS.'

'With what charge?'

'Section ten? Incitement to commit a sexual act. He tried to force her to touch him, there's no doubt about that.'

Ronnie raised her eyebrows. 'Sounds like the right call, but it's a tough one. What do we have exactly, apart from her allegation, which he denies vehemently?'

She flipped through the file until he stopped her at a page showing two photographs.

'Well, for starters, we have those scratches on his arm, showing that she must have fought him off, plus some bruising on hers – which is what you can see there.' He pointed at the second photo.

'Anything from forensics on that yet?'

'Still waiting for the DNA under her fingernails, but, assuming that comes through, it's pretty conclusive, wouldn't you say?'

Ronnie turned more pages of the file, scanning Foster's statement. 'He says there was an incident earlier when she fell, the one he reported, and he says that explains it. *She reached out and scratched me right down my arm.*'

'He would say that, though, wouldn't he?' Munro wasn't going to let this one go without a fight.

'I'm just saying it needs to be watertight.' Ronnie flipped the file shut. 'We need facts. Witnesses. Anything on his phone?'

'Search history showed the usual porn sites, but nothing child-related that we've located, so far.'

'Social media?'

'Interesting – he has a huge number of teenage girls following him on Instagram. The tech guys are going through it now, but it's looking like he's following them back, and some of their photos are, well . . .'

'Indecent? I wouldn't be surprised.' Ronnie had been shocked when Tilly had shown her the Instagram account of a school friend of hers – all bikini shots and pouting lips. 'When I see what the girls put on there to get attention, I think feminism has taken a bit of a backward step.'

'Some are more than indecent, I'd say.' He reddened. 'I thought these platforms took down anything like that, but apparently not, at least not until they're made aware of it . . .'

'Does he follow Amie?'

Baz nodded. 'Along with several other accounts that Amie follows and is followed by. Anyway, he said his following them was in response to them following him. Apparently that's modern manners for you. He doesn't deny having a bevy of admirers out there. He says it's normal, everyone does the mutual follow thing.'

'Why would anyone do that – just invite random strangers into their lives?' Ronnie wondered aloud.

'He follows thousands of people, doesn't really pay any attention to names.'

'Or ages.'

'As a user, you can do pretty much anything – look at whoever you like, follow anyone you like, whatever age they are.'

'What about message history?' She pictured Tilly sitting up in bed, in non-stop communication with half the world, it seemed, on some platform or other. 'On Instagram or whatever else he's got. My kids seem to move on to another app as soon as they get wind of the parents using it. So I definitely couldn't tell you what the latest one is.'

'Nothing incriminating, but he would have had plenty of time to delete anything before we got there.'

'The tech team might be able to dig it out. How about on hers?'

Munro seemed about to burst with excitement as he whipped out his tablet with a flourish. 'Ah, well, now that you mention it, there was this little gem . . .' He opened the photo app and revealed a screenshot of a direct message from danfoster365. It wasn't long, just a few words in fact, but a few words that could change a life, take away a future.

Can't stop thinking about how much I want you right now . . .

Sexting was a tricky area when it came to what was or wasn't inappropriate. She'd once found a message like this one on Eddie's phone: her boy of few words turned out to be quite effusive when the subject matter was right. But the leap between thought and deed was a substantial one, and these words of Foster's were hardly conclusive proof of assault.

Munro was still talking when she tuned back in. He had taken a stance that proclaimed self-assurance, propped up on the filing cabinet with one hand, legs casually crossed at the ankle, his other hand on his hip.

'From Amie's statement, we have a clear case of Section 10 incitement, and if we get the DNA . . .'

Ronnie read Foster's words again. 'What was his response to your finding this message on her phone?'

'Flatly denied sending it.'

Ronnie frowned. That didn't make sense. 'But if Foster had sent a message to Amie, he'd know she'd still have it on her phone. Why would he deny it?'

'I don't know, sarge. Maybe it's just panic time. Deny everything.'

'Any more on his history? Any disciplinary issues, past employers with something to say? Anything on his laptop?'

'Still looking into that, and trying to get the deleted message off his phone, or wherever it goes – that great dustbin in the clouds . . .'

'No stone unturned, DC Munro.' Her expression was mid-smile, neither serious nor joking. She didn't want Baz to presume she was either.

'He doesn't have a leg to stand on, sarge – I mean, he admits to spending time with her earlier in the day. Not just at lunchtime, either. Her father saw her talk to him by the gate when he dropped her off. He said they seemed friendly. Obviously, he had plans to get more friendly . . .'

Ronnie looked down at the statement again, and back at Munro. 'But he claims that at lunchtime he was just doing his job, taking her up to the Oasis or whatever they call it. He was following procedure, wasn't he?'

'The Sanctuary.' The hand went down from the hip and then both were clasped behind his back. She had rattled him. He took a few steps around the office, a lion trapped in a cage.

'Whatever,' she said. 'But he was doing the right thing at that point, I think. We need more.'

Munro stopped and faced her. 'She says he didn't need to be there; she told him he didn't need to worry, but he stayed. Isn't that overzealous?'

He was clutching at straws, but she appreciated his commitment. 'It wasn't Amie's call to make. And anyway, overzealous or not, that could point the other way. He could just be extremely law-abiding, obeying the rule book to the letter.'

'Good point,' Munro conceded. 'Tricky one to argue, I suppose. But his skin under her fingernails? That's a typical sign of a struggle.'

'Well, firstly, we don't have anything from forensics yet to confirm, and, secondly, he says she did it earlier in the day when she was trying to stop herself falling. I don't see how we identify which struggle we're talking about here. It seems to me that the defence would have a decent case of reasonable doubt.'

Munro frowned, his feathers still ruffled. Ronnie leant forward. The incident room was filling up, and the details of the case didn't need broadcasting to the whole force.

'I know what you're thinking, Baz. I share your impatience to put Foster away for this, trust me. But I also have an obligation to ensure that we have a solid case. We don't need to move any faster than it takes to do things properly. We need to wait for the DNA. And check the CCTV. There's nothing at the actual scene overlooking the bench where they were, but see if you can pick him up elsewhere on the campus, on his way there, on his way back. If we get him on that as well, we may be on to something.'

'Right you are.' She could have sworn he gave a little skip as he left.

Ronnie glanced at the clock on the wall. An hour left until she had to leave to pick up Serena and Alice, and she needed to clear her mind, put her thoughts in some sort of order. She spun her chair round to face the window. If she allowed herself a few minutes with her eyes shut, she could slow her mind to the point where her thoughts emerged more clearly from the fog of fast-paced discussion.

Here was a twenty-one-year-old man working in a school, accused of a sexual offence against a fifteen-year-old girl. So far, they had her statement and a text from him on her phone. There were scratches on his arms, and some on hers. Bruises on her elbows. He was a serial follower of scantily clad underage girls on Instagram. It wasn't enough. But with CCTV and a DNA match they would be nearly home and dry.

Unless there was something else here. Something they hadn't picked up on.

Munro was at the photocopier. She left her desk and stood next to him, watching the machine spit out sheet after sheet of witness statements.

'What if there had been a relationship between Foster and the girl that went bad? If he was indeed where she said he was, it could have been to finish the relationship, and Amie could easily have fabricated the story as some sort of revenge.'

Baz picked up his original from the feeder tray. 'But he denies there was any kind of relationship, consensual or otherwise.'

She nodded. 'Of course he would. Nobody wants to be caught out abusing a position of responsibility.'

He looked at her, examining her face for clues to her thoughts. 'What are you thinking, sarge? Something was going on? Long-term?'

Ronnie could only think of Serena. She was the connection, the reference point. 'Abused women and girls are the best keepers of secrets,' she said. 'That's all I'm thinking. Sometimes they keep them even from themselves.'

Munro seemed to be letting it sink in. 'An ongoing abusive relationship? But she was adamant nothing had happened between the two of them before.'

'And, with both of them denying it, it's unlikely to be what he goes down for. Evidence-wise . . .' she handed him the copies from the tray '. . . we can only work with what we've got.'

'So, we're back where we started?'

'I guess we are. Let's wait for the lab and the cameras to come back with something. And I need to go, or I'll be in trouble with the matriarch.'

Munro held open the door for her. 'Good luck today, sarge.'

'Thanks.'

Ronnie felt a rush of warmth towards Munro. It wasn't often she felt supported at work. At times, it had felt like a constant battle, looking over her shoulder to see who was judging her, who might throw her under the bus when it came to taking the flak for a mishandled operation or a suspect walking free. She had been wary of Munro at first, an eager young DC, keen to get ahead and climb the CID ladder. Who knew whose toes he was prepared to tread on to do that? But there were moments when she was forced to throw suspicion aside, and this was exactly one of those occasions.

CHAPTER 7

St Barnabas Church in Hackney was an odd choice of venue for the memorial service. Fred Delmar had never been a churchgoer and had very little time for anyone who claimed to be at the mercy of a higher power than the self. Having said that, he had never appeared to exercise much power over his *own* self, letting his gambling habits lead the family into dire financial straits on more than one occasion. Perhaps a little praying wouldn't have gone amiss.

Ronnie collected her mother at precisely the agreed time, but Alice was already hovering on the porch under the wisteria, looking anxiously at her watch. 'Veronica, at last. I was just getting worried. It's a long way across London.'

'Don't worry, Mum, we have plenty of time. Relax.'

A few roads away, Serena waved from her kitchen window and was out of the front door in seconds. She wore a dress that said more Druid priestess than grieving daughter, but then she had never owned a single item of smart clothing.

'Thanks, Ron, you're a star.'

Ronnie's self-esteem was restored, and she threw Serena a look of appreciation. 'You're welcome. Right, prepare for an exciting tour of the picturesque outskirts of Halesworth . . .'

There was nothing exciting or picturesque about Halesworth town centre, let alone the outskirts. But none of them had moved there for excitement. Free of dependants and commitments, Alice and Serena had followed Ronnie to suburbia a few years after her move. They had always been keen to do their bit with childcare support, and then, after the divorce, sisterly and motherly support as well. Ronnie had been adamant it wasn't necessary, that they shouldn't make such a dramatic move just for her and there was no risk of the twins losing touch with family, but Alice had been having none of it, and Serena had just looked at her as if to say, *It's actually me that needs propping up, please let me be near you . . .*

They arrived at the church with time to spare. A few cars were pulling into the car park and various dark-clad mourners hovered around the entrance. Switching off the ignition, Ronnie looked at her mother, then at her sister. 'All set? We can do this.'

'We can, for your father, God rest his soul.'

'It's the final chapter. Ten years of uncertainty and we're drawing a line under it all.' Serena didn't sound convinced, but the words were just right.

'Indeed we are.' Ronnie climbed out and held the door open for her mother. Serena was already there to take her arm. 'You still sure you don't want to say something, Mum?'

Alice turned to her with a horrified look. She had been adamant about not speaking – *I'd only cry, and that would*

59

set everyone off – and the vicar had been more than happy to read out her words, the memories of forty years together, which had ended so suddenly, so cruelly, without closure or resolution.

The church was filling up, but with very few familiar faces. This must be what happened when you lost your parent as an adult. When you were young, you lived with them, you knew their friends, where they went, who came round, what they talked about. It was hard to imagine them having a life outside the family unit.

'Who *are* these people?' whispered Serena, echoing Ronnie's thoughts.

Ronnie stole a glance backwards to assess the congregation. 'I can see a few old neighbours from Waterman Lane, and a few who I presume must be Dad's business colleagues. Mum seems to know them, thankfully. I don't want her paying for sausage rolls for the general waifs and strays of the East End. Perhaps we should make them take a test before they go into the pub – *How well did you know Fred Delmar?*'

Serena shifted uncomfortably in her pew, folding and refolding her shawl on her lap. 'It's been so long, I'm surprised there are so many of them still in touch.'

Ronnie squeezed her hand, imagining what must be going through her mind and willing it to go away. 'Looks like it's starting,' she whispered.

The congregation listened, noses were blown, eyes dabbed with tissues, as the celebrant listed Fred Delmar's idiosyncrasies, foibles and 'unique' world view. He had left school at sixteen to set up his own window-cleaning business and sold it twenty years later for a small fortune. What had happened to that fortune was another story. Alice and her daughters had been left enough to live in comfort, but Fred had enjoyed the good life, and had put that firmly at the top of his agenda.

At the pub after the ceremony, cheeky allusions were made to illicit affairs he might have witnessed when up ladders looking into people's bedrooms, to the incriminating Polaroids he must have collected, in case *one day, when times were hard* ... Middle-aged men stood around in tight groups, sinking their teeth into flaky pastry, nodding, slapping each other's backs, and Ronnie didn't recognise a single one of them.

'It's all in good spirit,' she reassured Serena, seeing her face fall at what she overheard of the Polaroids conversation. 'Let's face it, he was a bit of a wheeler-dealer, our dad. I'm glad they didn't feel the need to mention the gambling habit.'

'Thanks, Ron.' Serena squeezed her hand.

'What for?'

'Being there for me. And Mum.'

'Don't be silly. How are you feeling?'

'I'm OK – I took an extra Valium this morning.'

Ronnie winced. 'I hate that stuff.'

'I know you do, but it works, calms me down. Stops me thinking.'

'I hate that you need it. I hate that anyone could do something to you that makes you need it.'

'Don't even think about that. I feel so responsible for the way you feel about the male population sometimes . . . after what happened to me. You're always fighting my corner, but not just mine. You're fighting on behalf of all women who have suffered because of men.'

Ronnie looked over her shoulder, then back at Serena. 'It's not a fight – at least that's not how I see it. Remember what Dad used to say to us?'

'Well, his favourite piece of advice was *Trust your gut*. Not exactly original, but wise, I suppose.' She frowned. 'But wasn't there something else? His maxims always had a second bit that contradicted the first, like he was hedging his bets.'

'Sounds about right for Dad.' Ronnie took a sip of her water, wishing it was something stronger. 'But let's be clear. I don't hate men. I just find that my trust in them isn't automatic.'

Her phone pinged. A message from Munro. She patted Serena on the arm. 'I'm just going to step outside for a minute.'

DNA is a match.

OK. Anything else?

The message. They dug it out. It was sent from his phone.

CCTV?

No cameras facing the spinney itself but the CCTV from the side of the sports hall shows him leaving in a bit of a hurry.

I can send it over if you like. Oh, and we have some screen-shots of the Instagram girls, underage for sure, all of them.

Let me look at it and I'll call you in two minutes.

On the terrace, waiters were clearing the debris of lunch from tables. The sun was low in the sky and the air was cool. Pulling her scarf around her shoulders, Ronnie thought about Serena, a shadow of her teenage self, para-lysed by the pain of the past, her life on hold because of a man who thought he could get away with treating a girl like a piece of meat. She was the one who should be angry. And this might be Amie Slade in a few years' time, if she was let down by those whose job it was to protect her.

She sat down at one of the tables, let her eyes rest on the cheery laminated menu advertising a selection of unimaginably calorific puddings, and mentally reassessed the case.

The DNA under Amie's fingernails was a breakthrough, that was for sure. She had fought him off and he had the scars to prove it. The girls he named as witnesses were vague in their recollections and it wasn't a police job to put suggestions into their heads. One of the girls just said Amie was a loner and an outcast; a few others admitted to run-ning on past her just after she slipped in the corridor, but nobody had noticed anything else.

Then there was the CCTV that put Foster leaving the scene at the right time. Hardly conclusive, but in keeping with the big picture. And the Instagram message, which showed his intentions beyond doubt. She opened the screenshot Munro had sent her. The words seemed pretty harmless, almost romantic in a different context. But whether or not there had been an existing consensual relationship between the two of them was irrelevant. Foster was in a position of responsibility. Amie was a minor.

Her phone pinged again, this time with the images of Foster leaving the scene. A blurred figure, in a hurry, looking over his shoulder and upwards. At the camera? Of course he'd know where the cameras were. He was acting school caretaker. She replayed it, saw how his pace slowed after he'd looked into the lens. He must have realised he shouldn't be in a hurry. Being in a hurry would make it look as if he had something to hide.

The Instagram screenshots were provocative to say the least. It was never easy to pinpoint the age of a teenage girl, but the ones Foster was following were younger than the twins.

Ronnie zoomed in on one of the screenshots. A pretty girl, elfin features, wide grey eyes peering out from under a blonde fringe. Lips slightly parted, index finger on the lower lip, while the other hand was pulling her sleeve off her left shoulder. Another photo of what looked like the same girl sitting up in bed, as if she'd been surprised by someone coming into the room, naked except for a sheet pulled up just enough, but still revealing too much. Ronnie shuddered, imagining Tilly posting images like these, and not realising what she was letting herself in for when they fell into the wrong hands.

On Foster's phone – loads like this, read the message from Munro underneath the attachments. *Tech guys say highly Photoshopped, probably bear no resemblance to the girls whose accounts they are.*

What they had now was enough, if not for a conviction, then at least enough not to be laughed out of the CPS meeting. As for Baz, she couldn't fault him. However impatient he might have been to get going, his dedication and his attention to detail were actually spot on, and she rarely gave him the credit for it.

Dialling his number, she put the phone back up to her ear and spoke with certainty and resolve. 'OK, good work, Baz. Run it by the boss, then let's go to the CPS.'

'Roger that, sarge.'

And it was done.

Serena was saying goodbye to Simon in the doorway when Ronnie turned to go back inside, and she felt a surge of a thousand emotions jostling for place as she sat down next to her, fists clenched.

'What the hell is *he* doing here?'

Serena frowned at the retreating figure. 'I thought you'd invited him. He knew Dad pretty well, though, so I guess he just wanted to pay his respects.'

'Sorry.' Ronnie checked herself. 'I want to say that I'm learning to manage it and it's all good, but he's just so cocky and pleased with himself, it's hard not to rise to that.'

'Well, you're right about his manner. He talks down to me like I'm an invalid.'

'He's got such a nerve coming here today, not even saying hello to me. What's he up to?'

'Don't think about it, Ron, it's not worth it. Anyway, I remembered the other half!' She stepped on to the terrace and took a deep breath of fresh air.

'The other half of what?' Ronnie followed her, struggling to remember what they had been talking about.

'What Dad used to say. About gut feelings. *Always trust your gut. But sometimes it's not enough . . .*'

'Talk about covering your arse.'

'Exactly.'

Ronnie imagined her father being there now, passing on his wisdom. He was right that gut feeling couldn't get you far in life, and the need to dig deeper was the basis of her own *no stone unturned* mantra that Baz must have grown sick of hearing. But it was thanks to proper digging that they had their man.

The door behind them opened, bringing the sounds of indoors on to the terrace, and with them Alice Delmar, the *magna mater*, a glass of wine in hand. She held out her arms as she approached.

'My girls.' There was the hint of a tear in her eye. 'I'm so glad we did this, and I couldn't have done it without you. It was time to say goodbye.'

Serena and Ronnie let themselves be enveloped in Chanel-infused faux fur. Theirs was a small but perfect family.

CHAPTER 8

Summer came back around, like a fair-weather friend who could only stay for a cup of tea. No sooner had it arrived than the days started drawing in again.

They had pulled Amie out of Millhurst High. *Too many ghosts*, they said, and sent her to a private tutorial college to finish her GCSE year. She didn't mind. She felt more at home among the *misfits and dropouts*, as Maeve called them when she didn't think Amie could hear. Nobody at the college knew about what had happened to her at Millhurst. She just said she'd been home-schooled until her maths tutor had given up teaching to look after his daughter who had cancer. It was fun, inventing the detail.

But then they said she had to go back to proper school. They enrolled her in Merrymount sixth form. *A new start for you*. But she didn't want a new start. She wanted things to stay exactly as they were.

In July, Nana died from an infection she caught in hospital. Amie felt the loss like the amputation of an arm, but everyone else's lives seemed to carry on the same. She thought Dad might spend more time at home now he wasn't visiting the care home, but he was just as absent, just as busy.

Amie spent the month leading up to the new term unable to eat, unable to sleep. Her life was holding its breath. The house was a graveyard, curtains closed against the summer, and she was all alone, except when Daniel Foster crept into her dreams in the early morning.

It was the same dream every time. The bench in the spinney, the sun in her eyes, his skin on her skin, his hands gripping hers to stop her escaping, his breath in her ear telling her she wanted it, he *knew* she did. *I've seen the way you look at me.* She would wake with a start in a cold sweat, heart beating wildly. It was as real as the day it happened. And it was only a few weeks until his release.

What had happened to Amie was *one of those things that made you realise the importance of what you had.* She had overheard Dad saying that to Mum one night when they thought she was asleep. And for a long time after the incident, Amie had found herself at the centre of their world. It felt as if they were a proper family that stuck together through thick and thin. But, as the months had passed, the mask had started to slip.

Then, as if in a last-ditch attempt to rescue whatever might remain of togetherness, they booked a last-minute holiday to Corsica – a week at an all-inclusive five-star hotel. It should have been *the luxury break of a lifetime,* as it said in the brochure: *Watch your stress melt away as you relax by one of our three infinity pools . . .* But instead of fixing things it just highlighted all the ways in which they were masquerading in a freakish pantomime.

When he'd finished playing tennis with Andrew, Dad would stay on at the courts for more games with other grey-haired men, coming back to the pool all red and sweaty, to find Amie buried in a book under a palm tree or watching the volleyball that she never dared join in with. Andrew spent most of the day skulking around with his iPad, watching and listening to anything except what was all around him. Maeve swam endless lengths of breast-stroke, her head stretching up out of the water, hair as dry as a bone.

At mealtimes, cutlery clinked on plates and eye contact was avoided. Amie found reasons to escape early – a water aerobics class or a windsurfing lesson that she had no intention of taking – and waited for the day they could go home and stop pretending. She watched the normal families from behind the safety of her sunglasses, parents rubbing lotion on each other's backs, moving from the sunbed to the pool in unison to push toddlers around on inflatables, being part of something special, not a fragment of something broken.

Maeve was packing for what seemed like a whole day before they left. By evening, she was still moving slowly around the hotel room, sorting clothes in silence, folding and refolding Andrew's T-shirts and shorts while he went off in search of a good Wi-Fi signal. After dinner, Amie walked to the end of the jetty and sat mesmerised by the jumping fish, which came alive just as the sun was going down, a ball of red fire clinging to one sky before making a new dawn in the next. Dad found her there, deep in thought.

'So, this is where you run off to, Monamie. Can't say I blame you.'

He creaked down next to her, dangling his bare feet in the water beside hers. She smelt his aftershave and breathed it in, closing her eyes so all she could feel was him close to her, the warm breeze caressing them both. In the distance, the squawk of a gull, the hum of a boat engine in the bay and the tiny scratch of a plane in the reddening sky. They sat a moment in silence before he spoke.

'Excited about the new school?'

His words jolted her back into a reality that she couldn't bear to look at. She focused on the tiny beetle that was crawling towards her hand and imagined what it would be like to be that small, that vulnerable. One minute there would be a soft pink mountain in front of you and the next it would be hovering over your head, about to crush you to death. She let the beetle come to the mountain and watched it climb on to her finger, oblivious to the risk.

'I don't want to go to a new school. I hate change.'

The beetle scuttled over her knuckles and up her wrist without a thought for danger.

Dad was quick with his answer, as if he knew exactly how the conversation would go.

'I know you don't like change, but when the change has happened, and you start living a new life, things will fall into place.'

'I don't want a new life. I want my old life.'

'I know, but things just change whether we like it or not, and we can't stand in their way. We grow up, we grow old, we learn things and behave differently. Sometimes the new start is good for us, takes us away from memories and old habits, so we can be our best selves.'

'Are you your best self?' She looked away, because she didn't want to see his face when he answered.

'I probably haven't been, but I want to be.'

She let the beetle cross to her other hand. 'And how will you make that happen?'

'It's not about *making* things happen, Amie, it's about going with the flow, embracing change; it's about going where life leads you, shaking off what's holding you back and bravely stepping into the future. We need to live our lives to reflect who we really are.'

'I don't know who I am.'

'You will, in time.'

A gull swooped and caught a flying fish, skimming the surface of the water and turning back skywards.

'Are you going to get divorced?'

'What?' The question startled him, and he frowned as if she had uttered the most explicit of obscenities.

'I said—'

'I know what you said, but why do you ask?'

'Because you and Mum argue all the time, she's always upset, you never laugh, never spend time together. Do you even *like* each other?'

He looked skywards for inspiration. 'It's more complicated than that. Marriage often turns out to be different from what you expect. Your needs change.'

'And you don't need *us* any more, do you?' She hated how her voice sounded: desperate. But it was too late, the words were out there.

'Don't be ridiculous, Amie, it's not like that. Things just happen, and—'

'And you go with the flow. I heard you the first time.' She hardened at the use of her name. He never used her proper name. She wanted her other names back.

'Yes, to a certain point, you do.' He shifted slightly, looking straight ahead as if searching for a rescue ship on the horizon.

'So which flow are you going to go with?'

'What do you mean?' He sounded irritated, but he knew what she meant.

'I mean, are you going to leave us?'

'I will never leave you, Amie, you should know that.' Now his tone was angry. She should back off, but she couldn't stop herself from asking the question.

'Are you going to leave Mum?'

'I don't think either of us knows what's going to happen, but it's true, we aren't getting on well, and it hasn't been good for a long time. What happened to you . . .' He hesitated a second. 'Let's just say, it probably didn't help. The stress of all that . . .'

He was floundering, Amie thought. Because he was wrong. She stared at him in disbelief. 'Things got better. I thought we were happier, all of us.'

He looked up at the darkening sky and shut his eyes tight. 'It's been a strain, that's all.'

'I wouldn't like it if you left.' She should concentrate on the now, on the immediate problem, the one that was going to turn her world upside down.

There was a long pause as they watched the sun slip lower over the horizon.

'It's a beautiful world, don't you think? We are lucky people to live in it.'

He was changing the subject again because he couldn't say the words she wanted to hear. She leant her head on his shoulder so he couldn't see the sadness in her face. In a few minutes they would be in pitch darkness.

He stood up to leave, and walked a few paces before looking back over his shoulder. 'Coming?'

The beetle was still exploring her left hand, but its time was up. She plucked it out of the fleshy terrain and squeezed it with the fingers of her right hand until its body crunched. She flicked its remains into the sea and got to her feet.

They flew home the day before term started. The wheels hit the tarmac like the final cut. No more chances. No more edits.

CHAPTER 9

'It's been two years since he walked out, Ronnie. I would be thankful he's done it this way, not tried to blast you out of the water with some sort of *unreasonable behaviour* allegation.'

Susie was never one to mince her words. Ronnie took a sip of her gin and tonic, jingling the ice against the glass as she swirled it with the straw. She found herself looking around, mentally assessing the men at the bar – *would she or wouldn't she . . . ?* This was a recent thing, like waking up one day with a sense of smell you had learnt to live without. It had started when she'd met Stuart Slade for the first time. A reminder of what she had been missing, of what she could have again one day.

She turned back to Susie.

'I know, but it's still a shock. Getting the letter on the doormat, all official, wanting all this information from me. Feels like a burglary. I feel violated.'

'I can imagine it must be hard seeing it all in writing. I wonder what's brought it on. I mean, he seemed happy just being separated, I thought?'

'New girlfriend getting serious, I presume. Kids are there this weekend. Maybe I'll find out more after that.'

74

'Have they met her before?'

'I don't know. To be honest, I don't want to go down that road. Makes me feel a bit miserable.'

'Oh, come on, Simon's not worth it. You gave it your best shot. Maybe you both did.'

Susie was only being fair, but fairness wasn't always enough in a friend. They should be on your side totally and utterly, fighting your corner, crushing your enemies and putting your happiness at the centre of their world. Simon had *not* given it his best shot. He had got going as soon as the going got tough.

Susie read her mind.

'I know, that's not what you want to hear. He wasn't the best husband, he let you down, betrayed your trust and broke his promises. But you don't need the acrimony.'

They clinked glasses and Ronnie gave a sigh of resignation. 'Thank you, just for keeping it real. I don't need to become some bitter and twisted old hag, not just yet anyway.'

'In other news . . .' Susie glanced around the bar conspiratorially and leant over the table. 'I have finally finished my PhD., and you will soon be calling me Dr Marshall, if you please . . .'

Ronnie beamed and raised a glass. 'Oh, Suze, that's fantastic! It's been worth the hard slog, then?'

'I had my moments of doubt. But the clinical placement at Ferndale was great. My mentor was none other than the renowned Dr Craig Samuels himself. Remember the psychiatrist from that case at the Old Bailey last year?'

Ronnie's face lit up. 'Yes! Bit of a genius, seemed to have a mind that's police-trained as well as medically brilliant. Completely refuted the defence of diminished responsibility, which isn't that unusual, but he basically suggested he was making up his psychosis to get out of trouble. Brave, doing that.'

'He thinks that there's far too much leaning on mental health defences these days.'

'That's hard to say, without knowing the statistics, but I imagine he'll be in high demand with the CPS if that's the attitude he takes. And for you . . .' she raised her glass, 'an exciting new career beckons. You'll be a brilliant ed psych. I know it.'

'Well, as long as I toe the line, keep on the straight and narrow, and all those other clichés. It's an absolute minefield of professional conduct and safeguarding rules. Confidentiality is the linchpin, they keep telling me. So many protocols to remember and stick to or basically you're out on your ear.'

Ronnie winced. 'I can imagine. There must be times when that really goes against the grain. So, what are you doing to celebrate?'

'Well, I'm having a bit of a gathering on Saturday, if you can make it. At Hemingway's, the new bar on the High Street.'

Ronnie hesitated, then nodded vigorously. 'Sounds fun.' That was her standard answer to invitations these days, the one that was keen without commitment, and Susie spotted it. She looked at Ronnie questioningly.

'I feel a *but* coming. Or maybe an excuse on the night when it's too late to be persuaded?'

'No buts. Just that it's been so long since I had a night out, unless you count taking the kids to the cinema.'

'All the more reason to come along. You deserve it. And you never know, you might make new friends.' Susie's eyes twinkled.

'I'm fine, honestly. I don't need propping up.'

'I'm not talking about propping up. I'm talking about going out, having a good time, letting your hair down. Go on, Ron, I'd love you to be there.'

'Let me check if Simon can have the kids.'

She was flailing around for excuses and Susie saw straight through it. 'Didn't you say it was his weekend?'

Ronnie held up her hands, defeated. 'OK, well, barring any disasters, I'll come along. You're right. It's probably the best thing for me.'

'Wonderful. I really want you there.'

They clinked glasses as the deal was done.

'No regrets about leaving the police, then?' Ronnie took another sip of her drink and felt its warmth sink into her body and relax her.

'Not at any point. Feels like a lifetime ago now.'

'And where are you working?'

'I'm starting next week at a place on the High Street. They provide ed psych services to lots of schools round here, and I'm going to be on the team.'

'Hopefully we'll see a lot more of each other, then. I've missed you.'

Susie swirled the remains of her drink. 'Me too. I miss that whole scene, but I probably only remember the good bits . . . So, what news of the suburban criminal underworld?'

'Nothing dramatic for a while now, which is good in some ways, but I do like a challenge, and there isn't much of that. Baz Munro is still rushing around trying to please everyone and Lydia seems to be under his spell, rather annoyingly.'

'Ah, our illustrious detective inspector . . . So what is it with this Baz? Do you fancy him?'

'God, no.'

'So what, then? What have you got against him?'

Ronnie sighed. 'OK, so if you really want to know, he makes me feel a bit insecure. He doesn't have any commitments outside work that I know of, and I do, and it's just not a level playing field.'

'Doesn't sound like the Ronnie we know and love. Do you really think he's going to usurp you?'

'Not necessarily, but I feel like I'm constantly looking over my shoulder.'

'Let it go, Ron. What will be will be.' Susie sucked her ice cube and then let it fall back into the glass. 'I'm all for equality, but there's no point in assuming there's a threat around every corner. So much more important to get on with the job, let things play out. You're a great detective, and you have absolutely nothing to worry about, believe me.'

'Thanks, Suze. Just what I needed to hear. I obviously don't have enough going on elsewhere in my life.' Ronnie gave her a sideways look.

'Maybe, and let's work on that one. Sounds like my kind of challenge.' She clinked her glass against Ronnie's. 'I remember you saying how good he was on that case with the fifteen-year-old and the handyman. Has the guy done his time yet?'

'Almost. Eight months goes pretty quickly.'

'Sounds like a bit of a light sentence.'

'He pleaded guilty in the end, and, with remorse and no history of bad behaviour, all the mitigating circumstances in the book, it was never going to be a long stretch.'

'Sounds like a turnaround from when you first arrested him.'

'It was a surprise, but with the evidence against him it was his best option, and he'll be on the register for a few years, so no chance of a job around children, which was where he was headed.'

'It was lucky you got him before he did any more damage.'

'But I can't help thinking, well, you know, all that time behind bars won't have softened him. I get this prickly anxiety when they come out, thinking about the new friends they've made in there. It might be just the beginning. Who knows what his next plan might be?'

'Presumably he's got to check in every so often, prove he hasn't absconded.'

'He'll be monitored, but with technology the way it is, we're constantly playing catch-up. Sex offenders are grooming victims all over the internet. Just because he's languishing in his bedsit, it doesn't mean any girl out there is safe. Including mine.'

Susie squeezed her hand. 'I believe in you, DS Delmar.'

Ronnie pulled out her phone to check the time. 'Thank you, Dr Marshall! But right now I have to get home. Promised the kids we'd get a Domino's. Not sure why. Can't stand them. The pizzas, I mean, not the kids . . .'

'Oh, God, I haven't even asked about the twins. And there's me going on about being an educational psychologist. How are they doing? GCSEs this year?'

'Not too bad, I suppose. Eddie got into some trouble at school. Got caught smoking. There was a suggestion of drugs, but it didn't go anywhere, thank God – his mates were the ones with the weed. But we had to give him a serious talking-to . . .'

Susie rolled her eyes. 'And what about Matilda? What's she like these days?'

'Exactly as you'd expect, with that name. Full of character and brassy as you like, never uses one word where five will do, probably will end up a barrister like her father. Has to win every argument, you know . . .'

'Sounds exhausting.'

'I may be calling on your services. That's if they haven't died of starvation in the last few minutes. Do you mind if I dash?'

'Not at all.' Susie jumped off her stool and threw her arms around Ronnie. 'I'll get this. And seriously, do bear me in mind for any psych assessments, won't you?'

'Will do. See you Saturday. Text me the time and stuff.'

As Ronnie stepped into the street, rain began to fall. The days were drawing in and with darkness came that feeling of semi-despair. Every year Ronnie felt it more acutely: the dimming of the light, temperatures sinking, summer shaking itself down into autumn. It should have been a beautiful time. It *used* to be a beautiful time. What had changed? She made a mental note to get herself a SAD lamp.

CHAPTER 10

Merrymount Sixth Form College for Girls wasn't merry, nor was it on a hill, let alone a mountain. It was a purpose-built 1970s building, next door to a boys' comprehensive. Classes were small, the grounds were bordered by high fences, and this was all supposed to make Amie feel safe and contained, but it just made her wary. She tried to keep a low profile and chose a seat at the back of the class, but by the third day, Miss Emsworth, the form tutor and psychology teacher, had moved her to the middle, next to Mia Craven, saying she wanted to get her 'more involved'. Shiny new textbooks and timetables were handed out and the head teacher came in to talk about the importance of seizing opportunities for learning.

At the end of her first week, Miss Emsworth asked Amie to stay behind after school for a chat. The prose poem she had written for the school review sat on the table between them, and straight away Amie regretted writing it.

It slips through your fingers, summer.
Nature preparing for change, bracing itself to be stripped down and put in the freezer.

Leaves blow and skitter down the street, on the run from the cold, while lazy wasps hover around the windfalls, taking a last desperate feed before icy winds send them into hiding.

It's three for two on tacky-back in Tesco and they're shouting, 'New beginning,' when the world is getting ready to sink into coldest darkness.

The teacher looked at Amie with sad eyes. 'That is very moving, but also very bleak. Is that how you feel about the new school year?'

'I always feel like something good is slipping away, when summer's over.'

'What about the cycle of nature – new beginnings, green shoots and life renewing itself?'

'What about the futility of all that?'

'I see what you mean.' The teacher looked at her quizzically, trying to decipher her thoughts. 'But I don't find futility in the cycle of renewal. It might be just a personal viewpoint. I love what you've written, but it sent a bit of a shiver down my spine, I have to say.'

'Is that a bad thing?'

'I suppose not. It's a great skill to manipulate a reader's emotions.'

'I'll write something more cheerful next time.'

Miss Emsworth looked relieved. Amie kept her eyes on her, trying to work her out, but she just looked away again.

'How are you settling in here?' she asked, closing the folder in front of her.

Amie shuffled in her seat and stared out of the window. The sky was bright, as if to prove her wrong. No sense of foreboding about this day.

'Fine,' she lied.

'I just wanted to say that I know you have had time off school, so it must be a bit of a shock coming back. If you need anything, if you're struggling at all, just say the word. I'm here for all the students, not just academically. I'm here to support you in whatever you need.'

'Thanks.' Amie wondered whether she meant it. It was a big promise.

'Is there something else? You look . . . on edge.'

'Things aren't great at home.' Amie clenched and unclenched her fists, digging her nails into her palms until it hurt.

'How?' The teacher leant forward, tilted her head to one side.

'Dad's leaving us.'

Miss Emsworth listened in silence with tears in her eyes. And Amie hadn't even told her how it really felt, the proper detail that made it real. All that detail sat in her head like mud. The bitter, inescapable truth that there was no hiding from any more.

It had happened less than two weeks after they got back from Corsica. Dad had called from downstairs. Not Mon-amie, but 'Amie, Andrew. Please can you come downstairs? Your mother and I need to talk to you.'

She put her head round Andrew's door. 'Dad wants us.'

Her eyes were adjusting to the darkness while her other senses were hit all at once – the stifling warmth, the whirr of technology, the stale smell of socks. The blackout curtains were pulled closed against the evening light, but a single shaft reached across the room, a lightsabre in the darkness that struck the back of her brother's head. He lay sprawled on his stomach on the bedroom floor, knees bent, feet in the air swinging open and shut, open and shut, like clashing windscreen wipers, chin propped on the palms of his hands, face only inches from the laptop screen. That was how he tuned himself out of the real world.

'Andrew,' she hissed, 'why do you make everything so difficult?'

The carpet was invisible under a mass of scattered clothes. Mumbling something unintelligible, he pulled off his headphones, shook out his shaggy mane and staggered to his feet, big boots treading heavily on the multitude of cables and discarded T-shirts. He wore his shoes indoors all the time now, and nobody cared any more. Amie was forever taking hers off, trying to keep to the rules.

'This is all a bit serious, isn't it?' He crouched back down again to press a button on the laptop, to pause his game. 'I mean, what can be such a big deal?'

What followed sat in her head like a series of snapshots, as if to sew them together would bring too much pain.

Amie going down the stairs first, hand sliding down the banister, feeling the wood under her fingers, tracing knots and chips in it she hadn't noticed before.

Andrew following her, heavy-footed, slapping his hand on the wall and swinging his gangly body down the last steps.

Maeve sitting on the edge of the sofa, clasping the seat cushion with white knuckles. Lips pursed.

Stuart, stony-faced, gripping the back of the armchair like a shield.

Amie and Andrew having it explained to them in bursts and pauses exactly how their lives were about to be ripped to shreds.

What they said was probably a jumble of clichés that meant nothing to Amie. *It's not your fault* and *We love you, we're just not in love with each other.* Amie imagined there must be a law about what you said to children in these situations, so one parent could creep away from their responsibilities and promises with no accountability.

After it was over, Amie sat staring at her knees, not daring to look up until Stuart said her name. But it was her real name again, as if she wasn't his friend any more.

Raising her head slowly, she met his gaze.

'Please stay,' she whispered.

'I can't stay.'

Andrew stood up and left the room, muttering something that sounded like *Fuck's sake.* Dad's eyes followed him briefly, then flickered back to the middle distance.

'Where are you going to go?' Tears were pricking her eyes now. She fought them back.

'Only into the annexe. For now.'

'When?'

'Tonight.'

And, with that one word, the tidal wave surged and gathered pace as it headed for the shore. All Amie could see before her was unstoppable devastation. All she felt was rage. The hot, spitting rage of a volcano about to erupt.

Dad moved into the annexe, and everything changed forever.

CHAPTER 11

Someone must have been hovering in the corridor while she was talking to Miss Emsworth, because the news of Amie's parents splitting up spread around school like wildfire. Mia Craven, whose parents had got divorced when she was a toddler, did sympathy like it was a school subject you could get an A in. Amie was wrapped in cotton wool and carried through the day like the crown jewels displayed on a velvet cushion. *Look but don't touch.* She was suddenly the centre of attention again, but, just as it had been with Mum and Dad, it wouldn't last forever, and then where would she be?

The ending came sooner than Amie could have imagined when she overheard Mia talking to the other girls about her in the changing room after games. She was laughing and saying, *I know. I was only being polite and now I can't shake her off. She's like a leech.* There was a burst of muffled laughter, then whispers, followed by what might have been an impression of her, because they all laughed at once without even trying to cover it up. Amie cycled home alone and hid in her room all evening.

Sitting in bed, she scrolled through her social media feeds, trying to distract herself from the hurt, but all she found was endless evidence of how everyone else in the world was better than her. The girls at school had made that clearer than ever, and with Dad leaving and the nightmares about Daniel . . .

Tears rose behind her eyes and she blinked them away. She found a chatroom online where girls who had been through what she had were saying how desperate they had become and how they planned to show the world their pain. Just reading their messages, Amie felt she had been understood.

And then, like a miracle, along came Elisa.

Elisa wasn't like the other girls. She didn't go round liking every single social media post just to keep herself popular. She didn't come into school with a scarf round her neck to hide imaginary love bites, didn't obsessively watch YouTube videos on how to get the perfect eyebrows. She was OK being just her. She and Amie had gravitated towards each other from the start, but neither of them knew when the start was. Her face was familiar, but Amie couldn't place it.

'Have we met before?' Amie had asked, suddenly wary of what she might know, might have heard about her. At the time of the incident at Millhurst High, her identity had been a secret, because *the victim cannot be named for legal reasons*, and she had been grateful for that.

'Yes,' she said. 'Don't you remember?'

It turned out Elisa had been at Millhurst but in another class, and their paths had never really crossed. But, when she looked at her messy crop of blonde hair, Amie couldn't help but think of the girl reaching through the door, pulling Katie away. She didn't want to remind her of that day, because the memories were better left hidden, so she just said, 'Of course, yes, I think I remember now,' and that was enough. She beamed inwardly at the turnaround of loyalties and felt a new warmth inside that kept a smile on her face all day, until Mum's friend Celia turned up.

It was supposed to be a new start, with Daniel Foster all forgotten, but the adults in Amie's life couldn't just let her get on with it. Today, Celia Burrows came by after school on the pretext that she was *just passing*. She worked some evenings at the Birchwood rehab centre on the other side of the new dual carriageway, so it was a lie about passing by.

Amie was just getting her bike out of the racks when Celia appeared, in all her manicured finery, expectant and apologetic. Little Alfie was in tow as usual, kicking a ball around the playground. *My brave little soldier*, she called him. He was nothing of the sort.

'New school looks fab. How are you getting on?'

'Fine.' Amie hoped that was enough to get the message across that she wasn't in the mood for a chat.

'And how are things at home?' Celia persevered.

'Fine.' It was none of Celia's business. *Ask Mum. Ask Dad. Don't make me spell it out.* She yanked her bike free of the rack and turned to go. Then she turned back. 'Actually, it's not fine. They're getting divorced.'

Celia drew breath before continuing in a kind of new, gentle tone that didn't suit her. 'Oh, Amie, I am so sorry to hear that. But you'll be OK. Happens to so many families.'

Amie started walking away, hot and furious with Celia for being there, right in her face, talking about it as if it was *normal,* when to her it was an enormous swamp sucking her downwards. She made a pretence of accepting her words and forced a smile.

'I just want you to know . . . it's nobody's fault . . .'

Why was Celia saying this? Amie felt like saying, *Yes, it is.*

They both watched the soldier boy make a swipe at his ball and miss. Amie picked up her bag and slung it over her shoulder, put her hands on the handlebars, but Celia just moved to go with her.

'I'd better get going,' Amie said, turning away from her.

'Why don't you leave the bike? I've got the car just outside. I can give you a lift home.'

'That's kind of you, Celia, but no, thank you.' It was never-ending, trying to get rid of her. She was almost seventeen. She didn't need a babysitter.

'If you're sure?'

'I'm going back to Elisa's anyway.'

Elisa was half walking, half running across the playground, backlit by the lowering sun. Amie turned towards her, grateful for the rescue.

But Celia still hadn't finished. 'Wow, nice bike, Amie.' And Amie thought, It's not nice and you know it. It was bright orange, sprayed by Andrew on Mum's instructions. She had tried to explain that if they were that worried about her not having any friends, it would be better to have a bike that didn't make her look like an idiot. Dad had said that spraying it orange meant it would never get stolen, but it also meant that Amie had to ride an orange bicycle. She had screamed at Andrew when she'd come downstairs that day and seen what he'd done. She wished people would shut up about the bike, especially Celia, who was still calling after her. 'Well, we'll always know where to find you, won't we?'

Hopefully not, she thought.

'You looked as if you needed rescuing,' Elisa said, scooting with her left foot on the left pedal and swinging her right leg over the back. Amie cycled after her along the bumpy footpath, dodging lamp posts.

Elisa was the opposite of Amie: dark grey eyes and fair hair, a mix of her Italian mother and the Scottish father she had never met. She had that happy-go-lucky personality that you only found in books, a representation of all those mantras that hung in people's hallways: *Life isn't waiting for the storm to pass, it's learning to dance in the rain . . .* She had something to say about everything, came up with ideas you'd never think of yourself. Miss Emsworth had talked about going to see the school counsellor, but Elisa listened to everything Amie said, so she didn't need anyone else. Elisa understood. Elisa was enough.

They turned into Albion Road, along Larks Lane that led to the old Grayshott Road, and along the pavement under the fig trees, which drooped so low you had to walk on the road to avoid hitting your head. Elisa's house was at the end of a cul-de-sac looking over a park. Nobody came that way and, best of all, nobody else from school lived down there.

Her mother was out at work and it was just the two of them and Scamp the cat. Elisa put two brownies on the table in front of them and sank down next to Amie on the sofa.

'So, who was that woman who wouldn't let you get away?'

'Oh, just Celia, Mum's friend, wanting to know how things are at home, telling me it's all normal having your family break up.'

Elisa inhaled sharply. 'How dare she do that? It must be the most horrific thing.'

Amie felt the warmth of empathy soak through her body. She stroked Scamp, who was making a nest in her lap. The feel of his shoulder blades under his fur made her shiver. He was so vulnerable, so trusting. She wanted to keep him there, making her feel safe and warm. They could look after each other.

'So, am *I* allowed to know how things are at home?' Elisa gave her a nudge, making Amie smile uncertainly.

'Dad's moved out into the annexe. It's awful.'

'Will you have to move house? Are you going to end up with a wicked stepmother?'

Amie's stomach lurched at having her worst fears articulated. It made them real, made it all a horrible possibility. 'I hope not. To both.'

'How does it feel? Watching it all happen and not being able to do anything about it?'

That was a question Amie couldn't fathom, but there was one big feeling inside her that she knew the name of. 'It feels like failure.'

'How can it be failure? You haven't done anything?'

'I was born. I exist.'

'Hardly your decision. Maybe it was just wrong from the start, them being together.'

'Still, that makes me a mistake, which means my life shouldn't have happened. I'm just accidentally left over from the bit when they thought it was right, before they realised it was all wrong.'

'Don't be ridiculous. It's nothing to do with you.'

Elisa was doing her best to help, but in Amie's mind there was no alternative viewpoint. The way things were was the way she saw them and that was that. 'It meant they were forced to put up with each other. If I hadn't been born, they could have been free to live their lives. After . . .' She hesitated. 'After . . . what happened at Millhurst, there was a time I thought we were OK, looking after each other, you know.'

Elisa nodded. But Amie didn't want to go on, didn't want to remember Dad saying what he said on the jetty about the stress of it all.

Elisa read her mind. 'You think it was all too much, in the end.'

Amie just sat and stared at the wall.

'What about Andrew? You're always saying how awful he is. At least share the blame with him.'

'He's Golden Boy these days because he got into Oxford, and he thinks that gives him the right to be horrible to everyone, especially me . . .'

'Glad I haven't got a brother.'

'And you are yet to have the pleasure of meeting mine.'

'Can't say I'm in a massive hurry. There's the whole of the school next door to choose from. And I quite like that Josh guy. You know, the one with the dark hair who hangs around with—'

'I know who you mean,' Amie said quickly. Josh was the one everyone fancied. She didn't want to talk about Josh. Boys just reminded her of what she didn't want to remember.

Elisa saw her face change and reached out to touch her hand. 'Sorry.'

'It's OK.'

Amie looked at her, wondering whether she should tell her about the dreams. But to do so would give them life, would give Daniel Foster a seat at the table he didn't deserve.

Elisa seemed to understand, because she brought the conversation back to Andrew. 'So Andrew must be off to uni soon?'

'Not soon enough.' Amie tried to leave it there, but, once she started, the words came pouring out in a torrent. 'It's so *unfair* how he gets to see Dad all the time. They leave me at home with Mum while they go off to the driving range or football. And Mum likes things to be a certain way, or she goes to pieces, but he doesn't care and deliberately does the opposite. He leaves his shoes undone, doesn't wash his hair, grows it really long, plays music she hates. I have to work twice as hard to make things better. In the end, he's going to make life so bad for everyone that it will all fall apart. And if they take one of us each, he'll go with Dad, I know it.'

Her voice was reaching a crescendo.

Elisa interrupted. 'They won't do that. And you can come and stay here, if that happens.'

'Sometimes I feel as if I'm being sucked back from the beach by the current, you know? Never quite making it to shore.'

'I know what you mean, like a riptide.' Elisa could always articulate Amie's thoughts. She was grateful for that.

'Just like that. Andrew's the riptide.' Amie clenched her fists, forcing her nails into the palms of her hands. Scamp leapt off her lap and the next thing they heard was the cat flap swinging shut behind him.

Stuart was just opening the front door as Amie pushed her bike up the drive. He still had the key. That was good. It was as though he still had rights, still belonged. Maeve was at book club, so it should have been perfect, but they sat at the island making awkward small talk, avoiding the elephant in the room. Then there was a pause, one of those that you just say anything to fill, which was what Amie did.

'Celia turned up at the end of school today. She was waiting in the playground, wanting to give me a lift home. I had my bike, though, so . . .'

'That was kind of her, wasn't it?'

They stared out of the window now, each of them not understanding the other, as he went on.

'People *are* kind, Amie, we need to remember that. Sometimes we don't feel grateful, but we need to recognise good intent.'

'If you say so.'

'Look, it's not going to be easy for the next few weeks, and I realise that for you and Andrew there will be a lot of questions, a lot of frustration. But you need to remember that this isn't just about you. This is about your mother and me and resolving our difficulties. We have no choice here, Amie. Nobody wants to live in an unhappy home. When things settle down, you will be – we will *all* be – so much happier. It's hard to see that now, but you'll see what I mean.'

'I won't. And Mum won't either.'

'She will, believe me. She can't be more unhappy than she is now.'

'That's because you're going! If you stayed—' Her voice rose in panic.

'I can't stay, Amie,' he interrupted, suddenly stern. It was a slap in the face.

'You can. You haven't tried.'

'I have. God knows I have.'

There was a pause while she gathered her last armful of ammunition and threw it at him, piece by piece. 'Some people stay together for the kids.'

He dodged the bullet neatly. 'I know, but that's not necessarily the right thing to do, not every time. Andrew's finished school and you won't be long now either. You're not kids any more. You're young people, young adults.'

'But what about . . .' Her voice shook, as something inside tried to stop the words in their tracks before they polluted the space between them.

'About what?'

She let it out, all in a rush. 'Daniel Foster . . . What happens if he comes back for me and you're not here? What happens then?'

Dad put his head in his hands. The washing machine pinged its reminder that the cycle had finished. A lawnmower started up next door and reminded Amie of Mary Morrison. She wanted her back there, right now, telling her lovely things, not leaving her.

When Dad left to go back to the annexe, Amie went to her room, sat on the bed and stared at her reflection in the mirror. Her eyes were hollow, her face pale and expressionless. She rolled up one sleeve, ran her fingernails down the length of her arm, watched the blood rise to the surface, trickle down from where her sharpest nail had made the deepest cut. The pain in her arm dulled the pain in her head and her heart. It was different. This pain was visible. The other was a ghost that made her think the unthinkable. In the olden days, bleeding exorcised evil from the body. She wondered how much blood she needed to lose to make that happen.

She heard the footsteps outside her bedroom door just in time, pulled down her sleeve and picked up a book, sitting back against the pillows. Maeve pushed the door open and stood leaning on the frame, a glass of something in one hand. Her eyes were unfocused, staring into the middle distance.

'So, your father has bought a motorbike. I mean, can you believe it?'

She said '*your* father' as if he was Amie's fault, as if his motorbike was her fault. She hesitated, knowing whatever she said would be wrong, and Maeve just carried on. Her voice was slurred, like a record on the wrong speed.

'I don't know what he thinks he's doing.' She let go of the doorframe and turned to go, but made sure Amie heard every word. 'A motorbike, for God's sake. At *his* age!'

When she called them down for dinner, she had tears in her eyes. Amie stared at her plate. The food tasted of nothing. Andrew wolfed down his meal and went back to his room, taking the stairs two at a time, muttering something that sounded like, *I can't wait to get out of this fucking madhouse.*

CHAPTER 12

Simon tapped on the window just as Ronnie was about to drive off. She wound it down again. Tilly and Eddie had gone indoors. She'd see them on Sunday evening when he dropped them back.

'I was going to say, the guy who raped the schoolgirl last year, isn't he out of prison now?'

'That's a weird thing to ask. It wasn't rape anyway.'

'Well, whatever it was, I was just making sure he didn't live anywhere around here. I know you're not supposed to tell me anything, but I've heard that the first thing these paedophiles do is go out looking for another child.'

Ronnie looked at him in exasperation. 'You're right. I can't tell you anything.' She pressed the button to raise the window and saw his lips mime words she couldn't read. He lifted his hands in despair and turned back to the house. She waited a second, her eyes on the upstairs window where a figure moved a curtain aside and then let it fall. She caught a glimpse of dark hair. She wound the window down again.

'Oh, and Simon, don't forget to remind Eddie to go to Serena's. He said he'd mow the lawn and it's supposed to rain tomorrow.'

He gave her a thumbs-up and she accelerated away with as loud a roar as she could muster.

Ronnie didn't generally go out on her free Saturday nights. More often than not, she would settle down in front of a film, only to wake up two hours later as the credits rolled, having missed the whole thing. Weekends without the kids were for catching up on sleep, and she relished the thought of an empty house every fortnight. Finding herself single again at thirty-eight, she had managed to resist the pressure to *get out there and have a good time* and was more likely to be found sipping a flat white in a coffee bar than stepping on to a dance floor.

But if Simon could move on, then so could she. She threw open her wardrobe doors and surveyed her meagre collection of outfits. She hadn't bothered buying anything new for some time. It hadn't seemed worth it. She pulled out one piece of clothing after the other, holding it up against her, turning sideways, then flinging it on the bed, until she had exhausted the collection. Settling finally for a pair of jeans and a loose silk shirt, she pulled the front door shut behind her and steeled herself for whatever lay in store.

The cocktail bar was heaving when she arrived, and music pounded in her ears the second she stepped inside. 'Susie Marshall's table,' she shouted in the ear of a waitress, who showed her to the booth where the women had gathered. A sea of eager faces awaited her, and Susie greeted her with the broadest of smiles.

'Liz, Gen, Helen, listen up. This,' she announced, cutting through the thumping music, 'for those of you who don't know her, is the very wonderful Ronnie, also celebrating tonight because she is finally getting divorced from a loser who has run off with some floozy called Natasha . . .' She emphasised the important words *floozy . . . Natasha . . .* so everyone got the gist, then trailed off. She was already clearly several tequilas ahead of Ronnie, who found herself the immediate focus of attention. She was surrounded by a flurry of whoops and flashing white teeth, lipstick, perfume, air-kissing and shouting in each other's ears. Margaritas were ordered and poured, and she did her best to catch up and answer the interrogators.

Did he cheat on you? How did you find out? What did you say? Have you met her? The questions came thick and fast, and she realised she didn't know the answer to a lot of them.

Had he cheated on her? That was the question she had always done her best to avoid answering. When they'd split up, she had ignored the fact he always kept his phone hidden and went away for unexplained weekends of work. She hadn't questioned his assurances that there was no one else involved; she hadn't gone through his pockets, read his emails or abused her professional privileges to track his phone. What kind of detective did that make her?

When he moved out, she had told the children it was a trial separation, that Dad was feeling stressed and depressed, needed some space to think. She had told them they were loved, that nothing would change, and, luckily for them, very little had. She and Simon had remained civil to each other, on the surface at least, but perhaps that was the reason the divorce papers had come as such a shock. Until now, there had been no real severance; the emphasis had been on amicable separation, and she had been in denial that it would ever go further. Denial had been her means of coping.

Now, under the critical, quizzical eye of the sisterhood, and emotionally recharged by a strong cocktail, the truth hit her hard. Natasha had replaced her in Simon's life. She could do what Ronnie couldn't. She made him happy.

Ronnie took herself off to the bathroom to gather some vestiges of composure.

'Ron, are you OK?' It was Susie, knocking on the toilet door.

'I'm fine,' she sniffed.

'No, you're not. Get out here. Come on.'

She came out of the cubicle, letting herself be wrapped in the arms of someone who knew she was suffering much, much more than she had let on. 'I suppose I just haven't let go yet.'

'I know, Ron, I know. It will pass with time. Have another drink.'

When Serena opened her front door the next day, she looked slightly aghast.

'What happened to you? You look terrible.'

'Thanks. Girls' night out. A rare occurrence, not to be repeated for a long time.'

'Need a coffee?'

'Yes, and water, and maybe bacon and eggs. Whatever you've got.'

It was a cottage half the size of Ronnie's place, and the opposite in every way. Where Ronnie had convenience, Serena seemed to have made things deliberately difficult for herself. Ronnie's modern, architect-designed flat boasted state-of-the-art speakers sunk into the ceilings, a forty-two-inch plasma TV on the wall of the open-plan kitchen/living room and remote controls for all the lighting, heating and blinds. You could, and she often did, sit in one place and operate everything with the touch of a button, bewildering unsuspecting guests when lamps came on and a gas-effect fire leapt into life without anyone moving an inch. The residents of the gated development had complimentary membership of the gym and underground pool, where stressed commuters could pound up and down the lanes, slogging world-weariness out of their systems.

It hadn't been Ronnie's choice. She was more eclectic in her taste, preferring to live in a patchwork of old and new, of classic and modern, antique and hi-tech. It was Simon who had been determined to have the latest in everything money could buy. His career in the law had permitted this extravagant purchase, and his departure had left it in the hands of his less enthusiastic soon-to-be-ex-wife.

'Got any ibuprofen?' Ronnie pulled open the cupboard above the bathroom washbasin to see an array of pills of different colours in bottles and packets before her. 'Blimey, I didn't realise you had your own private pharmacy.'

'Here.' Serena was closing the door, handing her a packet of more familiar drugs and a glass of water.

Waiting for them to kick in, Ronnie sat in the kitchen, taking in the idiosyncrasies that defined her sister. Viewers of *Through the Keyhole* would be baffled by the incongruity of it all. A traditional kettle sat whistling on the stove and a jug of wilting delphiniums stood in the centre of the round oak table. On open shelves, rows of chunky glass jars holding mysterious grains stood alongside a pile of mismatched pans of various sizes. Some blackening bananas languished in a fruit bowl and a few eggs in another one that Ronnie recognised as having made at her pottery class. *Simon won't have it in the house*, she had said, handing it over. *Says it doesn't match anything*. The place was a mixture of cosiness and neglect. There was everything you needed, but you might struggle to find it.

Serena cracked two eggs into a pan and Ronnie watched them sizzle in the hot oil.

'So, tell me, how did you get this hangover from Hades?'

'Susie's fault, initially anyway. She's just qualified as an ed psych, and it was an excuse for a night out. We went to Hemingway's – you know, the bar just on the corner of the High Street?'

'That cattle market? Young men on the lookout for rich divorced women? Doesn't sound like your scene.'

'Blimey, is that its reputation? God, no, but apparently I had a blast.'

'Is that what it was like? A cattle market, I mean?'

'A bit, I guess, as in there were lots of men and women in a small, dark, crowded place.' Ronnie hesitated again, realising she was struggling to remember any detail at all.

There was an early part of the evening which still stood in sharp focus, but after a certain point, everything clouded over, like the gradual onset of blindness. She tried to focus on the beginning of the night.

'Lots of you?'

'Susie had invited everyone she knew, I think, and she insisted on telling them that I was a) wonderful and b) a right mess, so I had people buying me drinks and trying to get me to pour my heart out all night.'

'OK, so nice people, then, at least.'

'I suppose so, although I can't actually remember that clearly . . .'

'Ron, that's not like you!' Serena turned round, wide-eyed.

'No, I know. I just hope I didn't embarrass myself.'

'Don't give yourself a hard time. You went out for a few drinks. What's the problem with that?'

'I don't know. Just a nagging feeling, somewhere, that something bad happened.' She looked at her hands, turned them over, examined her knuckles. 'It hurts here.' She touched a bruise on her wrist.

Serena slid fried eggs on to the plate. 'It will come to you.'

'Not sure I even want it to.' Ronnie wolfed down her breakfast, while Serena pushed a bit of toast around her plate, chin in hand. Ronnie put down her fork and reached out to her. 'Sorry, all about me and I haven't asked you anything. I hope Eddie did a good job on the garden?'

'He did a great job, mowing, clearing leaves, all tidy afterwards.'

'And you? How are you coping?'

'Oh, I'm OK. I was just thinking, you know, when you said you couldn't remember. It kind of takes me back. You lock up all the unpleasant memories safely in the dark recesses of your mind, then you end up in therapy bringing it all up again, like vomit.'

Ronnie pushed her plate away. 'Good timing with that comment.'

'Sorry. I didn't mean—'

'I know. I meant . . .' Ronnie reached for words to explain that she meant the vomit, rather than the night they were both thinking about. They were silent for a minute, remembering the events that night in Waterman Lane that had bound them in secrecy for so many years.

Outside, rain was falling and the sky was heavy. Serena put a record on. She must have been the only person left with a record player from the eighties rather than a faux-vintage imitation. It was Bob Marley's 'No Woman, No Cry'. Ronnie had never liked the song. Surely it should have been the other way round? It was men who made you cry.

Serena read her mind. 'You're thinking about Simon again.'

'Maybe. I just worry that we made the wrong decision.' Ronnie felt her leg jittering involuntarily under the table.

'Ron, you know there's no point in going down that road. What's done is done, and I don't like to throw blame around, but he was the one who broke the wedding vows.' She gave Ronnie's arm a squeeze. 'Water under the bridge. Turn the page. Move on.'

'You're right. Any idea how I do that?'

'Just do it. You're always telling me to man up and manage my life without leaning on pills and therapists and then you get that *helpless victim* look in your eyes whenever you bump into Simon's new woman. Where's your spirit gone?'

Serena could certainly throw the mud back at her when she wanted to. It was a fair comment. She did really need to pull herself together.

Back home in the flat, Ronnie nursed the rest of her hangover on the sofa, cursing having wasted a whole day of freedom getting over a night she couldn't even remember enjoying. Simon dropped the twins home at seven, and there was an immediate row about who would have a shower first.

Ronnie's phone pinged. It was a message from Susie.

How are you feeling? Did you get home OK? Felt bad about leaving you but you were having such a good time . . . !

She didn't remember having a good time, let alone getting home, and why had Susie left her there?

She typed a quick response.

Am OK, thanks! Chat later.

Then she switched off her phone. It was time for more important conversations. She wanted her children with her, wanted to make the most of every second she had with them. She pulled Tilly down next to her on the sofa.

'So, tell me about Tilly's world. What's the gossip?'

Swathed in a towelling dressing gown and turban, Tilly let herself be cuddled, then looked at her mother searchingly and said, 'That's funny. I thought you were going to ask about Natasha.'

'Not at all.'

'I bet you're wondering, though – is she pretty, are they happy . . . ?'

'Actually, Tilly,' said Ronnie, settling down next to her, 'I don't give a monkey's about her. I want to talk about you.'

'Really?'

'Really. And I wish you weren't so surprised. You and Eddie are the centre of my universe. Don't make it sound like I've been neglecting you!'

'Ha! Don't worry, Mum, we're not calling Social Services just yet.' Tilly gave her a hug. 'Now, where shall we start . . .'

Tilly was still talking when Eddie finished his shower. Ronnie had heard about every girl in the class, what they said about each other behind each other's backs, who fancied whom and who had lost their virginity. Parties, alcohol, sex, drugs, it all poured out without reserve, without invitation, and all Ronnie cared about was not the facts and opinions being relayed, but that, throughout the break-up and the complicated years that followed, she had kept the lines of communication open with her fifteen-year-old daughter. That was the most important thing of all.

At that moment, Eddie came crashing into the room. 'Hope I'm not interrupting a girly chat.'

'Yes, you are,' said Tilly, throwing a cushion at him. 'But we'll let you off this time. By the way, I was wondering – how is Auntie Serena?' She got up and perched on a stool at the island, where Ronnie had just started chopping onions, suddenly stupidly hungry again.

'Why do you ask?' Ronnie played for time.

'Just that she's always, well, you know: distant, a bit odd, not quite all there. Eddie said—'

'Shut up.' Eddie glared at her. 'I didn't say anything.'

'It's fine to ask, though,' said Ronnie. Teenagers were perceptive. 'She is fine, she's been through lots of difficult stuff in her life, and sometimes that catches up with you and you have to get back on track.'

'You mean she's in therapy?' asked Eddie.

They knew so much more than you expected them to know. There you were, pussyfooting around difficult issues like sex and relationships, mental health, drugs, self-harm, and there *they* were, anticipating your every word, not just up to speed but further ahead, and often in a position to tell you a thing or two.

'I'm not going to discuss everything with you two, because I'd rather Serena talked to you herself, and she can tell you in her own words. But, yes, she is going to a thera-pist once a week, and it's all good. You youngsters should remember that. Don't resort to booze and drugs when things get on top of you.'

'Mum, are you hungover?'

'Tilly!' Ronnie raised the saucepan in mock anger and laughter filled the room. Her little ones were growing up. There was no escaping that.

CHAPTER 13

'I'm off to the Slades' to deliver the bad news. Any last-minute top tips?'

The smiling face around the partition wall again. The way he managed to maintain such a buoyant mood whatever the subject matter was verging on annoying.

'Sarge?'

Ronnie checked herself and forced a smile back. 'Sorry, Baz. I was miles away. No, I think you've got it covered. You OK to go ahead with Overton?'

'Of course. Ready for anything, sarge, you know me.'

He was nothing if not confident, even smugly so, Ronnie thought. But she needed to let it go. He was, after all, about to go and deliver a difficult message to a family who had been through hell.

'Well, thanks for doing it. But don't imagine it will be an easy conversation to have. There will be a lot of questions. They'll want to know exactly where Foster is going to be living, lots of stuff you can't tell them, but make sure they know he has strict conditions attached to his release and he can't go anywhere near her. He knows that any breach of the rules will land him back behind bars.'

'Got it.'

She lowered her voice. 'Oh, and give them my number, just in case.'

'Your personal number?'

'For emergencies.'

'But what about protocol? Lydia wouldn't agree to that.'

'I know. As I said, it's just in case.'

She watched him from the window, walking purposefully towards his car, climbing in and starting the engine. He swung out of the gates to the car park and disappeared, leaving her breathing long, slow breaths to calm the nerves that she couldn't explain. The twins were a year younger than Amie, and Amie had been in the wrong place at the wrong time. It could have been anyone.

She couldn't begin to imagine what it must feel like to be Maeve Slade, watching her daughter's assailant walk free. She needed to stay close, to make sure Amie was safe.

'DS Delmar?'

She spun round. 'Ma'am, hello. I was just—'

'Can I have a word?'

Ronnie followed her into her office. Since the DCI had moved to the top floor, Lydia had inherited his workspace as well as most of his workload. On her desk were three neat piles of paper and cardboard files and a hardback notebook with an expensive fountain pen placed on top. She sat heavily in her leather chair and swivelled to forty-five degrees from the table, just enough to not be facing Ronnie directly but still have her attention, then reached out for the fountain pen, which she held and twisted slowly, with the thumb and forefinger of each hand.

The DI's message was short and to the point. There had been a complaint against Ronnie by a member of the public. The information was vague and it wouldn't amount to anything monumental at this stage, but there were issues around misconduct, which, if proven to be true, might have consequences for Ronnie's career, at least on a temporary basis, pending further investigation.

It was one of those conversations where the words and their meaning were disconnected, like journalists talking about *collateral damage* as if it were a sprained ankle or a dent on the car bumper rather than the deaths of innocent people. Like *we're going to have to let you go*, which implied you were a bird trapped in a cage, desperate to escape. Lydia stopped short of firing her at least, so perhaps she was supposed to be grateful for that. But all Ronnie could feel was utter incredulity.

'Do you have anything you'd like to add at this point?' Lydia had swivelled back to face front. It was time for Ronnie to give her side of the story. 'Can you tell me what you were doing on Saturday night that might have given rise to this?'

Ronnie was too stunned to speak. It didn't make any sense. She stared back at Lydia in disbelief, looked right and left as if she was going to find an audience of practical jokers.

'Please go ahead. I'm listening.'

Ronnie took a breath to calm the fury that was smouldering inside her.

'On Saturday night I was out with some friends. We may have been a bit rowdy. It happens to everyone once in a while. But I don't think I did anything *wrong*.'

'Not what we've heard.'

'Well, I need details. What have you got? What exactly am I supposed to have done?'

'As I said, I can't disclose any more at this stage. Except that it is possible you will be charged with bringing the force into disrepute, if the allegations turn out to be true.'

'And I vehemently deny that I have ever done any such thing . . .' The words came out automatically. Denial was meaningless without memory.

'Unfortunately, DS Delmar, you aren't going to be the judge of that.' Lydia faced her now, giving her the look that always made Ronnie feel five years old.

She took another deep breath. She mustn't rise to it, but her gut instinct to do just that was fighting against her self-control, and winning. She exhaled slowly. 'No, ma'am, I realise that.'

'We should have some news for you when I've seen the relevant CCTV, but hopefully that will establish that this has been some case of mistaken identity or petty exaggeration. Meanwhile, I hear DC Munro has gone to see the Slade family to brief them on Foster's release.'

'Yes, he's just left.'

'Let's hope we can live up to our promises to protect that girl.'

'I'm sure DC Munro will give them the reassurance they need,' said Ronnie.

'Oh, I'm sure he will.' Ronnie thought she saw the trace of a smile on Lydia's lips as she turned to go.

Fuming, she forced her mind back to the weekend's outing. Something she had done or said had led to a formal complaint, and she was determined to remember what it was, however deep she had to dig.

The beginning of the evening was clear in her mind. She had joined the group, talked and drunk for an hour or so before heading off to the loos, for some peace and quiet more than anything. Susie had found her in there, sobbing, and brought her back to the group. There were men at the table who hadn't been there before, perching on stools inserted at angles between the women. She tried to visualise their faces.

Normally she prided herself on her recall skills. The number of times she had interviewed a witness who had no recollection of her attacker's appearance had taught her to observe everything with microscopic keenness. *Notice what's around you, who's around you*, she used to tell the twins, when they were still young enough to care what she did for a living. *One day it might matter.* But right now her mind wouldn't obey. Each time she tried to focus, relax her brain to let the detail flood back, the image closed down. It was as if she was being shut out of her own memory bank.

At the end of the day, she took out her phone and typed a message.

Can I pop round?

Serena was quick to answer.

Of course. I'll put the kettle on.

Ronnie didn't say she'd prefer a glass of wine. It seemed inappropriate given the circumstances.

As her sister poured the tea for the second time that week, she replayed her conversation with the DI.

'Bloody Lydia wouldn't give me the full picture. *And* I can't make my brain remember what happened. It's all a fog. I'm never drinking again.'

'What about Susie? She must have some idea what happened if she was there?'

'She just said I was drinking and chatting with people all night and she left before I did. Nothing to report.'

'Sometimes, if you stop thinking about something for a bit and then go back to it, the answer is suddenly crystal clear. Try it.'

So Ronnie went over the events of the evening again, and patchwork images reordered themselves as she questioned them and tried to bring them into focus. She set her mind on the early part of the night, hoping that the momentum of memory would bring the latter part trailing behind, unable to escape her mind's grasp.

The women in the group had been raucous, to put it mildly. She hadn't met that type for a while, and their sassy bravado and sense of entitlement, perhaps just entitlement to having a good time, had been unsettling. She couldn't engage with it, which might have made her come across as stand-offish. At some point, a few got up to dance.

She took a breath, let it out slowly, tried to let the memory wash back over her. The more you tried to remember, the harder it was. *Relax.* Then suddenly she saw him in her mind's eye, a man sitting too close to her, wearing a Burberry jacket, asking her questions, looking into her eyes. Then he was gone, like a deleted screenshot, and she had nothing. Was he the one who had sent in the complaint? And, if so, what could she possibly have said or done to warrant it?

'Can't you go on the system to find out who made the complaint, or exactly what it was?'

'That would be too risky. I'm sure they will tell me eventually, but they're *investigating*, apparently.'

'Couldn't it just be a pack of lies, a practical joke, or someone with a grudge?'

'All of those, in theory.'

Serena stirred her tea, watching the tiny whirlpool in the cup. 'What's at stake for you, worst-case scenario?'

'Well, a misconduct charge could lead to me having to step down, go back to uniform.'

'And the absolute worst-case scenario?'

'Gross misconduct. That's a whole other ballgame. I'd rather not think about it.'

'What's the defence? Can you claim diminished responsibility, like with a murder charge?'

'I'd be on dodgy ground saying I wasn't responsible for my own alcohol intake.'

'Unless your drink was spiked. It happens more often than we think.'

Ronnie put her head in her hands. 'Which I can't prove now. Any traces of anything would be out of my system.'

'How did you get home?'

She closed her eyes, shaking her head. 'I don't know. I don't have any memory of getting home at all.'

'Fuck.'

Serena never, ever swore.

CHAPTER 14

What struck Amie most at home was that there seemed to be less of everything, especially talking. On the rare occasions Stuart was around, he and Maeve spoke to each other just the minimum amount, like, *Have you paid the milkman?* and *Can you pick Andrew up from football training tonight?* and the minimum seemed to get even less by the day. There was one less place set at the table every night after he moved out, and no beer in the fridge. She didn't remember the last meal they'd eaten all together, but she was glad she hadn't known at the time that it was the last meal. Maeve started having migraines, going to bed in the afternoon and sometimes not getting up till the next day.

Stuart's presence was announced by his motorbike in the drive, gleaming and powerful, leaning at a jaunty angle on its stand, a symbol of his new life. Maeve refused to look at it and turned away when she walked past it. You might not have noticed her look away, because she'd suddenly be frowning at a smear on the car window or picking up a leaf that had blown on to the drive, but Amie noticed it every time.

Then, one day, two police officers came to the house. Dad was late for the meeting and Mum refused to even look at him as he sidled into the kitchen, making whispered apologies. They told Amie she had nothing to worry about, that Foster had served his term and was going to be living a long way away from her. He'd be working for the local authority under strict supervision. They smiled empty, kind smiles, asked if she had any questions, and left together, swinging symmetrically into the front seats of their car and pulling away with a wave.

Amie crept upstairs. Andrew's door was open.

'What just happened?' he said without turning round from his screen.

'They came to say he was out. He's free.'

'Has he got a tag or something?'

'He's not allowed within twenty miles of Millhurst. They know what he does all the time.'

'OK, but what if you go somewhere else, and he's there?'

He always had to spoil everything.

'I'll just have to make sure I don't go too far from home.'

'And what if he gets a phone and finds your number?'

'Shut up!' She slammed his door, then her own, sat down on the bed, trying to calm her racing heartbeat.

The seeds of doubt had been sown. She pulled the curtains closed, then opened up her phone and disabled all the location settings, just in case Daniel Foster was cleverer than they thought. She forced herself to remember his face, so she'd recognise it in a crowd, imagined it with glasses, a beard, all the different things he could do to disguise his identity.

That night, she dreamt about Daniel asking what was the matter with her, why had she ruined everything, what was she going to do to make it right? – and telling her how he was going to punish her. She woke in a sweat, heart pounding, rigid with stress.

The next day, Miss Emsworth stopped Amie in the corridor and asked her to come by the staffroom after lunch. Elisa was off school with the flu, so the alternative was making conversation with girls like Mia Craven, and it brought Amie out in a sweat just to think about it.

Miss Emsworth took her into a classroom and shut the door. Amie tried to smile because she knew it was expected, but it was more of a grimace. She was probably going to be asked how she was feeling again.

'Don't worry, Amie, this won't take long.'

She pulled up a chair and motioned for Amie to sit down.

'So, Amie.' She adjusted her seat and clasped her hands. 'I just wanted to check that you're OK, at school, at home, everything like that. Lots going on for you, lots of changes, and I'm just making sure you're coping with it all.'

'I think I'm OK, so far. Thank you for asking.'

'And is there anything you want to talk to me about? I mean, anything at all?'

She was hot, under the intensity of the teacher's gaze. 'No, I don't think so. I'm fine.'

I'm fine. The lie must have shown through this time, though, because Miss Emsworth inclined her head, with the tiny frown that said, *Carry on . . . I'm listening . . .* and Amie found herself spilling out a bit of the truth, a few heavy raindrops from the enormous thundercloud that was taking up space in her head.

'Don't worry. Everything is confidential.'

She meant the Daniel thing. Nobody could say the words.

'He's out of prison,' she blurted out.

'How do you feel about that?' Miss Emsworth's eyes were wide and full of sympathy.

'I'm scared. In case he comes looking for me.'

The teacher nodded slowly with a trace of a frown between her wide eyes. 'But you do know he will be monitored very carefully. He can't come anywhere near you.'

Amie looked beyond her face to the blue autumn sky outside. A pigeon flapped past the window.

'I always used to have nightmares about what happened,' she whispered, 'and now they're about what might happen if he finds me again.'

'It must be awful. And what you went through. I can't imagine . . .'

Amie bit her lip hard and blinked back tears. 'He wants to punish me.'

'He has nothing to punish you for! He admitted what he did, didn't he? Expressed remorse?'

'That was just to get a shorter sentence. I looked it up. He said all that so he could get out earlier and it worked.'

She clenched her hands together to stop them from shaking. 'I know he's coming for me.'

'How do you know?' Miss Emsworth leant forward, head inclined.

Amie breathed a deep breath in and out to calm herself. 'I just know.'

Miss Emsworth looked as if she was about to cry, then a thought seemed to occur to her.

'Is there anyone you talk to, in school or outside?'

'Why?' She was trying to pass the problem to someone else, Amie thought.

'I mean, the girls in the class can be a bit cliquey, but they are a nice bunch.'

Amie shifted in her seat and looked at the clock. 'I'm not really much of a clique person. One friend is enough for anyone, isn't it? And I kind of prefer being on the edge.'

Miss Emsworth raised her eyebrows and nodded, looking slightly sad. 'OK, if you're happy like that, of course, we're all different, and school isn't always very forgiving of that fact.'

The attention was unnerving and it was a relief when Miss Emsworth wrapped things up a few minutes later, shuffling papers on the desk in the way that says, *We're done here*.

She tilted her head one last time, and almost whispered, 'Well, I'm here if you need to talk about anything. Please remember that. And I mean anything. About the nightmares, about schoolwork, whatever it is.'

The bell went and Miss Emsworth held the door open for the first returners from the fresh outdoors, rosy-cheeked and dishevelled, glowing from their secret lunchtime assignations at the fence that separated the two schools.

Amie slipped back into her seat. Mia Craven raised her eyebrows at her and turned to whisper to the girl behind her, who stifled a snigger.

The topic for the afternoon's double psychology lesson was determinism versus free will. For a while, Amie was absorbed by something other than what her classmates thought of her, what was going to happen to her family, and what Daniel Foster was planning. The question at the heart of it was whether your life was mapped out at the start by your genetic make-up, or whether you were free to live it as you chose. Determinism sounded like an excuse for doing whatever came into your head, but then Amie wasn't aware of having made many decisions herself. Most things that happened were because of other people who, presumably, were acting according to their own programme. It made sense. But it meant you should be able to predict the future as well, if you had all the information.

She cycled past Elisa's on the way home, not consciously, but drawn in on an invisible thread to a place of solace. Elisa was sitting on the doorstep, throwing conkers into a flowerpot.

'Thought you were ill?'

'Not that ill. Sick with boredom. Come and sit down. What did I miss?'

Elisa wanted to hear everything about everything, especially where it concerned her. Amie told her about the chat with the teacher and Elisa jumped on the subject of friendship. She seemed pleased Amie wasn't keen on getting in with the in-crowd, but she wanted more.

'So, what do you think are the essential qualities of a good friend, then?' she asked. It was an innocent question, her face all angelic as if to say, *Just describe me, that will be fine.*

'Well, not someone who's stuck at home, ideally,' said Amie, without thinking.

'What? You mean you've found a replacement for me already?' Elisa prodded her in the ribs in a show of humour, but Amie saw something else in her expression that made her suddenly wish she had gone straight home.

'I need to go.' She picked up her bike and swung her leg over the saddle. 'See you at school when you're better.' She meant *a better friend.*

It was almost dusk as she turned into Pine Walk. The damp, intoxicating perfume of autumn filled her senses. The last of the cut grass and the first bonfires. There was a new chill in the air. Lights were coming on in the houses which stretched into the distance like cruise ships hovering on the horizon. Perhaps if she swam out there the crew would haul her in, wrap her in blankets and feed her hot chocolate with marshmallows. She could pretend she had suffered memory loss, and some nice family would take her home with them and give her a new life, a family who wouldn't leave, which she didn't have to fight to keep together, and fail every day.

She turned her key in the lock and took one last greedy breath of freedom before stepping inside. They were in the kitchen, Andrew slouching on a stool at the island playing on his phone, Maeve pouring boiling water on to something in a saucepan while sausages sizzled in a pan. There was a smell of burning meat and boiling vegetables.

Amie pushed open the back door to let the smoke and steam out. 'Mum? Are you OK?'

Maeve hadn't heard Amie come in at all and jumped, scalding herself on the kettle, then rushed to the sink, where she held her hand under cold water for ages, and Amie wished she had kept her stupid mouth shut.

She couldn't eat the sausages, because she was full of darkness again and there was no room for food inside her as well.

Andrew ate quickly in silence and stood up, scraping his stool back, slicing through the silence like a guillotine. Maeve stood by the sink, leaning back against the granite, watery eyes staring out of the window into the distance, in a trance.

'Mum . . .' Amie reached out to touch her hand. *Don't all collapse around me*, she thought desperately.

But it was all too late. Maeve pulled her hand away. 'It's fine, Amie, all fine. What's done is done. You have nothing to worry about.'

The reflection of her face in the window said the opposite.

Amie was still awake, lying rigid on her back, when the front door creaked open and clicked shut. Her eyes popped open, heart beating. She slid out from under the duvet, pulled open her bedroom door and crept downstairs to the kitchen, where a figure was standing motionless, half turned away next to the dark window, tapping on his phone.

'Dad?' she whispered, trying not to make him jump. 'Why are you here?'

'Amie! Don't creep up on me like that!' He slipped his phone into his back pocket and turned towards her.

'Sorry . . .' She hesitated, fighting rage because he'd called her by her proper name again. She waited for him to correct it, say something nice. She didn't want to go back to her room until he did, but at the same time she didn't want it to be like a warning: *I'll stay here until you do.*

'No, *I'm* sorry, Monamie.' He held out his arms to her. 'I came in to pick up some post. Why are you up so late?'

She relaxed, felt the stress drain away. But he smelt of somewhere else and she felt a pricking behind her eyelids. She felt an overwhelming need to make him stay.

Reading her thoughts, he pushed her away slightly, holding her by the shoulders. 'You look all worried. What's wrong?'

She wanted to tell him everything: that it wasn't working for her, this life without proper parents. She wanted to tell him that she couldn't eat or sleep, that she didn't want to live like this any more, and that sometimes she didn't want to live at all. She wanted to tell him how she'd been abandoned and bullied, even Elisa was being weird, and she was having nightmares again.

She wanted to tell him that Daniel Foster was coming back for her.

But instead she told him happy things, listing them like the shopping in 'I went to market and I bought . . .'

He sat down, eyes on her now, all attentive, and she glowed inside.

'What are you doing in psychology this term?' he asked.

'Free will versus determinism.' She bit her lip, wondering again whether this whole conversation was part of destiny's grand plan. 'It's about whether we are responsible for what we do, or can we just say it's all out of our hands?'

Stuart's face lit up briefly. 'And what do you think, Monamie?'

Amie traced the pattern of the granite worktop with her finger. 'I think things just happen, because of other things. It makes sense, if you think about it. Isn't that what you used to say – go with the flow?' She was remembering their conversation on the last night of the holiday. She was showing him that she'd listened, that she'd taken on board everything he'd said.

'So you're coming round to my way of thinking, then?' He was tapping his phone again.

'Depends what you mean.' Amie went hot inside. 'Not about you leaving.'

Stuart put his phone down and looked at her with a hint of exasperation. 'We've been through this.'

'I know, but . . .' Amie scrabbled around for the right words. 'Sometimes you might *think* something is inevitable, but maybe it isn't. You can always change your mind – if it turns out to be the wrong thing to do, I mean.'

It was no good. It was all coming out wrong, and his reply was proof of that.

'It's not the wrong thing to do, Amie. It may seem wrong to you right now, but it will turn out for the best for everyone. Trust me.'

But she wasn't sure if she trusted him, or anyone else.

CHAPTER 15

It was just by chance that Ronnie was walking past Baz's empty desk when the phone rang.

'CID.'

There was a pause, then a female voice answered. 'Oh, I was expecting DC Munro.'

'He's away from his desk just now. Can I help? It's DS Delmar.'

'Yes, I hope so. I mean . . . It's Maeve Slade here.' Her voice was jumpy.

'What's happened? Is Amie OK? Did DC Munro take you through the process?'

'Yes, I mean, he did, and it's not that, just that something happened at school. And now there's something else . . .' Her voice was muffled, then clear, then muffled again.

Ronnie picked up a pen and looked around for a notebook. 'Go on,' she urged.

'It's Foster. I think he's been in touch with Amie.'

Ronnie's blood went cold. 'I'll be straight over.'

She picked up her bag and headed back to the car park. She should call Baz, or send uniform, shouldn't be wasting resources on a routine visit, especially having been

131

told she was officially the subject of a misconduct investigation. She could feel Lydia's frown on her already. But this was an exceptional situation, and she felt a connection with Maeve that she couldn't ignore. They had both known the hopelessness of not being there for someone, the guilt of not being able to protect a girl who needed protection, who had a right not to be violated. If she could do something to help, she would, because it felt as if helping Maeve was somehow, in some bizarre way, helping herself.

Maeve was smaller than Ronnie remembered, slighter, looked as if she had missed a few nights' sleep. There were bags under her eyes and her hair was in disarray. She ushered Ronnie into the kitchen and pulled up a stool for her and another for herself, reaching out for a second as she almost lost her balance. Ronnie's arms went out to save her, but Maeve gave her a look. Her hands were shaking.

'Water? Coffee?'

'No, I'm fine. Tell me what happened,' said Ronnie, pulling out her notebook.

As Maeve talked, Ronnie took in her surroundings. All was exactly as it had been a year before, but even tidier, more spartan. The white marble worktops were spotless, the windows sparkled, and there was that familiar odour of bleach that she remembered from their first visit. Simon could live in a place like this. Not a thing out of place. A show home ready for open day.

'I'm sorry for calling CID. It's just . . . well, I didn't know who else to call.'

'You didn't have my number?' Ronnie remembered the conversation with Baz and felt the resentment come pouring back.

'No. Should I have . . . ?' Maeve looked nervous, and Ronnie tried to calm her own fury at Baz for ignoring her instructions.

'I asked DC Munro to give you my mobile number, and I'm sorry if he didn't, but I'm glad I'm here now. So, tell me . . . ?'

Maeve looked hesitant, then breathed in deeply and spoke on the outbreath, in a lowered voice. 'I may have made a mistake . . .' She faltered.

'A mistake?' Ronnie imagined Baz and Lydia shaking their heads and reminding her not to waste valuable police time. She should have sent uniform. That was what she'd be told when they found out.

Maeve twisted her wedding ring on her finger, one way, then the other. Upstairs, a door slammed, and they both jumped.

Ronnie tapped her pen on the worktop. 'What do you mean, a mistake?'

Maeve spoke almost before she had finished, but her answer made no sense in the context of mistakes. 'He's been in touch. Foster, I mean.' She was stumbling over her words, glancing occasionally towards the staircase as if expecting Amie to come running down at any moment. Her face was white.

'In touch how?' The mistake could wait.

Maeve lowered her voice. 'She said she's had a message from him.'

'What?' Ronnie felt a sharp pain in her head, as if she had been stabbed. She was suddenly hot all over, her heart racing. 'Have you seen it?'

Maeve sighed. 'She deleted it.'

Ronnie's heart sank. 'Can I talk to her?'

'She won't come out of her room. I've tried.'

'She's not at school, then?'

'No—'

Ronnie didn't let her finish. 'What else did she say about the message? How was it sent? Was it on text, email, Instagram?' She heard her voice getting more impatient. There was no point in that. The more in a hurry you were, the more slowly things went.

'I don't know. I don't use social media. Does it matter?'

Maeve was picking up on her agitation. Ronnie tried a calmer approach. 'Well, we may be able to access deleted material from her phone if it was backed up somewhere. Meanwhile . . .' She took another deep breath. She needed to sound convincing. 'You have no reason to worry. Any breach of the conditions of his release could destroy his whole future.'

'Do you know what – I'm exhausted with all this.' Maeve leant forward, head in her hands, rocking gently back and forth. Ronnie recognised that feeling. Parenting *was* exhausting. But it was what you signed up for. There were no guarantees it would run smoothly.

'What about Amie's father? Stuart, isn't it?' Ronnie remembered his handsome face and easy charm and wondered if he'd bailed when things got difficult. Serena had a theory that it was always the good-looking ones who wandered off. Perhaps they were spoilt for choice, or perhaps it was the women falling hook, line and sinker for good looks without any regard for compatibility.

Maeve heaved herself back upright and looked at a spot somewhere outside in the distance, beyond the garden wall. 'We're separated now; he's living in the annexe. Are you married?' Her eyes were suddenly on Ronnie, unnerving her, making her want to look away, but she held her gaze.

'Divorced. Or in the middle of it, at least.' She remembered the papers that she needed to sign. Simon had texted her about it again that morning and yet again she had put it out of her mind. Denial.

'It's been so hard. Sometimes I don't think I can take it any more. It's like I've lost touch with myself, who I really am.'

Ronnie looked around the room for clues as to who Maeve Slade really was. Everything about the kitchen shouted conformity and compliance. There wasn't a jar of coffee in sight to disturb the smooth emptiness of the work surfaces. Not a scratch on the chrome splashback. Not a smudge on the window. Perhaps she was polishing her way into some sort of oblivion every day, erasing what she couldn't bear to see and not allowing a trace of imperfection, even in her children.

Maeve's eyes went glassy, then cleared. Tears would be out of place in a show home.

Ronnie glanced at the door. 'Can I go upstairs? Try to get Amie to talk?'

'You can try.'

Maeve showed her upstairs, and went back down to the kitchen, leaving Ronnie to tap on the door.

'Amie? It's DS Delmar, Halesworth CID. Can I have a word?'

No reply.

'You saw my colleague DC Munro the other day, and I'm just following up to make sure everything's OK. Can I come in and have a quick chat?'

Still no answer.

Ronnie hesitated. If Amie wasn't going to play ball, she could just get the question out there.

'Your mum says you had a message from Daniel Foster.'

No answer.

'Is that true, Amie? If it is, we need to talk about it.'

Still no answer, just the slow creak of a cupboard door clicking shut.

'What did it say?'

She left the same pause for Amie to respond, but there was nothing.

'I want you to know that we have taken every measure possible to ensure that he will never come anywhere near you again, but nowadays it's a race to keep up with the technology underworld. So, if this happens, if he does manage to get in touch, we need to see your phone, straight away.'

The door opened so suddenly, Ronnie jumped back in shock. Amie stood before her, barring the way, one hand on the doorframe, the other on the door. She was smaller than Ronnie remembered, thinner, paler, her hair wilder and more tousled.

'Thank you for opening the door. I realise you've probably had just about enough of the police visiting your house.'

'It's OK,' Amie whispered, eyes wide and sad.

'Can you show me your phone?' Ronnie held her hand out, like a teacher confiscating a packet of chewing gum. Amie looked downwards, the admonished pupil.

'I deleted the message.'

Ronnie's heart sank again. She had been hoping, against all hope, that there might be a chance she hadn't.

'What did it say?'

She regretted the firmness in her tone when Amie's eyes glassed over, and tears began to form. 'It said he would find me.'

'Find you?' Ronnie lowered her voice, to combat her utter incredulity as to how it could possibly have happened, how on earth a convicted sex offender had managed to contact his victim the very week of his release. If this were Tilly, she would be in touch with Police Complaints, campaigning for tougher penalties for offenders.

'Yes. Nothing else. Just that.'

'Well, if he tries to get hold of you again . . .' She held out her card.

Amie took it, but didn't let her finish. 'I'll tell you. I promise.'

The door shut again.

Ronnie went back downstairs, feeling drained. She had hoped for more, or less. A traceable message, or some kind of misunderstanding. But there was nothing but a brick wall in her path.

Maeve was waiting for her in the kitchen, eyebrows raised questioningly. 'Well?'

Ronnie perched on a stool and clasped her hands, the way she did when she delivered bad news. 'She agreed to let us see any message that she gets from Foster in the future. That's the best we can hope for right now, and with any luck she's heard the last of him, because we're watching him like hawks.'

'Thanks. I suppose that's all we can ask for.'

Ronnie gathered her things and brightened her tone, trying to sound decisive. 'My first priority is to send someone to see Foster, check out his phone. We'll get the tech guys on the Instagram trail, see what they can dig out.'

Maeve nodded, her expression serious now. 'Thank you.'

'Has Amie had therapy, in the past year I mean?'

'Not, as such.' Maeve seemed unsure.

Ronnie let it go.

'Why don't I have a chat with one or two of Amie's teachers, just to see how things are, and to see if any of them would be willing to keep an ear to the ground, let us know if they pick up on anything?'

'Fine.'

'Anything else, let me know straight away.'

'I don't think I could cope with anything else.'

There was a pause then, as Maeve looked out of the window, the way a child might do when they say something they know has pushed the boundary, waiting for the bomb to fall. Ronnie followed her gaze towards the swaying pines that gave the road its name. Something about her words set Ronnie on edge.

She slid her notebook and pen back into her bag. She should get going. At that moment, the priority was investigating Foster's access to the dark web before he took things to the next level. Carrying out his threat of finding Amie wasn't going to be hard, if he really wanted to. But she couldn't leave the house, or its occupants, without doing something to alleviate her nagging unease.

It was a flash of inspiration that made her pull out her wallet and flick through the cards.

'I may know someone who could help with all the stuff that's going on with Amie. I can see there is a lot more to it than meets the eye, which isn't surprising.' She handed Maeve a card. 'Susie Marshall. Give her a call. She's an educational psychologist, formerly in the police. One-to-one attention might be what Amie needs.'

Maeve nodded, her face impassive. 'I'll call her.'

As soon as she had turned out of the private estate, Ronnie pulled over into a lay-by, relishing the silence as she processed what had just happened. *I may have made a mistake*, Maeve had said, but what about? Calling CID about a deleted text message? Marrying a man who couldn't stay the distance? Or something else?

Her mind flashed back to the police complaint. A thought dawned on her that left an unpleasant taste in her mouth. Had Maeve taken things into her own hands when Amie got the text from Foster, thinking CID hadn't done their job? Had she realised, when Ronnie had dropped everything to respond to her call, that she shouldn't have done what she did?

She forced the idea into abeyance. It was too much. The affinity she felt with Maeve precluded this idea entirely. How could she even have known Ronnie had been at Hemingway's on Saturday night? But then who else could be the informer who wanted to ruin her career? If it wasn't Maeve, that mystery would just have to sit on the back burner for a while.

She called Munro and got voicemail, and was about to – reluctantly – try Lydia, when Baz called her back. She poured out the latest developments and he agreed to follow up with Foster. 'I'll get over there right away, see what's happened. Can't believe we've lost control of him that quickly.'

'That quickly? We shouldn't lose control of him *at all*,' Ronnie pointed out.

'It's very unlikely he's stepped out of line, given the consequences he'd be facing.'

'Do whatever it takes, Baz.' She was glad he couldn't see the look of exasperation on her face.

'Copy that. Oh, and I'm sorry, sarge, for not giving her your number.'

Ronnie was momentarily startled at the apology. So, it wasn't a case of adherence to the rule book after all.

'It wasn't deliberate,' he went on. 'Although I'm sure you must have thought it was.'

He knew her better than she realised. 'Not a problem. Now go and check out Foster's tech skills. I'll see you back at the station tomorrow.'

Next on her list was salvaging her career. She couldn't allow a few drinks on a night out to destroy her future, as seemed more than likely just at that moment. Lydia had given her the impression that a decision would be made at any moment. If she was going to do anything about the allegations against her, tomorrow might be too late.

CHAPTER 16

When DS Delmar visited, Amie had been at home because of what they thought she'd done to Jess Fleetwood, but what happened to Jess was just the result of what had happened to Amie that morning. Determinism. Fate, or whatever you wanted to call it.

Mum and Dad had met the Fleetwoods at the Open Day before term started and since then asked about her way too often – *What did Jessica Fleetwood get in the maths test?* (100%) and *Where did Jessica Fleetwood go on holiday?* (somewhere in the Caribbean). It was like being a spy, reporting on everything she did, everywhere she went. Elisa said they were weirdly obsessed and she should tell them it was upsetting, but Amie never did, nor did she say anything about what had happened with the boys at the school next door.

The boys from Grayshott College prowled round the gates like hyenas at the beginning and end of school. Amie would do anything to avoid them, and fear surged through her body at the thought of having to even cross their path. But that day, arriving a few minutes later than usual, she saw them swarming around the entrance. As she steeled herself to walk past them, one of the boys whistled, but, as she looked up, a half-broken voice said, *Not you, ugly*, and then there was a burst of manic laughter. Jess Fleetwood, a few steps behind her, shouted back to him, *Hey, Josh, see you at lunch break*. And he said, *Come on your own, won't you, babe – don't bring that freak*. And Jess laughed, a raucous belly laugh that brought cries of *What did he say?* and more laughter.

Amie went straight to the bathroom and made herself sick. She went back and sat there again all through break time, digging her nails into the skin on her arms until it bled. The physical pain would numb the pain in her stomach, which turned over every time she thought back to the scene at the school gate. It brought it all back, Daniel Foster and the nightmares, and her heart was pumping with panic. Hurting herself brought distraction and relief, but, when the bell rang, she had to pull down her sleeve and go back to maths with Mr Brunsdon.

Algebra got much harder at A level. Now it was equations that looked more like Chinese proverbs than maths problems, with more symbols than numbers, and no real words other than 'if' and 'prove' and 'show'. Jess Fleetwood was hunched over her desk, busy proving what n was, and probably x and y and z as well, just to beat everyone else. She was clever, beautiful and popular, and she had done nothing to deserve it.

Jess also had the longest, blondest, straightest hair, which must have taken hours to blow-dry every morning. It was the kind of blonde you saw on hair-dye boxes, glossy and thick and poker-straight, and the opposite of Amie's. She had to stare at it all through maths lessons, this hair that made boys fall at her feet, and girls fall over themselves to be in her gang. She'd read about Samson and Delilah. Hair had power.

She wondered what Jess would look like if her hair only went as far as her shoulders, stopping in a neat line just where it met the back of the chair. That would make her more real-life, less fairy-tale princess, and, most importantly of all, she, Amie, would have justice.

Her hands hovered around her pencil case, fingering the scissors, stroking the blades but keeping them hidden.

Elisa was at her right elbow. She could almost feel her breath on her neck. She nudged her with the lightest of touches. 'Go on, do it!' she whispered. 'I dare you.'

Amie glanced up to check where Mr Brunsdon was. He was leaning over Mia Craven's shoulder, pointing at something and waiting for her to work it out.

'Go *on*!'

'No!' It was a crazy idea. She took her hand away, horrified. It could never work out well.

But Elisa's eyes were on her like bullets.

She slid the scissors out of the pencil case. Reaching forward, she lifted the helpless snake of hair with her left hand. It was just another part of Jess, a part of her she didn't need, didn't even notice Amie touching. Then suddenly her vulnerability struck Amie so powerfully that she just wanted to let go, stop things in their tracks right there. There must be another way.

'Go *on*.' The order was clear and angry, and a prickle of fear burned in her stomach.

'No. I can't.'

Amie didn't know if she had whispered out loud or just thought it, but Elisa just leant across her desk and snipped, hard and fast.

Then Jess turned and screamed, staring at her hair lying on the floor, a whole ruler's length of blondeness, and Amie's heart started thumping *run away, run away,* but she was paralysed.

Maeve came in at lunchtime to collect her. Her face was blank and cold. Miss Emsworth looked her in the eyes with a look that hurt to see, a look that said *you have let me down.* Amie didn't say it was Elisa who did it.

At home, Maeve spat out her fury, said how ashamed she was and told her to go to her room. Then she shut herself in the sitting room and Amie could hear her sobbing like a child.

She lay on the bed and stared at the ceiling, finding little patterns in the shadows cast from the landing light. Her mind was numb. She got up again and messaged Elisa.

You shouldn't have done it.

> *Rubbish. She deserved it. Little Miss Perfect needed bringing down a peg or two.*

> *And it's made your mum and dad sit up and take notice finally.*

I'm not sure it was a good way of doing that.

> *And maybe your dad will realise you need*
> *two parents . . .*

She had a point, but Amie couldn't agree with her about it being OK. She couldn't put her hand on her heart and say it was the right thing. She felt a twinge of discomfort as she closed the chat with a thumbs-up emoji.

She stared out of the window at the street beyond the back garden, where little huddles of nursery children gathered fallen leaves for an autumn collage. She wanted to be one of those padded toddlers, podgy hand held high to reach the grown-up; wanted to go back to that time when everyone looked after you because you were small and helpless and it was against the law not to.

CHAPTER 17

Hemingway's looked strange in the daylight – a naked shadow of its night-time self. Ronnie walked past it once before retracing her steps and steeling herself for what lay ahead. She pushed the door open and stepped into the gloom. Her eyes took a few seconds to adjust before identifying a slight figure behind the bar, cleaning optics. He heard the door swing shut and turned around, a bright smile on his face.

'Can I help you? We're actually closed at the moment.'

Ronnie flashed her badge. 'Halesworth CID. We're investigating a complaint against a police officer from a customer on these premises last Saturday evening. Would it be possible to have a look at your CCTV footage?'

'Last Saturday? Sure, I'll ask the boss. I wasn't on that night, didn't realise there had been an incident.'

'We're not sure ourselves yet, but the cameras should be able to shed some light on it.'

'What's your name, can I ask?'

'DS Ronnie Delmar.'

He disappeared and came back a second later with the boss in tow. She was in her mid-thirties at a guess, heavily made-up, wearing a tight red dress more appropriate to a nightclub, Ronnie thought, before remembering that it *was* a nightclub.

She did a double-take when she saw Ronnie. 'Sorry I was expecting . . .'

'A man? Don't worry, happens every day.'

'Amber. Nice to meet you.'

Ronnie shook her hand. 'Likewise. Did your young man explain . . . ?'

'You want to see the CCTV of Saturday night?'

'If that's OK, yes, please. We just need to check the facts behind an allegation.'

Amber looked slightly alarmed. 'There wasn't anything unusual going on. It's usually pretty tame in here, even on a Saturday. I used to work in the City and that was a different story – drugs, fights, everything. You wouldn't imagine it, would you, all those posh lads with their fancy jobs and cars, behaving like hooligans?'

Ronnie could easily believe it. What she found harder to accept was that her own behaviour at any point on that evening had warranted any kind of investigation. The sooner she saw the footage, the better. She glanced out of the window, half expecting Lydia's forensic team to appear, dressed head to toe in white crime-scene suits, looking for clues that would put a nail in the coffin of her career.

'If you come with me, detective, I can show you how the cameras work. They're linked to my laptop in the back office.'

Ronnie followed her out of the bar and down a tiny staircase to a room half the size of a police cell, stacked almost floor to ceiling with files and papers.

'Around what time are you thinking?' asked Amber, clicking on the link and fast-forwarding through a video of blurred grey figures around a bar.

Ronnie thought for a second. 'Let's say nine-thirty onwards.'

Amber stopped the video as the ticker turned to 21.29. 'Shall I leave you to it?'

'That would be great. Thanks, Amber, you've been very helpful.'

'Well, I hope you find what you're looking for,' Amber replied.

I hope I don't, thought Ronnie, as the Barbie doll disappeared back upstairs.

The video was poor quality, even for CCTV. Darkness and the angle of the camera conspired to make it impossible to pick anyone out with any certainty. Ronnie flicked through the different angles, looking for herself. The table where they had sat came into view from time to time, but it was impossible to see who was sitting at it. The camera on the bar was clearer, the light was brighter, but she could only see the tops of heads, and only a rough idea of height and build unless anyone turned around, and, even then, the direction of the light meant that the faces were indistinguishable.

She rewound and studied more of the figures at the bar. A group of young men were buying rounds of pints with chasers in tiny glasses, tequila slammers to give them the courage to talk to women.

One man seemed to be on his own, nursing a pint, looking this way and that but with no obvious companion, even fifteen minutes later, by which time anyone who had gone to the loo would have come back.

She zoomed in, but the angle was still wrong and she couldn't see any of his face at all. She rewound again, studied his physique, the way he held himself, turned his head. There was something familiar about him.

Lydia had said to her once, *The reason you can't place someone that looks familiar is usually that they are not where you expect them to be. Loosen your mind. Untie yourself from expectations.*

She took a deep, slow breath and pulled out the bottle of water from her handbag. Unscrewing the lid, she glanced around the room, took in its contents, emptied her mind of everything to do with the night in the bar. She took a sip of water, counted the pens in the mug that stood on the shelf, read the back of a dusty instruction manual lying next to it. Then she turned back to the screen and clicked on the mouse to bring the picture back.

She stared at the blurred image, zoomed in and back out again. And fury rose inside her like a monster. There was no mistaking the man at the bar. She'd know him anywhere. How far would he go to get what he wanted? How could she ever have been in any doubt?

Hearing Amber calling from upstairs, Ronnie was dragged back to the real world.

'Just finished,' she called back.

'Got what you wanted?' asked Amber.

'As I thought: nothing there to worry about. And thanks again for your time.'

'No worries.'

'Oh, and Amber . . .' She turned back. There was one more thing she needed to say. 'Don't say anything to anyone about my visit, if they ask.'

'I won't.'

As she stepped out into the bright street, she caught sight of Lydia's Volvo pulling into a space a few metres away. Panic rose in her stomach as the door opened. She had seconds to make her escape, and just had to pray that they hadn't seen her car in the next road, and that Amber would keep her word. Putting her faith in universal justice, she turned on her heel and walked fast in the opposite direction, heart thumping. The more distance she put between her and the DI, the more her fear faded and gave way to seething, uncontrollable rage.

The fallout in terms of her career wasn't any better or worse than Ronnie expected, just sooner. She came into work the next morning to find a note on her desk saying she should clear her belongings by midday and stay away from the station until further notice, at least until the committee had come to a decision.

Baz wasn't at his desk. He would be sitting at hers for the next week as acting DS. He was probably already off buying posters for the partition walls. She texted him asking for an update on Foster, and the reply was immediate.

Nothing on his phone but the tech team are on it. I'll keep you posted.

It was a relief, but a confusing and frustrating one. The *tech team* was a glamorous description of one former DC who sat in the basement hacking into people's internet search history, but if that was all they had, then it would have to do. Lydia had made it clear, with metaphorical flourish, that flogging a dead horse in a blind alley was not what she wanted their scant resources spent on.

CHAPTER 18

On the second day of Amie's suspension, the weather got worse. The concrete sky stood like a colourless backdrop to the onset of winter. Leaves came down in flurries as the wind gusted around the trees, carpeting the pavements with brown mess. The sun came out less, they turned the lights on before dinner, and she had to wear socks over her tights because Maeve wouldn't turn the heating on before November.

On the third night, there was a thunderstorm. The tallest, oldest tree that had headed the line of conifers between the garden and the neighbours' driveway blew down, crushing part of the fence. It lay like a murdered soldier, scattering pine needles and cones across the perfect front lawn Maeve was so proud of. But she wasn't upset. She just said if only it had been a few more inches to the right, then it would have hit Dad's motorbike.

Amie screamed at her then, with the full force of her lungs, and it came out as a roar, an unintelligible garbled mess of words, but she poured it out, how she couldn't work or eat, or sleep at night because of everything that had happened, that she was getting threatening messages from Daniel Foster, who was determined to find her and punish her. And yet, even with all this, some stupid motor-bike was more important.

That was probably the reason they said they needed her to see a psychologist. Nothing more was said apart from that Amie was to make the most of it because these things cost money and money didn't grow on trees, in case Amie hadn't noticed.

Susie Marshall wasn't what Amie expected. She imagined psychologists to be grey-haired bespectacled ladies, who smelt of mothballs and lived with cats. Susie arrived at the house wearing leather trousers and biker boots with a floral blouse and chunky silver jewellery. Amie liked her.

The first thing they talked about was confidentiality, because nothing they spoke about would go any further unless Susie believed there was a danger to life. That was a relief.

Then Susie wanted to know about what made Amie happy and sad, the things she did that made her feel good. She drew arrows that went from thoughts to feelings to actions, then back again, to show her how everything was linked, then went on to talk about how everyone had things in their life that made them more fulfilled.

'Let's think about what makes you *you*.' She pushed the pad of plain paper towards her. 'And what helps you make sense of the world.'

Amie had to draw pictures of places, people and activities that meant something to her. It was supposed to be a collection of images that she could look at and remember the good things. Memories of Nana were in it and so was Dad, but not Andrew or Mum, because, as she tried to explain, in stutters and half-sentences, they made her feel stressed and not good enough. It was the same with the girls at school.

While Susie asked questions about her relationships with her classmates, Amie doodled on the paper. Most of it was a mess, and she wasn't sure it was really working, but Susie seemed satisfied. She took the page and looked at it from different angles. Somewhere in the top corner, the number 41 had emerged from the swirls and lines, and Susie asked what its significance was.

'I don't know. It's just a number.'

'Anything special about forty-one?'

Amie rolled her eyes. 'Not exactly special. It's the thirteenth prime number, the sum of the first six prime numbers. Can we move on now?'

Susie was turning the drawing around again, telling her she didn't mean *mathematically,* but Amie just reached for the pad, scribbled it out and started drawing more numbers in swirly style. Soon 41 was surrounded by 35, 57 and 83.

Susie made some notes and took a photo of the page in front of them, then asked Amie why she had cut Jessica Fleetwood's hair.

Maeve must have said something to her. Amie took a deep breath and gripped the sides of her chair.

'I didn't do it.'

Susie looked surprised. 'Really? But you were sent home because of it.'

'I know, but it was Elisa who did it,' Amie said.

'Who's Elisa?' Susie asked.

'A girl in my class.'

'Why did she do it?'

'To get revenge for me, for what happened in the morning. She did it for me.'

The cat was out of the bag. She stared at the table. Muscles tensed all over her body.

'Have you told anyone this, Amie?'

'No. It's easier if I just let them think it was me.'

'Easier? Are you sure?' Susie was looking at her with incomprehension, then her expression turned gentle, sympathetic even. 'Did she *make* you take the blame?'

Amie bit her lip. 'Not exactly. I was about to do it, but I got scared at the last minute, so she took over. She just did it for me – she did what I wanted to do but couldn't.'

'It sounds like she's quite a powerful friend, as friends go?'

'Do you mean she has control of me? Because she doesn't.'

'I wouldn't suggest that.' Susie's voice took on a much gentler tone, as if Amie were a startled animal she needed to coax back home. 'Nobody has control of you except you. But to me this sounds a bit like bullying.' She gave Amie a long look then, right into her eyes and beyond, as if scanning her for whatever alien presence was taking her over and making her do things. 'What do you think?'

Amie felt her insides go hot and cold. She tried to piece together the logic but there was no escaping the fact that she was down a dark cul-de-sac of reason and would have to backtrack.

'In this case, maybe she was being controlling, but that's not what she does normally, or we would never be friends.' She said it with as much certainty as she could.

Susie let her words sink in before asking another question. 'Does anyone else try to control you? Your father?'

'No.' The answer just happened before she had time to think. 'He just goes with the flow.' She let out a laugh, and Susie looked alarmed for a moment.

'How about your mum?'

'Yes, a bit. But I know what she wants. I know how to keep things the way she likes them. Andrew doesn't. Or he won't.'

'How do you two get on, you and Andrew?'

Amie clenched and unclenched her fists under the table. 'We don't. He just does things his way, all the time, and nobody stops him.'

Susie made a note of something, then changed tack. 'Tell me about the incident in the morning. The one that Elisa was encouraging you to get revenge for.'

Amie sat and stared at the table.

'Fair enough. You don't have to talk about anything you don't want to,' said Susie, 'but as you know from all this . . .' she reached over to tap the psychology textbook that lay at the other end of the table, 'the mind is a powerful tool that doesn't always lead us in the right direction. Friends can do the same thing. They try to persuade us to act in certain ways sometimes, but I think the better friend is the one who acts in your best interests. Elisa must have known there was no good outcome for you there, so what was her motivation, I wonder?'

'You mean, she wanted me to get into trouble?'

'Well, she must have known that would happen.'

'But she knew I was upset about what had happened earlier.'

'Upset?' Susie paused. 'Have you heard the expression *the red mist*, Amie?'

Amie shook her head.

'It's what we say when we feel real anger, the kind that stops you seeing things clearly, makes you do things you wouldn't otherwise do.'

Amie let the idea sink in and stared down at the table. 'Elisa knew how I felt and she knew what would make it right.'

Susie looked at Amie searchingly. 'Make it *right*? Do you really believe that?'

'I don't know. I think I did at the time.' She couldn't remember now what she believed, or what she was supposed to believe. Beliefs were mostly futile.

'I don't think you do believe it. And then there's your response to it, Amie, which *is* in your control, because you have free will. You have a choice. You can say *no*, you know.'

Amie's mind flashed back to the day she didn't want to remember. Susie must have sensed it because her expression changed. 'I'm sorry, Amie, that might have been the wrong thing to say.'

'It's OK.'

'Do you think about it a lot, what happened last year?'

'Mostly when I'm asleep. I have dreams, that he's coming back for me.'

'That must be very disturbing for you.' Susie's gaze was on her, intense and searching. 'Is there anything that makes you think he would try to do that?'

Amie stared at her phone on the table. 'I got a message. But I deleted it.'

Susie straightened up. 'What? He has your number?'

'Found me online. I've made my account private now, but there are still requests to follow me from people I don't know.'

'Can you delete your account completely?'

Amie nodded, but that way she'd be isolated in the virtual world as well as the real world, and she wasn't sure she could bear the loneliness.

When Susie left, Amie texted Elisa, because she needed to make the best of the one friendship she had. Elisa told her everyone at school was talking about what happened, that there was almost a sneaking admiration for Amie, that she had taken on the image of some kind of fantasy Robin Hood-type figure. Another rumour going round was that what she'd done was the ultimate feminist act, proving women didn't need long blonde hair to survive in the world. There was even the suggestion that she had done Jess Fleetwood a favour, shown her there was another way.

Then Amie told her about her chat with Susie, and immediately regretted it.

You talked about me? What did you say? Nothing incriminating, I hope . . . ? ☺

Emojis were like the final seal to get rid of any doubt. But underneath it there was a kind of warning that the smile might not be forever.

Nothing incriminating, don't worry ☺

But Amie was worried. She needed Elisa. But she needed her to be on her side, not getting her into trouble. Susie might be right. She was taking Amie over. She was out of control.

CHAPTER 19

Ronnie spent the days that followed her suspension cleaning the flat ferociously, deriving a peculiar sense of satisfaction from scrubbing the fridge and wiping down skirting boards. How ironic that with her determinedly feminist outlook on the world she should take out her stress on J-cloths and bleach. She could be out on the golf course or putting her feet up, and yet here she was in her rubber gloves listening to catch-up episodes of *The Archers*.

With three sparkling bathrooms and the whole flat filled with the scent of Toilet Duck, on the fourth day she collapsed on the sofa and, even more unusually for her, began to cry.

Tilly was first home, bursting into Ronnie's melancholy like a foghorn, only to suddenly retract in shock as she saw her mother stretched out on the sofa, sobbing into the cushions.

'Omigod, Mum, what's happened? Are you OK?'

Ronnie sat up, wiped her face with her sleeve and pulled her in for a hug. You couldn't be sad for long with teenagers around. 'Yes, I'm fine, just things got on top of me, briefly.'

Tilly wrapped her arms around her in a tight embrace. Mother became child and daughter became mother, in a

161

strangely comfortable swap. Ronnie wondered if fathers and sons ever did the same thing, but couldn't picture Eddie comforting Simon and making him a hot chocolate.

'Is it just the work thing,' Tilly asked, 'or . . . ?'

'Why, what else would it be?' At that moment, Ronnie had forgotten anything else existed. Even Simon's new girlfriend peering out from behind the curtain had faded from her worry list.

'Oh, I don't know, other stuff – Dad?'

'What about him? Is there something I should know?' If there was, she might as well hear it now; it couldn't make her feel any worse.

'No! It's not that. I just thought, maybe you were sad about the divorce and stuff. It's OK to be sad. At least that's what you're always telling me . . .'

'Thanks, Tilly Maravilla.' It was a coded tribute to Ronnie's father, that she would use Spanish terms of endearment to remind her children of their heritage, but it wasn't always welcome.

'You can stop calling me that now I'm nearly sixteen.'

'Oh, go on, humour me just a bit longer. Where's Eduardo Bombero?'

'Cadet training. Don't let him hear you call him that either. He's finished his fireman stage.'

'Playing soldiers now instead.'

'Don't let him hear you call it that. He'll be furious!'

They laughed. It was a special comfort, having a child you were close to. She thought about Maeve Slade, who lived in a fortress of her own making, of clean lines and spotless marble. Did she know the joy of hugging her children?

Tilly looked at her phone. 'I've got a ton of homework. Phone Susie. I don't want you to be alone.'

It was a good idea. At least Susie could enlighten her about what on earth had happened on Saturday night.

Tilly was right. Susie was exactly who Ronnie needed. She arrived with an armful of lilies and a bottle of sparkling wine.

Ronnie put the flowers in the sink, reached for some glasses and poured the wine. As she did so, it occurred to her that alcohol might have become a little too much of a prop in her life just recently, but she swept the thought away. There was nothing normal about *just recently,* and needs must. 'Cheers, my friend.'

Susie raised her glass and took a sip. 'So, what's the story, exactly? I got your message about the complaint, but I have no idea what it was about.'

'I interfered with the investigation into myself. How crazy is that? I checked the CCTV at Hemingway's to see if there was anything on me – and to see who might have reported me. And you won't believe who it was.'

'Oh, Ronnie, why did you do that? You were bound to get pulled up for going behind their backs. Sometimes I wonder how you ever got into the police.'

'My passion for justice, observant eye, analytical mind?'

'Yes, but there's this thing called upholding the law.'

'I do that. That's the whole point.'

'And obeying the rules.'

'Yes, but there are the decent rules, and then there are those that actually prevent the functioning of the whole organisation. Anyway, the guy on the CCTV, the one who must have made the complaint . . .'

'Who was it?'

'Only Baz Munro.'

'What? Your DC?' Susie did a double-take. 'I didn't see him there that night.'

'Nor did I, but then I wasn't looking for him. And it was dark, and he was on the other side of the bar.'

'Do you think he'd stoop that low, make an anonymous complaint, get you suspended from duty? Did you tell illustrious Lydia?'

'She wasn't there to tell, and she must have seen the same video recordings I did because she was there seconds after I left. I'm raging inside that anyone could do it at all, but if Baz has a grudge I don't know about, or just wants me out of the way, it makes sense.'

'Oh, Ronnie, I wish I hadn't left that night. You seemed to be happily chatting to a guy at the table when I went home. Didn't even look up when I said goodbye.'

'Would you recognise him? Could you describe him?' She was clutching at straws to retrieve any clues that might trigger her memory.

'I saw the back of him sitting down, couldn't even take a guess at his height.'

Ronnie put her head in her hands. 'I'm just going to have to let this one play itself out, aren't I?'

Susie hugged her. 'I think so. But let me distract you with some other news. Maeve called me, and I met Amie yesterday.'

'Good. What did you think? Is she hiding something?'

Susie looked taken aback. 'Oh, my God, Ron. Don't tell me I'm your plant so you can pick up some inside information. You're incorrigible.'

'Not at all,' Ronnie protested. 'You said to put your name forward where I could, so that's what I did. I can't believe you think I'd do that. I'm just curious!'

'You're smiling. You're trying not to, but you can't fool me, detective.'

'But, seriously, have you had any thoughts so far? That you're allowed to divulge?'

'Not many, but solving mysteries in people's heads takes time.'

'Is it PTSD, after what happened? Foster's release must be making it worse.'

'Possibly, although she doesn't fit a pattern. It's interesting listening to her talk. What's the dynamic like with her and her mother? I only saw them together for a minute or two, when I arrived.'

Ronnie thought back to her meeting with Maeve. 'It's almost as if she and Amie are scared of each other, somehow. She seems to see Amie as a threat, but Amie comes across as almost mouse-like, as if she's frightened to go out in the world. I can't work out what's going on there.'

'It's not surprising there's some tension, with the divorce going on, but I agree with you, something's not right with those two. Even just from the few things Amie said, I think there's something between them I can't put my finger on. Hopefully, in time, I'll get through to her and understand it.'

'And apparently there was an incident at school.'

Susie hesitated under Ronnie's questioning gaze before replying. 'I know. Amie was sent home for cutting another girl's hair off in the middle of a lesson.'

Ronnie sat up in shock. 'That's why she was home when I went round there on Wednesday?'

'That's the official story, but I've spoken to Amie and there may be more to it. Unfortunately, confidentiality rules until the law says otherwise, as you know . . .'

Ronnie's heart sank, partly at the thought of her instincts being right, partly at Susie's reminder of her duty of care. 'Even if it helps the case? Come on, Suze. I'm only trying to safeguard her, as you are. We're on the same side.'

Susie grimaced. 'You know the rules. I'd be struck off. But I promise that if there's any reason I feel that something should be passed on, I won't hesitate. Trust me?'

Ronnie let out the breath she was holding. 'Of course. Let's just hope it's Foster's release causing a temporary glitch in family relations.' Ronnie listened to her own words and didn't believe them. 'And it just reminds me to follow up with Amie's teachers. The more witnesses we have to her behaviour, the better.'

'You don't sound convinced,' said Susie.

Ronnie took another sip. The wine was going down easily and the stress was melting away. 'I remember when I met Maeve a year ago – she had this look, as if she were a kind of alien controlled by an extraterrestrial power.'

'What?' Susie slid Ronnie's glass back over to her side of the table and sniffed it. 'What have you put in here, girl?'

Ronnie laughed, then her face settled into seriousness again. 'It was a kind of blankness, as though she was waiting for instructions before moving on to the next facial expression.'

'Like when your eyes get fixed on something in the middle distance and you can't move them? Completely normal. We all do that.'

'Maybe. But it's the way she is in the house, the way she looks nervously at the door when she talks about Amie, as if she's seen a ghost. When I was there last, she had called the direct line to CID, but then she was saying she'd made a mistake. As though she shouldn't have called us at all. And with that complaint against me . . .'

'You think it was her?'

'Not any more. But it crossed my mind.'

'So you're back to thinking the mistake she mentioned was to do with calling CID?'

'I assume so. She wasn't going to elaborate, so I can only guess.'

Susie frowned. 'It's what abused women do: withdraw their testimony.'

'You think Stuart . . . ? But they've split up, haven't they? He's moved on.' Ronnie was certain of that, but Susie wasn't keen to discount anything.

'You can never be sure *why* they split up. He's hardly going to wear a T-shirt saying *wife-beater*.'

'I just don't think it's him, Suze.'

'You've met him, I take it. What's he like?'

Ronnie thought for a minute and realised she had no idea. 'He's strikingly attractive. Almost disconcertingly so. Distractingly so, anyway. But I'm not sure there's more to him than that.'

'Not sure . . . so it's possible.'

They shared a moment of silent contemplation before Susie offered another explanation. 'So if it's not him she's scared of, then who else? It's not Amie. She's like you say, a little mouse creeping around trying to do the right thing. Seems terrified of upsetting her mother. How about the brother?'

'Did Amie say something about him?' Ronnie glanced around for a notebook, thinking that perhaps she should be writing some of this down.

Susie exhaled deeply. 'Well, she may have hinted that he's a piece of work . . .'

Ronnie slumped back on the cushions. Her mind was on Andrew now and what he might be capable of. 'You don't think he's the practical joker type, do you?'

'I don't know. Why do you ask?'

'I don't necessarily think he'd do this, but apparently Foster has contacted Amie and threatened to come for her.'

'She told me. What are you thinking? It was a prank of Andrew's?'

'I didn't see the message, so I can't guarantee it wasn't a malicious fake from a resentful sibling.'

'A malicious sibling, or *classmate*, after what happened at school. What did she do with the message?'

'She deleted it. All I got from her is, he said he would find her.'

Susie was twiddling the glass again, this time with an expression that said her thoughts were racing. 'And why did she delete it? Surely she'd want him back behind bars where he can't hurt her.'

'Fear I guess, of it being real. You delete it and it doesn't exist any more, never happened.'

'Have you considered that she might be in his thrall somehow?' mused Susie. 'You know what teenage girls are like. And she doesn't seem to have any friends, apart from one girl who seems to have rather too much influence over her.'

Ronnie raised her eyebrows. 'Influence? What kind of influence?'

Susie made a face and was about to speak when Ronnie saved her from her excuses.

'Don't tell me, confidentiality again.'

Susie looked relieved. 'Sorry, shouldn't have said anything. But I'm wondering if there might be a pattern of behaviour: submitting to the desires of others, letting them take over, absolving herself of responsibility.'

'It's the kind of thing that only goes on for so long.' Ronnie was thinking aloud. 'I mean, no one can live like that forever.' She poured the last of the wine into their empty glasses. 'What kind of things do you do with her?'

Susie watched the bubbles dissipate. 'All sorts. But she's happy doodling with a Sharpie, so I let her get on with that while we talk. Seems to be her way of expressing herself.'

'I feel so frustrated,' Ronnie sighed.

'Well, as soon as they've finished investigating your investigation tactics, you can get back to it.'

Ronnie didn't say that it made no difference to her whether she was on or off duty. She had lived and breathed her work since the first day, and nothing could change that.

Susie drained her glass. 'You'll work it out, Ron. I trust your instincts. And you made a real impression on my friends the other night. I think you came across a bit like Superwoman, running a family single-handed alongside your job. I definitely picked up a bit of regret about career abandonment.'

'Tell them they're not missing much. My job may have cost me my relationship, and now some attempt at trying to find a new relationship has cost me my job.'

'Ronnie! That's so not true. Your relationship broke down because Simon was an arse. And besides, if going to a bar was an attempt at finding a relationship, then we need to have a chat.'

'Bloody Baz Munro. I'm furious. Why can't Lydia see through it?'

'Are you going to confront him?' Susie looked worried. 'I mean, you need to be *really* sure.'

Ronnie felt her stomach lurch, the way it did when she was caught out.

Gut feeling isn't always enough.

The sound of a key in the door pulled her from her thoughts.

'Hi, Mum, what's for dinner?' asked Eddie, exploding into the room. 'Smells peng.'

'Smells *what?*' Ronnie turned to him. 'Is there no end to these random invented words you teenagers come out with?'

'It means good, like *really* good. But you mustn't use it.' He looked a little alarmed at the thought.

'I don't think I will, unless the situation requires it. Anyway, the answer to your question is spaghetti Bolognese.'

CHAPTER 20

Back at school on Monday, things were different, but not in the way Amie expected them to be. Instead of crowds of admirers lining up for the autograph of their new feminist icon, she was met with icy stares and given a wide berth by everyone. Jess Fleetwood had had a proper haircut and it was all smooth and straight again, just a whole ruler's length shorter. It made her look grown-up, and the way she looked at Amie now was just the way Maeve did, as if she was an irritation, a loose thread she wanted to cut off but couldn't in case the whole jumper unravelled.

Even Mia Craven barely spoke to her any more, not even polite small talk. There was no mistaking the fact that Amie had been frozen out. What was worse was that Elisa seemed to have had the opposite happen. The other girls had sucked her into their mass of whoops and giggles at lunchtime, leaving Amie marooned and full of uncertainty.

She did her best to carry on, smile at everyone and keep out of their way, tried to ignore Elisa's booming popularity, and hushed a voice in her head that said this girl was not to be trusted.

Susie had suggested relaxation videos on YouTube, but she didn't trust the man telling her to relax. Once she was asleep, he might do something bad to her, or, worse, bring her face to face with Daniel again. In her dreams, paralysed and powerless, she was trapped in a horror film happening all around her. The ending was coming, and it wasn't going to be a happy one.

She cycled to school a different way each day, imagining Daniel Foster would be lying in wait for her if she took the same route twice. The changes she made were tiny: timings, taking different left and right turns through the network of avenues on the estate, taking longer than she should, occasionally coming out on the wrong side of school altogether. At night, she would check the windows were locked before she went to bed, even though they were never unlocked. At school, she hung around the classroom at break time, feeling safer in the presence of an adult than the other girls. Normally there were pencils to sharpen, desks to straighten, while the teacher sat at her desk marking books. It was peaceful, perfect: both engaged in tasks, neither disturbing the other, both working towards the same goal – the righting of wrongs, correction, improvement.

Then suddenly Miss Emsworth put her pen down and called Amie over. Amie was thinking she might have more jobs for her, some photocopying or worksheet-trimming, but it was something completely different, completely unexpected.

'Amie, remember that creative writing piece you did on autumn?'

Amie nodded. 'The bleak one.'

Miss Emsworth looked embarrassed. 'Well, actually I think it showed a lot of promise, and a lot of imagination you don't see in every sixteen-year-old these days. It was with that in mind that I was wondering if you'd be interested in entering a writing competition.'

'Oh . . .' Amie leant against a desk in the front row, slightly disappointed. She was happy doing jobs around the classroom. She didn't need anything else.

Miss Emsworth slid a magazine towards her and she recognised the familiar flimsy pages and the bright, busy images that crowded them. It was one of those magazines intended to inspire teenagers to get off their phones and start appreciating literature.

'The *Book Planet* run this competition every year, and I thought perhaps you should enter it.'

'Oh. OK. If you want.'

'Would you consider it? I think you'd stand a good chance. Nothing to lose.'

Amie scanned the page in front of her. 'I'd be up against the whole country. That's a lot of people.'

'It's national within age groups, yes. They usually get several thousand entries. Sounds like a lot, but between you and me, most of them won't be any good. I'm sure you're up to it. You need to apply in the sixteen-to-eighteen category, which I think gets the fewest entries. Sixth-formers are all too busy painting their nails and getting boyfriends.'

Amie absorbed what she'd said. Obviously, she wasn't going to be bothering with either of those things.

'What would I have to write about?'

'The theme this year is "Confession".'

'Confession?' Amie let the meaning of this sink in. She was being offered the opportunity for some kind of redemption for attacking her classmate's hair with scissors.

'I know. Slightly unusual as titles go. I think you can take it with a pinch of salt.' She had turned the page back towards her and was scanning the rules. '*A short story or poem on the subject*, it says here. So that's quite wide-ranging. I think you could tackle it from a new angle, thinking outside the box. Just as you did before.'

'Mum used to go to confession, as a child.'

'So did I. There's more to it than the Catholic ritual, though. You could think of a different perspective.'

But Amie's imagination was already in full flow. What if a priest took it into his own hands to administer justice, right the wrongs he'd heard about? If people knew what he was doing, they might even feed him false stories to get the outcome they wanted. She nodded thoughtfully. 'OK, I can have a go.'

Miss Emsworth beamed at her. 'You won't regret it. I have very high hopes for you.'

'Thank you. That means a lot.' It did. Not many people had high hopes for her.

She felt a rare sense of exhilaration as she cycled home without a thought for Daniel, or where he might be lurking to ambush her. She had a new focus, and it didn't depend on anyone else.

She browsed Amazon for books on confession. There were all sorts, some funny – confessions of chocoholics, shopaholics – some more serious, about the Church thing Maeve had talked about. She had never been very forthcoming about what it meant to her, if anything. A silver crucifix hung around her neck, but no mention was made of Jesus in the house, except by Dad when he was really angry.

She clicked on one of the book icons and downloaded it on to her phone. The first story in the collection was about a teenage boy whose eventual confession led to him being blackmailed and abused by the priest he had trusted. The boy in the story, Alan, had grown up in a children's home. He had got hold of some porn magazines and hidden them under his mattress, but ended up being so terrified that what he was doing was sinful that he hid them under his room-mate's bed and the room-mate got a beating for it. Alan felt so guilty, he confessed everything to the priest, who sexually abused him for years afterwards, telling him this was his penance, and this way God would forgive him and free him from sin.

Amie shared his rage. I know how it feels, she thought, when the people who are supposed to look after you do the complete opposite.

There were other stories with happier endings, about people who had kept dark secrets all their lives and were tortured by nightmares and unable to function until they finally confessed to the person they'd hurt and were able to live again. Confession was like a new sunny day giving them a chance to be better people than they were yesterday. It was God saying he was going to rub out all the mistakes and let them start again. Which was fine if you believed in God.

In Alan's case, it was clear that the blame for the whole thing lay with whoever it was had abandoned him and put him in a children's home in the first place.

Elisa disagreed.

Oh, come on, Amie. If you go down that route, nobody is to blame for anything. Your parents are breaking up because of something their parents did to them. Responsibility goes back to the beginning of time. We have to be accountable for who we are today.

Whose side are you on?

Amie pressed send and regretted it. Her heart thumped in anticipation of the reply, which came immediately.

I think we have to make the best of what we've got, not look around to see who we can pin it on. Maybe you need to do that too.

She didn't reply to the last message. It sat in her head like a meteor, radioactive and sparking. Elisa was goading her again, but this time Amie wasn't going to be the one getting into trouble. She would show her the meaning of accountability.

And then, before she knew it, the story was written, and the title.

My Confession
By Elisa Mead.

CHAPTER 21

A new girl called Charlotte had arrived in Amie's class. She seemed friendly enough and Elisa was off on a field trip that day, which made it easier for them to get to know each other one-to-one. They sat in the locker room talking about her old school and Charlotte showed Amie photos of her friends on her Instagram account. Amie didn't tell her about the Jess incident because she would probably find out in good time and that day didn't need to be brought forward.

Charlotte was allergic to nuts. She had to carry an EpiPen around with her everywhere, just in case.

'What happens if you don't have it, or it doesn't work?'

Charlotte looked surprised at the question. 'Anaphylaxis.' Then, when Amie frowned in confusion, 'I die.' She zipped the EpiPen back in its case and threw the case into her locker. 'Come on, let's go outside. I don't want to talk about miserable medical stuff.'

'Sorry, I shouldn't have . . .' Amie stuttered.

'No, no, it's fine, it's just that it really isn't a big deal for me, and I don't want it to be a big deal for anyone else, you know?'

Amie knew. They went out into the field and she pointed out the fence between Merrymount and the boys next door. They laughed at the clusters of teenagers that dotted its length. Amie explained how she timed her arrival in the morning to avoid the whistles and jeers, and Charlotte said, 'Thanks for the warning.' But Amie saw her smile, as if it was all just a joke.

Charlotte had come to Merrymount after her mother's job relocation. 'She's a doctor, works in Halesworth A&E.'

'Oh. That's useful – for you, I mean.'

Charlotte did one of those exasperated smiles, no teeth, nodding and looking the other way, which even Amie knew meant OK, *that's enough now.* She was about to say something to make up for it, take it away from medical things and back into how stupid the boys were, but she never got the chance, because it was then that they came to take her away.

While they had been chatting, in the middle distance Amie could see Jess and Mia loping towards them. Jess was in front, gaze focused ahead like a lion approaching its prey, smiling the most welcoming of smiles, but not at Amie. Within seconds they were upon them.

'Hey, Charlie, how's it going?' Jess looked cutely out from under her new fringe.

It was unnerving, Amie thought, how one moment you're in the middle of a group, then suddenly you're alone again. Jess and Mia were already leading Charlotte slowly away, laughing at things Amie couldn't hear. Arms went around her shoulders, hands stroked her hair. Once at a safe distance, they perched on the bench together, Charlotte in the middle, Jess and Mia on the arms at each end with their feet on the seat, princesses with their new toy, vultures circling the sick dog. There was some whispering, lots of flicking of hair and a few glances back at Amie. She pretended not to notice but couldn't take her eyes off their lips murmuring her name and listing the things she had done to deserve their contempt.

Elisa was sitting on the wall outside school when Amie left that evening. She was throwing conkers again, this time at a tree stump a few metres away. Her third one hit the target and she whooped.

'Good shot.'

Elisa jumped down. 'Let me walk with you.'

They walked together down towards the playground on the corner. The air was chilly and the pale sun hung just above the trees ahead. As she pushed her bike, Amie kicked the piles of fallen leaves that littered the pavement. Underneath was a carpet of mulch glued to the ground, impossible to shift.

She told Elisa how the others had taken Charlotte from under her wing, from right under her nose, how Charlotte had gone with them without the slightest protest, just walked into the enemy camp without even a backward glance.

'Oh, Amie, Jess is such a *bitch*! I can't believe she did that!'

'I suppose she thinks I deserve it,' Amie said, pointedly, because she didn't deserve it and Elisa knew it.

'She needs to get over herself.'

'What about Charlotte, though? What do you think she's said to her about me?' Amie wrung her hands, digging her nails into her palms again to dull the pain.

'Don't worry about Charlotte,' Elisa said. 'You've got me.'

'Yes, but still . . .'

She should have just said yes and stopped there. Elisa was running towards the swings. She took the nearest one, gave herself a push off and threw her head back. 'But still what? I thought we were all each other needed? Last week, when you didn't even know Charlotte existed, you and I were like *that*.' Taking one hand off the chain, she held up two fingers crossed, a symbol of inextricable relationship.

Amie didn't say anything, just looked down and kicked leaves.

'What's changed?' Elisa's voice was suddenly like Mum's. 'You're being off with me, Amie. Why? Has something happened?' Her feet touched the ground and she waited for an answer, but Amie just stared at her feet.

'Nothing. It's nothing.' She was learning to hold things back now. Maybe Elisa didn't need to know everything. She perched on the next swing just as Elisa jumped off hers.

'Are we good? You and me?' Elisa was standing in front of her, hands on hips.

'Of course. It's just . . . I don't want everyone against me, ganging up on me. You know what I mean, don't you? I just don't want anyone to hate me.' It sounded like a mess.

She dug the toe of her shoe into the ground while Elisa steadied the swing by holding the chain still. 'Amie, you're blowing this out of all proportion! Charlotte's new, and she's not going to take sides just like that; she doesn't want to make any enemies either, does she? She needs to find out what everyone's like in her own time, then decide. She'll come round in the end, although I have no idea why it matters if she does or not.'

Amie wasn't confident that Charlotte would even get the chance to make a choice. This was a mistake, telling Elisa how she felt.

'Amie, we have each other, and that's enough.' Elisa wanted to be the only voice, the only friend that counted. 'Unless of course it isn't . . .'

'Of course it's enough,' Amie said quickly. Elisa was holding both chains of the swing now, pulling her forward, then letting her go and catching her as she swung back.

'Then there's nothing to worry about. Is there?'

The light was dimming and clouds were gathering as Amie climbed back on her bicycle. Rain began to fall as she waited in the filter lane for a gap in the traffic. A van came to a halt and she raised a hand to wave her thanks, but then she saw the driver's face, through the wet glass, slashed intermittently by the windscreen wipers. Sandy hair, the shadow of stubble on his jaw, his eyes narrowed, fixed on hers. A wave of fear rose inside her and her feet struggled to connect with the pedals. Then, finally, she was off again, rain in her face, her heart beating its way out of her body.

CHAPTER 22

When she burst through the front door, panting and terror-stricken, Susie was waiting for her in the kitchen. She stood up in a hurry, scraping her chair back and nearly knocking it over.

'Amie! What's happened? You look as if you've seen a ghost. Come and sit down.' She pulled out the chair next to her and passed her a glass of water.

'I thought I saw him driving a van just now, with ladders on the roof. That means . . .' She was gasping for breath. Susie held her shoulders and told her to breathe with her, but the gasping wouldn't stop, tears started pouring down her face and everything came rushing out, unstoppable.

'He's going to find me. I know it. He wants to punish me.'

'Punish you for what?'

Amie was shivering now, even though the house was warm.

Susie waited until the panic passed.

'We need to go to the police, if he's breaking the terms of his release,' she said gently.

'No. I don't want that.'

They sat in silence for a minute before Susie said that they could talk about something else. She suggested Amie tell her more about Andrew, whether they'd ever got on in the past, whether there had been any happy times, but Amie said she couldn't remember any. Then she asked about Elisa, how they were getting on since the incident. Amie hesitated, sensing a trap.

'Can I see a picture of her?'

The question made Amie jump. 'Um . . . OK.' She pulled out her phone and scrolled down her Instagram feed. 'Here you go.'

Susie looked at the screen, then back at Amie, nodding. 'It's good to put a face to a name, I always find.'

When her phone alarm signalled the end of the session, Susie looked frustrated, as if she'd planned to talk more and hadn't got through it all.

The window was open when she left and her footsteps crunched on the gravel outside. Then they stopped and Amie heard Susie on the phone to someone. 'Ronnie? It's me. Not urgent, but you might want to give me a call back when you can.'

Ronnie? Surely that couldn't be a coincidence. What had happened to *confidential*?

When Susie had gone, Andrew came upstairs and pushed her door open without knocking.

'Who's this woman who's always coming round? Some sort of therapist?'

'None of your business.'

'She trying to get you sectioned for being a total headcase?'

Amie felt the red mist Susie had talked about. It was swirling all around him as he carried on.

'That hair-cutting thing was fucking weird. Don't you care about having mates? What was going through your head?'

'Getting my own back,' she said under her breath, and he laughed and shut the door, shouting out from behind it.

'Blimey, I'd better watch myself, in case you trim my fringe in the middle of the night.'

Celia Burrows came round on her way back from working at the Birchwood Centre, with Alfie in tow as usual. He shouldn't have been up so late, but his dad wasn't around, babysitters were too expensive, and her work didn't mind her bringing him as long as he stayed out of the way. Amie wondered whether she left him in the waiting room with all the addicts, but Maeve said not to be so stupid, that it wasn't like that, and that they were lonely and went there to do social activities together like painting and pottery.

Celia Burrows was the last person in the world who should have been looking after lonely people. Her perfect, shiny, blow-dried hair and long red nails made her look like just the kind of person they were trying to escape from – pushy parents and perfect mothers who kept being disappointed with them. That was probably why they ended up at the centre, feeling not good enough, not coping with life. Celia would have just been a reminder of all that. But Maeve said not to be so rude and that she was kind and generous to do it and they were grateful to have her.

Amie stayed in her room until curiosity got the better of her and she went to the stairs to listen to them talking. She heard the fridge door open and shut, then Celia's voice.

'I'm sure it's nothing, you know – it's easy to imagine these things. All married people do at some point.' Celia knew about everything and everyone, of course. Whatever it was, she would be able to tell you all about it, and loudly.

'I know . . . a midlife crisis.' Some of the words were indistinct.

'Exactly. I'm sure it's just that.' Celia didn't sound sure.

A short silence, the draining of glasses, and the barely audible thud as they were replaced on the table.

'Maybe he just needs some space.'

'Not that old excuse. Spare me.' Maeve wasn't falling for Celia's platitudes. Good for her.

'People do, though. It's a tough job, being married.'

And what would you know about that? Amie thought. And Maeve must have found it just as irritating, by the sound of her reply.

'Are you saying he's got it hard here with us, living in the lap of luxury, holidays twice a year, private schools for the kids, a son off to Oxford? What more could he possibly want?'

There was a pause. Just about everything that mattered wasn't on her list, but who was going to tell her? Then the voices were quieter again until Celia said, a bit louder, 'As I say, it's just space. Time and space.'

'Well, he's got that now. As much of it as he wants.'

186

'Mama!' Alfie's voice came from the lounge. He had finished his toast, probably leaving buttery crumbs down the side of the sofa.

There was a scraping sound as Celia pushed her chair back to leave. Amie crept back up to the landing, her heart pounding so loud she was sure they could hear it. Celia said, 'I'm sure I brought my pashmina . . .' and then went back to give Maeve her last nugget of wisdom. 'Whatever's going on, you've just got to trust it's for the best. Things will work themselves out in the end.'

Then there was a click of heels on the hall tiles and the whining of a little boy who had had enough. But Amie was too far away by then to hear whether Maeve agreed or not.

CHAPTER 23

The next morning, Amie came downstairs to find Maeve and Stuart standing in the kitchen, waiting.

She couldn't remember the last time she had seen them in the same room together. They weren't really in the same room even now, not in spirit. Maeve was facing the sink, holding a pan and a scouring pad, staring at a spot on the wall. Stuart was standing near the French windows, dressed in a suit for work, blue shirt, yellow tie. He stood with his hands in his trouser pockets, rocking on his feet and staring at the leaves which already almost covered the lawn, blotting out the greens and yellows of summer with a carpet of brown. A gust brought down another blast, and there was a second or two of silence as they settled on the grass.

Andrew trailed down the stairs after her, pushed past, looked this way and that, and asked the obvious question, the question that was hovering on Amie's lips, terrified to voice itself.

'What's going on, man?'

Stuart turned to face them all, glancing at Maeve, and cleared his throat.

'I'm moving out of the annexe next weekend.'

For a torturous moment, Amie thought he meant he was moving back into the house, back into the family, and, for that instant, her heart soared. Then, like a buzzard spotting a mouse on the ground a hundred feet below, it plummeted again.

'I mean I'm moving out, away.' He must have sensed the confusion.

'Why?' she asked, crash-landing from her millisecond of hope. 'What's wrong with the annexe?'

'Nothing. It's just that I need a bit more space . . . And Mum doesn't want me hanging around here all the time.'

'But *I* do!' Amie hurled herself into his arms, and he almost overbalanced with the force of it. Maeve saw them and winced, turned back to her scrubbing.

'I know, Amie, I know.' He was extricating himself.

'Where to?' asked Andrew, casually kicking a non-existent football. Why did he care? He was going to university, leaving the family cut in half. Down from four to two in a matter of days.

'It's OK. I won't be far. We'll see each other often; we'll have whole weekends together.'

He stroked Amie's hair, a tender farewell before being dragged away. She was losing the tug of war once and for all.

The silence that followed was interrupted only by the clink of Andrew's spoon in his cereal bowl, the banging of the dirty pan against the sides of the sink, and the sound of Amie sobbing into Dad's suit as she clung to him, marking her territory with salty tears before he took it away for good.

Parents didn't give children sad news just before they went to bed in case they had nightmares. But bad news in the morning – that made the whole day go wrong.

Charlotte went off with the others at lunch break, so Amie pretended she had to stay behind to catch up on homework, but all she could think about was Dad packing up and going, leaving home forever and leaving her to clean up the mess. Miss Emsworth let her stay in the classroom, where she ate her sandwich staring out of the window, watching all the fun she wasn't a part of. It left her cold now, because there was no more pain to feel.

When the rest of the class came back for the afternoon's lessons, Amie was buried in her book. She didn't look up as they took their seats, dragging chairs back noisily and pulling folders out of bags, or even when Charlotte, who sat at the end of her row, put her hand up to say she wasn't feeling well. It was only when Miss Emsworth shouted at someone to move out of the way, then, 'Charlotte, are you OK? I think you're having an allergic reaction,' that Amie raised her head. Charlotte was convulsing on the floor, her lips blue and swollen.

Amie stood up, heart thumping in fear. 'EpiPen. She needs her EpiPen.' But Miss Emsworth was already there, riffling through her rucksack.

'It's not here.' It was almost a scream.

'I'll call the ambulance.' With shaking hands, Amie pulled her phone out of her bag and dialled 999.

What happened over the next twenty minutes was more shocking than anything she had ever witnessed. The paramedics took Charlotte away, sirens blaring, and the girls were taken into the school hall to be addressed by the head teacher.

There was one of those long waits that teachers did to really get attention. Miss Emsworth had gone to stand by the window. The windows were a few inches open and through them wafted sounds of running footsteps and laughter. Then Miss Hanbury spoke.

'Charlotte's mother has assured us that her EpiPen was in her bag when she left for school this morning. So it would make sense that one of you here . . .' she did one of those pauses for effect, her eyes moving across the class before she continued, 'knows she has done something . . . utterly unacceptable.'

She gazed evenly round the assembled faces before continuing. Amie's heart missed a beat.

'Something entirely inappropriate to your age, your maturity and your humanity. Something which this school utterly condemns. Now is your chance to own up. If you do, then you do so with complete confidentiality. If you don't . . .' she left a long pause, 'there will be serious consequences.'

It was the longest silence. Then she explained what was going to happen next in a voice just like Maeve's – a colourless tone that spoke volumes. There was so much to convey, nothing could come close to showing it. They were to remain seated until all lockers and drawers, coat pockets and gym bags had been checked. Miss Emsworth stood leaning against the wall, arms folded, sad eyes moving round them until they rested on Amie, who couldn't meet her gaze. She couldn't bear to see what lay behind that sad look in case it was, *Please let it not be you again, Amie . . .*

It didn't take long to find the EpiPen in Jess Fleetwood's rucksack, although there was no sign of its yellow case. That must have been cast aside like a handbag by the thief who is only interested in the cash inside.

Jess denied all knowledge, her face reddening and her eyes swelling with tears. She said someone else must have put it in her bag, because why would she take something like that? She had no reason to. But nobody had seen anyone do it, so she remained the prime suspect.

It was on the way home that Elisa suddenly said, 'I wanted to show you that you could trust me.'

'What?' Amie stopped and looked at her.

'I wanted to show you I was on your side, because I know you were worried that I wasn't.'

'You mean, *you did it*? You planted the EpiPen in Jess's rucksack?'

'I didn't want you to think that I actually liked any of those girls. I mean, I know they like me, and they certainly don't get why I want to hang around with you . . .' Amie flinched at the words. 'But I wanted to do something to actually show you where my loyalties lay.' She turned to look at Amie. 'What's the matter? Don't say you didn't enjoy seeing Jess Fleetwood get the blame?'

'But what about Charlotte? She was the one who went to hospital. What did you do to her?' Amie was flustered. This wasn't how things were supposed to happen.

'A tiny smear of peanut butter on her desk was enough.'

Amie felt sick, but Elisa didn't seem to feel anything. She just smiled as if she'd got top marks in something.

'I think we should stop this now. You're scaring me,' Amie whispered.

'Stop what?'

'Punishing people.'

'At least I'm not a coward. I'm not afraid to fight for justice. I'm a pretty loyal friend, I'd say. You are completely out of the picture, blame-wise. And Charlotte's not going to be friends with Jess after that, is she? So, your problem has gone away.'

But, as it turned out, the problem hadn't gone away. Charlotte had. Her parents moved her to another school and there was a space in the class again where she used to sit.

So now, once again, Amie just had Elisa.

CHAPTER 24

The ping of her phone alerted Ronnie with a start. There were two text messages on her home screen. The first one was from Baz Munro. She clicked on the message, trying to suppress a wave of fury towards him as she did so.

Checked out the van story. Foster's doing some labouring work for the council and drives a transit van but all evidence puts him ten miles away at the time she says she saw him. Must have been her imagination.

She felt a pang of disappointment mixed with relief. When Susie had told her what Amie claimed to have seen the previous day, she had put the call in to Baz straight away, and he had been as good as his word, on this occasion, but the result was just another dead end.

The second message was from one of Amie's teachers, called Louisa Emsworth. She couldn't make a meeting that week but was happy to answer any questions or chat on Skype. That would do for now. Ronnie called her at once.

Louisa had one of those faces that made you smile. She was all lightness and positivity, bright-eyed and youthful –

untouched by the trials of life, Ronnie imagined, like Baz Munro.

'Hi, Louisa, thanks so much for getting back to me. As they will no doubt have told you, it's about one of your students, Amie Slade.'

'Yes, she was a new arrival at the school this year, so I haven't known her that long but I'll do my best. How can I help?'

'I'm just trying to assess what her state of mind might be at the moment. I heard she was suspended from school for an incident with another girl in her class two weeks ago . . .'

'I know, I was astonished. Not like her at all. Totally out of character.' Louisa's face showed a pang of distress.

'What's she normally like?'

Louisa inhaled, then let the adjectives flow on the out-breath. 'Quiet, unassuming, timid, diligent, compliant, eager to please.' Her face softened as she spoke. Talking about the good in people came naturally to her.

Ronnie wrote it all down, thinking how well it fitted with the girl she had met after the assault, and again in her bedroom doorway. 'Anything else?'

'Perhaps a little bleak at times? As in her view of the world. She doesn't see the joy out there.' Louisa's expression was sad now.

Ronnie let the word *bleak* roll around in her head. 'OK, makes sense, after what happened.'

'You mean . . . the assault.' Louisa obviously didn't want to say the words.

'It's bound to have scarred her. I wouldn't be surprised if the world looked like a less sunny place since that happened. And now he's out of prison . . .'

'Of course. But it still doesn't fit with taking the scissors to her classmate's hair. I still don't understand what was going on for her there.'

Ronnie nodded. It was one of those blind alleys of thinking where the only option was to reverse and try the other fork in the road.

'How does she get on with the other girls?'

'Hard to say, not having known her very long. She's definitely not one of the in-crowd. Then again, she says she's happy with that, and good luck to her. We can't all be top dog.'

'True.'

'The hair-cutting thing could have been a one-off, and it's not just her behaving out of character.' Louisa hesitated, as if wondering whether to disclose something. 'We actually had another incident today. An EpiPen went missing, stolen by one of the other girls, it seems. It was found in her rucksack.'

'And this was nothing to do with Amie?'

'Nothing at all. Well, except – it turned out to be the girl whose hair she cut.'

Ronnie sat up and replayed in her head what the teacher had just said, as she went on.

'So it may be something else. Not a reaction to Foster's release, but just a pattern of behaviour we're seeing among this group of girls. They can be nasty, and nastiness can spread like a virus.'

'It can.' It was true: once bad habits or friendships became ingrained, they would pass from individual to individual. 'The thing is, Louisa, we think Foster may have tried to contact her.'

'Oh, my God. What kind of contact? What did he say?' She looked horrified.

'A message. She deleted it.'

There was a silence as Louisa took it in. 'OK, so what are you thinking could be going on? She should be running to the police with the evidence, not deleting it. Could she be trying to protect him?'

Ronnie took a deep breath. 'That's what I'm trying to establish. I need as many ears to the ground as I can get. All we can do is stay alert, look out for anything that appears unusual.'

'Of course. What can I do to help, if anything?'

'I'd appreciate it if you'd keep me in the picture about anything you notice, positive or negative. And, if she confides in you, I'd like to know.'

'Understood. Actually, there has been one positive development.'

'Oh, yes?' Ronnie filled a glass with water from the tap and sat down at the table.

'I suggested she might like to enter a writing competition. I thought she needed a focus away from the difficulties she was having at school, as well as the whole family break-up thing. She seemed happy to be involved, so I let her get on with it. She has a definite creative streak, and I think she'll enjoy the escapism.'

'Sounds like a good distraction for her right now.'

'I hope so. The topic they have to write on is confession.'

Ronnie frowned. 'Gosh, that's a big one. Well, creativity is the best therapy, they say. Talking of which, is she getting any support in school at all with reintegration? She was taken out of the previous school almost straight away after the assault, so there could have been some trauma associated with coming back into the setting.'

Louisa was nodding in agreement. 'I expect there is some of that. But she won't see the school counsellor. I don't suppose her parents are very into that sort of thing.'

'What makes you say that?'

'I met her mother when she came in after the hair cutting incident. She seemed very cold, distant, disengaged. Like mother, like daughter, I suppose.'

'So it seems that Amie could be disconnected on all levels, at home and at school.' Ronnie tried to imagine what it might feel like, being unable to relate to anyone. The resulting loneliness would surely be intolerable. Could that state of disconnection arrive as a result of past trauma, or was it in your DNA? She should remember to ask Susie.

'I think you're right. I'll let you know if I hear anything. I'm not sure the form teacher is traditionally the sixth-former's first choice of confidante, but I'll do my best to keep an eye on her.'

Ronnie was about to say her goodbyes, then hesitated.

'So, Louisa, just to sum up, if I were to ask you for your gut feeling about Amie. As an observer, rather than a teacher, off the record. What do you make of her?'

Louisa didn't take long to reply. 'I think she's a vulnerable, lonely young woman, traumatised by a past sexual assault and feeling lost and abandoned since her parents split up, perhaps looking for attention.'

Ronnie scribbled some final notes, then closed her notebook. 'Thank you. And sorry for keeping you from your work.'

'I'm always here for Amie – for all the girls, if they need to talk. We do remind them they aren't alone, and I have checked in with her a few times to make sure she's OK. Can't say I'm any the wiser afterwards, but at least the channel of communication is open.'

'Well, thanks for taking the time to talk.'

'No worries. Before I go, can I ask you the same question? What's *your* gut feeling?'

'My gut feeling?' In Ronnie's head was Serena, and the events that lay behind all this, behind this very day and this very conversation. The details started pouring into her head, uninvited. 'I suppose I just feel responsible for Amie, and for what happens to her. I don't want to let her down.'

Once the door was open, the memories flooded back. When she finally ended the call and closed her laptop, it was right there, the night she was filling every waking hour not to remember . . .

It was two weeks before Christmas. Fred and Alice Delmar were off sailing for a week and Ronnie was supposed to be looking after her sister.

'Serena can look after herself – she's fifteen, for God's sake,' she'd protested, keen to stay up at college and party for the last week of term, but Alice had put her foot down.

'Just in case. Please, Veronica, I'd feel so much happier.'

She'd done it, she'd gone back home to babysit, and it was only the one night that she'd gone out. One night, and only to a gathering of her old school friends a couple of miles away. Serena had been more than happy to stay in watching trash on TV. Ronnie would be back by midnight, or soon after, she had promised.

She remembered seeing the missed calls on her phone, trying to call back, but the signal wasn't good enough. She'd let them persuade her to have one more drink, one more dance. Alcohol had fogged her brain. It was after one. Serena must be wondering when she'd be home. She should go.

When the cab dropped her off at Waterman Lane, the house was quiet and dark. There was a rustle in the bushes. Rabbits, squirrels maybe. The wind was up. Sounds were always more acute at night. Ronnie felt a shiver as she put the key in the lock, and looked over her shoulder just in case, as she always did, before going inside and clicking the door shut behind her. She switched the lights on and let out a breath she didn't know she was holding. It was then, with the night noises shut out, that she heard the tiny sound of sobbing.

Serena was huddled in a corner of the sitting room, half-naked, shivering and clutching the legs of the armchair in front of her. There was blood on the floor, and on her lip.

A bruise on her cheek. Tears rolled down her face. Her eyes were wide and frightened.

Ronnie fell to her knees at her side.

'What happened?' Her words came out in a whisper and sobriety landed on her like a brick.

Then Serena told her what he had done, the man she had let into the house thinking Ronnie had forgotten her keys. She could smell the alcohol on his breath and the sweat on his body; he kept saying he'd get what was owed to him, but she didn't owe him anything.

When he'd finished, he pulled up his jeans and walked out.

Ronnie sat cross-legged, holding her sister's hands. It was a few minutes before she could bring herself to speak.

'I will never forgive myself for not being here, you know that.'

'It's not your fault. I shouldn't have opened the door.' Serena seemed to be in another place, as if she had abandoned her traumatised body and was floating somewhere above, disconnected.

Ronnie had pressed her, gently, for details of her attacker, but she wouldn't, or couldn't, tell her any more than that it was a man she recognised from the poker nights.

'One of Dad's friends?' The thought was unbearable, and Ronnie's head was resisting the truth at every step. It couldn't be real. It couldn't have happened.

'Don't say anything. Promise me?' Serena was begging her, tears rolling down her face. 'Please, please don't tell Mum and Dad.' She was adamant that it would do no good, that Ronnie would be blamed, and that the family would fall apart.

Ronnie was torn between fighting for justice and doing what her sister was imploring her to do. When she graduated with a first-class degree in law, Fred and Alice Delmar were over the moon. In their eyes, their daughter was on track to become a partner in a city firm, or a famous QC. They showed her off to their friends and planned out her whole career.

Which was why it was such a shock, to everyone except Serena, when Veronica Delmar, with a glowing future as a successful solicitor or barrister, turned their expectations upside down and signed up to join the police.

CHAPTER 25

It was Saturday morning and Dad was out taking Andrew to football. They were usually there for hours, and when she was younger, Amie used to go along to watch, which she liked because Dad was so different on his own. He seemed more at ease, relaxed, laughing at stuff he wouldn't find funny at home. That was her time with him, or had been. Nowadays he didn't always want her to come. *Stay and look after your mum*, he would say, or, *Haven't you got any homework to do?*

Today it was the homework thing. She emptied the contents of her rucksack on to her desk and slumped on to the chair, staring out of the window at the bleak sky. It was like a knife in her heart that he didn't want her to go with him that day: the day before he moved out completely. He was taking away the only little bit of time they had left; but she didn't want to say anything that would make him resent her. She had to *suck it up*, as Andrew kept saying.

Dad stuck his head round the door before they left. Seeing her disappointment, he came in and stood behind her, his hands on her shoulders. 'There's no point coming to watch it today anyway. It's an away match, long drive, and I've got some work to do while Andrew's playing. How about we go on a bike ride later? Along the river maybe? Get some air in our lungs. Give you something to look forward to after solving all these Chinese puzzles.' He was looking at her open maths book.

She turned to see his reflection in the mirrored wardrobe. 'That would be fun. Yes, please.'

'Well, when you're done, pop into the garage and check the tyres, I think yours are a bit flat, then we can go for a ride this afternoon.'

'OK.'

Maths was easier after that. She finished it in half an hour and went downstairs to sort out her tyres. She was about to put the pump away when a thought crossed her mind and wouldn't go away. It wasn't exactly mean, or dangerous in itself, it was logical and self-preserving. She wanted to go on a bike ride with Dad. She didn't want there to be any risk of Andrew trying to join in. He had had his Dad time. It was her turn – maybe their last chance to hang out together before he left.

The pump let out air as easily as it let it in. Enough to put him off coming with them. If she hid the pump, then even better . . .

It was still ages till Dad and Andrew would be back, so she texted Elisa to see if she wanted to meet up. The growing tension between them sat like a tumour in her heart. It needed to be cut out. The damage needed to be repaired, differences resolved, because she was all Amie had.

She wheeled her bike out of the garage. The sun was streaming through the gap in the conifers where the tree had fallen, flooding the front garden with light where there used to be darkness at this time of the morning. Orange didn't seem such a bad colour on a day like this. She waved to Maeve through the window, but she turned away, her hands over her eyes. Another migraine perhaps.

Pine Walk was wide and quiet, each house nestling in its own leafy fortress, protecting invisible families from the horrors of the real world. Sports cars and seven-seaters crouched on gravel drives, waiting to ferry children to ballet, horse-riding and karate, and their parents to the golf club and Waitrose. Each house was set back from the road, so it was hard to see through the gates, over the walls, behind the hedges. Anything could happen in there and no one would know.

Amie cycled down the middle of the road, trying no-hands, but only managing a split second before she lost control and had to grab the handlebars again. Unswept leaves crunched under her wheels and her breath escaped in tiny clouds of fog, mingling with the smell of invisible bonfires. She passed Mia Craven's house, a little bungalow on the corner of Whitstable Avenue with a bird table in the front garden and a conservatory at the side bathed in honey-coloured sunshine.

She took a turning into Riverside Place and dared herself to go past Jess Fleetwood's brand-new red-brick palace, with all her A grades safely locked up and guarded by dogs that ran up to the electric gates snarling if you spent too long going past.

A few hundred metres further on, next to a new housing development, was Celia Burrows' huge detached mock-Tudor mansion, with big low windows at the front and no trees, gates or hedges, so you could see right in. Through the window of Celia's house, Amie could see Alfie perched on the sofa opposite a giant TV, transfixed by some cartoon. Sometimes he slipped off the sofa and climbed back up, then just leant against it, banging back and forth as he stared at the screen, fingers in his mouth, agog.

As she watched him, something disturbed the stillness of her gaze, making her lift her eyes away to the room beyond, and it was then that she glimpsed him, just in the background at first, a shadowy figure, outside the reaches of the sun's rays, silhouetted against the back window.

Someone might have described him as just an average-looking man, if they didn't know him the way she did, tallish but not too tall, well built, strong arms. He was leaning against something, the kitchen worktop maybe, or the table. She couldn't see exactly, but she was sure it was him, if he'd only move into the light. He was in no-man's land, her blind spot. She needed him in the sitting-room area where he would be lit from the front, exposed. She struggled to penetrate the darkness and identify the person whose presence in that room her mind couldn't fathom, couldn't comprehend, couldn't accept.

He moved forward, slowly, then a few steps back again. No, she thought. Come back. Let me see you. He stepped towards her again as if he heard her willing him on, turning briefly backwards, saying something to someone? Then forward again as if she was pulling him on invisible cords, a marionette, coming because she was calling him to her. Then it was all a rush: he was suddenly there, in front of Alfie, scooping him up in his arms and saying something she couldn't hear or lip-read, but Alfie made a happy face, a chortling face, and seemed to forget all about *In the Night Garden*. He swung him high into the air, making him grin and wave his stupid legs all around. He lifted up Alfie the way he used to lift up Amie.

The rest was a blur, a flurry of hugs and kisses and Celia Burrows handing him a cup of something and kissing him on the lips. He turned to face her, his back to the window now, and that was when Alfie saw her. He pointed his fat little finger and his mouth opened to say something, but by the time Stuart turned around, if he did turn around, Amie was gone.

CHAPTER 26

She didn't remember leaving. Her head was a mess of information that she didn't want but which she couldn't delete. She didn't see the road, or the cars that hooted at her when she veered in front of them. She took a wrong turn, then had to cycle back down the same road, getting more and more panicked as the roads closed in and held her there, trapped in their web. Elisa called her but Amie was too breathless to speak, so there was no sound except the tick of the wheels turning before she managed to pant a barely audible, 'Help.'

'What's up, Amie? Has something happened?'

Her lungs clamped tight and closed, forcing her to fight for breath. Her heart was beating so hard she thought it would jump out of her chest.

Elisa met her on the corner of Pine Walk. 'Jesus, you look terrible! What happened?'

'I saw him. In Celia's house.'

'Who? You saw who? Daniel Foster?'

'Not Daniel – Dad. It was my dad.'

Amie pushed her bike on the pavement and Elisa had to put one hand on the seat to steady it because she was so shaky. At home, she pulled open the garage, sending the heavy door clanking up and over their heads. There they sat, on the cold concrete floor with the bikes and the smell of petrol and tools.

Elisa was very clear on the subject of lying. She said, 'Everyone lies, because everyone has secrets. We all have things that we don't want other people to find out because we don't want to upset them.' She pointed out that Amie was as guilty as anyone when it came to lying. 'Are you going to tell your mum what you saw?'

Amie's head was churning with possible outcomes, but there was only one route to getting Dad back. That much was clear. 'Of course not!'

'There you go, then. You don't want to tell her because you know she'll get upset, right?'

'Right . . .' said Amie hesitantly, but she wasn't thinking about that, just that to announce the betrayal would be to put an end to any dream of him coming home, any possibility of the family unit being repaired.

'So you're going to keep a secret too.'

'But that's not lying, that's just not saying.'

'So if she asks where you've been, will you tell her?'

'I'll just stay quiet and she won't know, so it doesn't count as a lie.'

'OK, but you've lied before, about other things . . .'

Amie frowned, wishing she had never told Elisa anything, willing back a time when she'd still had the choice about how far to let her into her life. But it was too late now. She was a fixture.

'You have, haven't you? To make people think about you differently? To make people like you more?'

'*SHUT UP!*' Amie screamed at her, losing control of everything for a horrible long second, as the world closed in on her.

Suddenly Elisa was beside her, arms around her. 'Sorry, Amie, I'm really sorry. Forget I said that. I wasn't thinking.'

But Amie was crying because she knew Elisa was right. We lie to make people like us. We pretend to be better than we are so we don't disappoint other people, so that they don't change their minds and walk away. We lie to make people not worry, and we lie to make them worry, to make them take notice of us, appreciate us more. We lie to manipulate people and situations so we get the best outcome. We lie to stay in control. Because we're scared of losing.

'So is that what you think my dad's doing?' The confusion stung her mind like poison.

'Think about it. He doesn't want to come home and say where he's really been because he wants you and your mum to like him. He doesn't want you to be angry with him, disappointed with him.' Elisa looked at Amie warily. 'And you are angry, aren't you, now you know the truth? And disappointed. So you can kind of see why he lied.'

Amie clung on to self-delusion for one last desperate time. 'I don't exactly know the truth, do I? I mean, I just saw him in Celia's house. Could've been anything. Maybe she needed help with something she couldn't do herself. Maybe he was fixing the dishwasher.'

'Do you really think that? They're kissing in full view in the front room and you think he's round there doing the plumbing?'

Amie hung her head.

'Face it, Amie, he's in love with Celia. Look at the evidence. What else can it be?'

Amie forced herself to be calm, and spoke quietly at first, but her tone gained force and pitch as the words poured out. 'If he is,' she began, 'if you're right, then it's because she's *made* him fall in love with her. He wouldn't leave us. We're his family, not her. He wouldn't do this to us. She must have forced him, blackmailed him, given him no choice. That's the only explanation.'

'Does it matter how it happened? I mean, if he loves her, that's the main problem, isn't it?' Elisa stared at her.

There were daggers in Amie's chest, hearing that. She was clutching at straws now.

'But he can't love her. He can't have everything, everyone. We've got to come first. We'll always be more important. We're the proper family.'

'I don't know. Maybe he thinks she's his family too. Maybe Alfie does,' Elisa said quietly.

Amie turned away, stomach and heart clenched like rocks. 'Alfie?'

Elisa looked downcast, as if she'd had no choice but to deliver the death knell. 'This thing could have been going on for years and years.'

A chasm opened between them, full of the reality of what was not being said. Every word pulled Amie lower and lower. She fought against it, grappled for rescue.

'He should have told me.'

'Told you what? That instead of watching Andrew play football he dropped him off and went off to see his girlfriend? He thought he was protecting you by lying about it. You didn't want the truth. You still don't.'

She didn't want the truth, but she didn't want the lie.

'You need to let him know how angry you are. I mean, you can't let him get away with it, surely?'

Elisa reached up to touch one of the racing bikes hanging on a hook on the wall. She spun the front wheel and the spokes blurred as the whirr built up to a crescendo then faded to silence.

'He said we could go for a ride later,' Amie said absently. It had sounded like the best idea imaginable, but now her stomach was sick with dread at the prospect.

'Probably likes that idea. He can cycle ahead of you. No need to chat, talk about stuff, tell the truth.'

Amie hadn't thought of it like that.

'I think you need to remind him that you're his number one priority.'

'Which I clearly am not.'

'But you want to be, right? You should be. He's your dad. Maybe he's forgotten what being a dad means. You're doing him a favour. Think of it as just shaking him up a bit, shaking him out of his sleep, back to reality.'

'What do you think I should do?'

She spun the wheel again. A whirr and a blur.

'The thing is, it's OK while he's in the annexe, but tomorrow when he moves out, that's going to be final. Once he's gone, it's going to be much harder to do anything. It's got to be now.'

'But what do I do? What are you talking about?'

'You've got to make it difficult for him to leave.'

It sounded logical enough, but it was harder to imagine how that could possibly be done.

'You know when something happens and people say it's a bad omen, like you trip over the front step walking into your new house – it's a sign things are going to go badly?'

'You want me to make something bad happen?'

'Just something that makes him think, makes him realise . . .'

Amie put her head in her hands. 'No. I can't.'

'But you would if you could, right? If you were brave enough? It's your chance to get him back. To get your family back, to make things normal.'

'You do it.'

There was a silence as Amie let her words sink in. She didn't know if she'd said them or thought them, but if she sat there, in a kind of trance, she wouldn't be responsible. When she opened her eyes again, Elisa was sitting next to her, staring ahead, pensive.

Dad came home as if nothing had happened. A cheery whistle hello, then, *Off you go, jump in the shower and get all that mud off*, and Andrew grunting, *OK, Dad, I'm not a kid,* and then Dad striding off to the shed to get the lawnmower. He gave Amie a quick grin and she just stared at him, unable to speak, unable to move, unable to let him see the fury that was coursing through her veins. *Liar, liar.*

There was no mention of the bike ride. Even the smell of cut grass that crept into the kitchen made her feel sick as she stirred her soup, lifting spoonfuls of it and pouring them out again. Elisa finished hers, but Andrew was even ruder than usual, said nothing to Elisa at all. When she asked him when he was off to Oxford, he just slunk out of the room, and Amie hated him more than ever.

Wait till he knew about where Dad was instead of watching him play football. Then he'd have a proper reason to be angry.

CHAPTER 27

Sunday came too soon. Not just any Sunday but the last Sunday morning with Dad at home. He came into the kitchen looking for some tools and tears stung the back of Amie's eyes. He was angry and distracted but didn't say what about, just rummaged around in a drawer, impatiently, as if what he was searching for was deliberately hiding from him.

'Are you going straight away?' It came out in a burst.

'No, late afternoon probably. I've got a few things to do first.' He shut the drawer and turned to face her. His face spoke pity, confusion.

'Can I help?'

'No, Amie, but thank you for asking.' He looked at her uncertainly before carrying on. 'There was an attempted burglary last night. A couple of roads away. I'm just helping patch up some of the damage.'

'Oh, no. Who?' Her mind raced back to Daniel Foster, moving closer to her, trying to frighten her.

'Just a work colleague.' He zipped up the bag and got to his feet. 'Right, that's it. I've got to dash.'

He didn't even look back or smile when he closed the front door. He just revved his motorbike and drove off, leaving Amie feeling empty.

Maeve stared out of the kitchen window, silent and glassy-eyed. Amie looked at her and wondered what was in her head, what she knew or didn't know, whether she should keep her secret or whether it was too late. Dad had his new life and family with Mum's best friend. He would never have had the courage to tell her that.

Amie went over to her, put her arms round her waist and her cheek against her back, and Maeve turned round and hugged her back, just quickly, as if it wasn't really allowed.

'I'm sorry,' Amie breathed.

'Oh, Amie,' was all she said.

The next morning, in form time, they talked about the migrant crisis and racism, and everyone had an opinion about how the government should tackle the problem. Lines were drawn in the sand and views were laid bare. *We haven't got room for them here . . . It's none of our business what's happening in Syria . . . What happens when they steal our jobs? They'll commit crime to get money to live . . . They might try and take over our country, break into our houses, steal all our stuff . . . Terrorists will get in, disguised as homeless migrants. What then?*

Amie was glad none of her classmates were in government. Mia Craven was usually the most reasonable when it came to things like this. She liked things to be all calm and friendly, a reflection of her report card, and the classroom discussion had clearly disturbed her. She was the last one to speak up.

'I think we need more police around, because . . .' She looked around to make sure she had everyone's attention. 'Someone round the corner from us was burgled on Saturday night. They smashed the window of her little boy's bedroom and he woke up screaming, all covered in broken glass.'

There was a stunned silence. Miss Emsworth drew breath.

'How awful, Mia, I'm so sorry to hear that.'

'There were no police on the street, and nobody saw anything, except one person, an old lady opposite, who thinks she saw someone running away.'

'At least someone saw something. We need to look out for each other.'

There was a nod and a hum of agreement, then another voice piped up. 'She should go to the police. It must have been one of the junkies that go to the addiction centre down the road.'

But Mia still held the stage. She hadn't finished.

'That would be weird, because the woman whose house it was, she actually works there, with the addicts.'

'So who was it, do they think?' another voice chimed in.

'The old lady opposite – she thinks it was a girl. With a ponytail.'

There was a mass intake of breath, followed by some urgent whispering and murmuring. Jess Fleetwood said, 'Well that rules me out,' with a sidelong look at Amie, who held her breath, wishing herself elsewhere. Heads turned to look at her quickly and away again. Then the bell rang, and an unusually subdued line of girls filed out of the classroom.

Everything went wrong that night. Everything had been going wrong ever since what happened with Daniel, but now the speed of the going wrong was accelerating. Amie had been floating through space without gravity and suddenly she was in the Earth's atmosphere and being sucked downwards faster and faster.

It was about six o'clock in the evening. Dad had come to the house because he was supposed to be taking Andrew to the station to catch the train to Winchester. He said he was going to see a band with a mate and was staying over, so he had a sleeping bag and a rucksack and that was why he needed a lift. Amie wondered if he was telling the truth because she didn't think he had any mates, but she could see he was getting stressed about being late – not saying anything but just frowning and then dropping all his bags on the floor when Dad couldn't find his keys. Then he made a big fuss about wanting to go on the back of Dad's motorbike, but Mum refused and said if Dad wanted to kill himself that was his choice but he wasn't going to take her children with him. Andrew shouted back, *Forget it, I'll just cycle to the station*, and Dad was all apologetic and uncomfortable, as if he couldn't even make his own decisions any more.

When Andrew shouted from the garage that he was taking the Trek because his own bike's tyres were flat, Stuart shouted back that it was fine, and to go ahead, and then it was quiet for a little while.

Sometimes Amie knew what other people were feeling even when they weren't actually saying it. She felt sorry for Maeve, peeling potatoes in the kitchen, always disappointed, and for Stuart, the cause of all that disappointment.

But then, at other times, there was just a great yawning gap where her empathy should have been, and what happened to Andrew that night left her feeling nothing at all.

Andrew never got to the band. He never got to his friend's house, or even the station. It turned out there was something wrong with the brakes on the Trek, and he came off trying to avoid the car coming towards him. He called home and Maeve was off like a shot in the car, screaming at Stuart, who was about to go back home but ended up sitting at the kitchen table with his head in his hands.

'I can't believe the brakes failed. There was nothing wrong last time I rode it,' he mumbled.

'When *did* you last ride it?' Amie asked. 'You're always on the motorbike nowadays.'

'A few weeks ago? I don't know. Maybe longer.'

Amie swallowed the lump rising in her throat. 'Maybe the brakes had worn out or something,' she offered, lamely.

He muttered under his breath as he left the house, but she could just make out the words. *It should have been me.*

They said he'd been very lucky, and if the car had been going any faster it would have been a different story. But he came home covered with cuts and bruises, bleeding from his cheek which had scraped on the tarmac. Stuart left, and

Maeve just shut herself in the kitchen. It was the same as it ever was.

Amie wondered whether Maeve would have gone rushing out to pick *her* up off the road. She sat down on her bed and stared at herself in the mirror, larger than life. She pulled the turquoise duvet up around herself until she was just a little mermaid head sticking out of the sea. That would be an easier life. In this one she felt like an impostor, a misfit who belonged on the outside with the others, living on the edge.

All was quiet in the house. It was as if their story was over, and the stage managers were about to turn up to take down the set.

She checked her phone, then unravelled the quilt and reached under the bed for her rucksack. It was time to leave. Time to go to the one place she could be herself, the one place she felt safe.

The kitchen door was shut and she was about to go in to say goodbye, but she didn't want to see Maeve's tears, didn't want to hear her vitriol or her criticism, didn't want to know how alone she really was. She pulled on a pair of trainers and slipped out of the front door.

Her bike was chained up at the side of the house. She clambered on and cycled off quickly down the road. The sun was low in the sky already. Her heart was fluttering, but she focused on the destination. She looked over her shoulder as she approached the house, just in case, because you never knew, and propped her bike up against the wall.

The door opened before she had a chance to knock.

CHAPTER 28

Until that Tuesday morning, each day of Ronnie's suspension had begun like the one before, an empty expanse of time during which she was expected to twiddle her thumbs, stare at walls, watch paint dry, anything but go into work. The torture of it was unbearable.

Her mother had been more condemnatory than supportive, however hard she tried to dress it up. 'You know I support you, darling, but you need to take responsibility for yourself. What will happen to the children if you can't work?'

Ronnie had put the phone on speaker and carried on trying to match Tupperware boxes with their lids.

'What kind of behaviour are they talking about? And why can't you remember? You must have had an awful lot to drink . . .'

The evenings seemed interminable. She went to bed as early as she could justify, but then spent hours tossing and turning. When she eventually got to sleep on Monday night, it felt like only a matter of minutes before the early-morning message from Maeve Slade sliced into her dreams and dragged her back to reality.

Amie's gone missing.

She wasted no time getting on the road, but the traffic was heavy. It was over half an hour before she was pulling into the manicured private road where it was clear that money wasn't enough to keep children safe. There was a patrol car parked on the grass verge. The neighbours wouldn't like that. Next door, a middle-aged woman dressed in gym gear scurried indoors, presumably not wanting to be involved. Where was the spirit of community in this place?

The front door of Amie's house stood open. Maeve was standing on the step, in some sort of trance that was a cross between fury and devastation. Stuart stood behind her, his face blank and empty.

Ronnie hurried over to them. 'I got here as soon as I could.'

Overton came over from his car and looked from her to Maeve and back again. 'Sarge?'

'You can leave this to me.' Ronnie nodded at him and held out her hand to Stuart, who had aged more than the year that had passed since their last meeting. His hair looked greyer. There were more lines around his startling blue eyes, and he looked more like a lost little boy than the head of the family.

'Thanks for coming so quickly, detective.'

The hallway was less clinical than Ronnie remembered. Junk mail on the floor; someone, Stuart perhaps, had slung his jacket over the banister, and a discarded pair of trainers and a bunch of keys lay on the bottom stair. There was a smell of aftershave mixed with cleaning products that made Ronnie want to open a window.

She was ushered into the kitchen, while behind them came the *tap tap* of heels on the tiles and an agitated Maeve pulled out stools at the island. There were bags under her eyes and her hands were shaking. She folded her arms when she saw Ronnie notice.

'How long has she been gone?' Ronnie was pulling out a notebook, waving away the offer of a seat. In the hallway, she could hear Overton on the phone to Lydia. She might not have long before the doors were closed on her involvement and she was ordered home.

'I don't know . . . Her bed hasn't been slept in.'

'She didn't mention anything, something you might have forgotten, a sleepover with a friend?' Ronnie thought of her last visit to the house, when Amie had refused to come out of her room. They weren't a communicative family, that was certain.

'No. She didn't say anything. I just found her room empty.' Maeve's voice was rising in volume and tone as panic set in.

Stuart hovered in the background, as if unsure whether it was appropriate to comfort his ex-wife. He looked down at his phone. Perhaps he was googling what to do. All thoughts of his attractiveness evaporated as it dawned on Ronnie how ineffectual he was.

'Has she taken anything with her, do you know? Packed a bag?'

'Not that I can tell. But I haven't looked. I just thought to call the police. I was expecting it to be you. I didn't expect the whole force.'

Ronnie smiled. If only she knew what had happened since they last met. 'Well, technically I'm off today, so my DC is on his way. But, in the meantime, let's go through as much as we can. Is Andrew home?'

'I just got him up. He says he didn't see her go out, but he's locked in his room most of the time. He's off to Oxford today.' She looked over at Stuart, and he looked up suddenly, as if sensing her eyes on him.

'When was the last time any of you saw Amie?'

Maeve hesitated. 'Last night, sevenish? She went upstairs after Andrew came back home, saying she didn't want dinner. I didn't see her after that.' She looked at Stuart again, who shifted awkwardly, playing with his phone. 'Stuart no longer lives with us,' she said woodenly.

'I saw her around six, when I was supposed to be giving Andrew a lift, but he ended up going off on his bike, and came off it – which was my fault, I know.' He gave Maeve a warning look.

Then Overton was back in the room, trying to get her attention. His face was grim. Lydia had clearly instructed him to stay put until Munro arrived.

'She said you weren't authorised, boss,' he said, in a low voice, which Ronnie appreciated.

'This is an emergency. I'm sure we can make an exception. Munro will be half an hour away at least.'

'Yes, sarge.'

Ronnie's phone was ringing now, with Lydia's name on the screen. She switched it to *do not disturb*.

'Can I take a look at her room?'

Maeve nodded. Her eyes were wide and staring.

It certainly didn't look like the room of a runaway. The wardrobe was full, pyjamas on the pillow. Above the bed hung a Van Gogh print in a heavy wooden frame. The curtains were half-closed, the non-committal way people often left them if they were going on holiday. You couldn't get much from a child's bedroom these days and this one was no exception. She pulled open a drawer and was about to go through the contents when a voice in the doorway made her jump.

'Looking for anything in particular?'

Stuart was smiling a half-smile that might have accompanied an offer to help, which was the last thing Ronnie wanted. She did her best to give him an answer without encouraging him.

'Just information about Amie – interests, friends, that sort of thing. Teenagers' walls are often plastered with photos of their besties.'

'She's not a terribly sociable girl,' Stuart offered, glancing round the room as if some clue might magically jump out at them.

'I see. Well, give me a few minutes and I'll come back and join you downstairs. We need to take statements from you all, but it shouldn't take too long before we're out there looking for her.'

225

She turned back to the open drawer, but he didn't seem ready to go anywhere. She raised her eyebrows, sensing he had something more to say.

He lowered his voice conspiratorially. 'Detective, would it be OK if I left you to it? I mean, I have a bit of an emergency of my own to attend to at home – my new home, I mean.'

'OK . . .' Ronnie frowned, wondering what emergency could be greater than the disappearance of his own daughter. 'As you can imagine, most youngsters come back hungry and cold in a few hours, or they're at a mate's house and didn't notice the time . . .'

Stuart was nodding in agreement, probably letting himself believe her just because it was easier than contemplating anything else.

'And, meanwhile, please do let us know if you think of anything.' She handed him her card, suddenly filled with a rush of pity for this man who didn't belong and didn't seem to be handling his life with much success. 'Anything at all.'

Back in the kitchen, Overton was making tea for Maeve, who was slumped over the island, hands clenched against her forehead. He was doing his best to reassure her, in his own awkward way.

'In ninety per cent of these cases, young people turn up alive and well the next day. Secret parties they don't tell their parents about, hangovers, arguments, sulking . . .'

'But this isn't just your average case, is it?' Maeve looked up as Ronnie came in. 'With what happened to her, surely she's more likely to be in the other ten per cent.'

Overton looked relieved to be rescued. Ronnie didn't answer Maeve's question. There was no point in catastrophising. It was up to her to keep the mood buoyant.

'I'm going to need the names and addresses of any friends, family, anyone she might run to in times of trouble.' Her pen was poised and ready, but Maeve just stared at her helplessly, tears forming behind her eyes, as if she was imagining the worst things.

The doorbell rang. It was Munro, out of breath and looking suitably apologetic, slightly wary even. Ronnie just about managed to keep her composure, but her eyes were on him, her head full of disbelief all over again at what he could have done to her career.

'Morning, DC Munro,' she said through gritted teeth.

He shook hands with Maeve, then turned to Ronnie. 'Sorry, sarge, but you're supposed to be off-games, I think?'

Ronnie bristled with rage. *And whose fault is that?* she wanted to say, but she managed to swallow her anger enough to reduce it to, 'Fair enough.' His face gave nothing away, so she made sure hers didn't either.

'I'll take over from here,' he said. 'Overton and I can take statements from the family.'

'You'll need to put a call in to her school, contact any family friends, neighbours.'

Munro was nodding. He knew all this, but she couldn't leave without saying it, just in case.

She turned back to Maeve. 'You have my number. Let's talk later.'

Munro followed her into the hall. 'Good to see you, though, sarge.' He lowered his voice. 'Hope it all blows over soon. A *storm in a teapot*, as my mother would say.'

Suddenly Ronnie couldn't picture him as the stranger at the bar. He was too soft, too guileless to stoop to underhand tactics. But then she had seen the footage. You couldn't disbelieve evidence like that.

It was disconcerting how her instincts took her one way, then swung violently in the other direction: about Baz, about Stuart, and also about Maeve. The woman was a mass of contradictions. But then again, how would she behave if Tilly vanished from home? It was something she had nightmares about every time a teenager went missing.

On the journey home, she thought through the situation logically, trying to assimilate everything she knew about Amie to work out what might have happened. Had she been taken, or had she gone of her own free will? If the latter, then where would she have gone? Maeve and Stuart had been less than forthcoming on that front. Susie had mentioned a school friend. If she could get a name for the girl, then Munro could follow that up as well as carry out the usual enquiries.

All she could do at this point was follow avenues that others wouldn't. She needed to think like Amie, get into her head. How did her mind work? Who could help her find out?

Back home, she made herself a coffee and dialled Louisa Emsworth's number, which went straight to voicemail. She'd be in school by now.

Then she remembered the one person who at this moment might know more about Amie than anyone. Her number was easy to find on speed dial and the call was answered almost before it rang, with a generic *Hello*.

'Susie?'

'Early for you, Ron, thought you'd be having a lie-in, enjoying your freedom.'

'Sorry to bother you, Suze, and this is a little bit off the record, but—'

'Haven't you had enough of living life on the edge?'

'Look, hear me out. I've been at the Slades'. Amie disappeared last night.'

'Disappeared? Hang on, what were you doing there? You're on leave.'

'Looking out for the family, as I told you I would. But don't worry about that. I just need you to do me one favour. You know the drawings Amie was doing for you in your sessions with her?'

'Yes, what about them?'

'Can you send them to me?'

'Give me one good reason why I would do that. I told you, I'm treading a fine line in my role here as it is, without sharing stuff with you and possibly the whole of CID.'

'Look, I promise you it will go no further than is strictly necessary. But I need to see the pictures, just in case they can give me any clues as to where she might be. And who with.'

'In case it's something to do with Foster?'

'That's what's on my mind. But I need to get into hers.'

'You've got him covered, though, right? I mean, it would be impossible, wouldn't it?'

'Theoretically, but we don't have eyes on him every minute of every day and night. It's not unheard of for offenders to find ways of getting past the boundaries, and if there is any compliance on the victim's behalf it's even easier.'

'You think she might actually be in on it?'

Ronnie was trying to keep the thought of it at arm's length. 'We have to keep an open mind. We're contacting the school, of course. And you mentioned a friend in her class. We should talk to her too.'

'Ah, that would be the famous Elisa.'

Ronnie sat up. 'Famous?'

Susie hesitated. 'Well, not only is she Amie's only friend from the sound of it, but she seems to be quite persuasive, gets Amie to do things she wouldn't otherwise do.'

'Controlling, you mean.'

'Yes, you could say that. Seems to be working her way into Amie's life. Amie . . .' Susie paused, as if to get the courage to make a decision to continue. 'Amie says it was Elisa who cut her classmate's hair, not her. She just took the blame.'

'She *what*? Why would she do that?'

'Influence, power, fear – who knows. Listen, Ronnie, you know I'm telling you this outside the boundaries of protocol now? I really shouldn't give you any more information.'

Ronnie breathed deeply. Now wasn't the time to lose her patience. She needed Susie, and she needed to give her whatever reassurance was required. 'Of course.

I completely understand. Only give me what you feel comfortable sharing.'

'Well . . .' Susie faltered, still unsure. 'She showed me a photo of her. Shortish blondish hair, I think, and a fringe. Amie has moments of wanting to shake her off, do her own thing, but friendships are pretty scarce in her life, as you know, so it's hard for her to break away, I imagine.'

'A better-than-nothing kind of friend.'

'That's it. Beats loneliness.'

Ronnie thought of Maeve again, scrubbing her kitchen worktops within an inch of their lives, and Amie's brother skulking off up the stairs. The absent hapless father. It was a house full of lonely people. It wasn't surprising that Amie needed to escape.

'And the pictures? Can you send me those?'

'Honestly? They're nothing but a bunch of scribbles. I wouldn't read too much into them.'

Ronnie laughed. 'That sounds odd, coming from a psychologist. Can I have a look anyway, just in case? There's almost nothing else to go on, after all.'

'OK, fine, I'll send some photos, but seriously, this must go no further, or I'll be joining you on the job market.'

'Deal. Thanks, Suze, you're a legend.'

There was no point sitting at home. The twins had gone off to school and she couldn't concentrate on anything while Amie was missing, whether or not she was officially on duty. She climbed into the car and headed back to the Slades' estate. Where would Amie go? Where could Foster have taken her, if it was Foster? Who was this Elisa, and what was the story behind their relationship? Could that be where Amie was hiding?

Still waiting for Susie's message to arrive, she parked a few doors away from Amie's house and watched a woman dressed in Lycra jog down the road, a sports bag slung over her shoulder. Ronnie couldn't remember when she had last been to the gym, and it was only downstairs in the basement. Even now that she had some free time on her hands, it was the last thing on her list of priorities. Perhaps it shouldn't be. Perhaps girls like this one and Natasha hung on to their relationships by taking good care of their bodies.

The thought sent a familiar wave of self-doubt through her, the one that threw all the questions up in the air so they landed in a chaotic pile in her lap. Should she have gone part-time and joined the green-smoothie-drinking gym crowd? Would that have saved her marriage? The idea that she might have got it all wrong only needed a chink in her armour to come seeping through, and now there it was, taking root in her mind and making her unsure about everything. She took another deep breath and closed her eyes. The feeling will pass. Let it pass, she told herself. Now was not the time to give in. There was a missing child to find.

Finally, her phone pinged.

Sorry, had to retrieve from my laptop . . .

Five pictures had come through from Susie and Ronnie flicked through them, feeling a pang of disappointment.

They were, as Susie had warned her, nothing but doodles and scribbles. There were patterns of infinite circles, winding round and round until they reached a black hole which seemed to go right through the paper. Lines came out of the black circles like legs on a spider, surrounded by symbols, plus and minus signs, square roots and brackets. It was a mess. Susie was right. There was nothing to see, and if a psychologist couldn't make anything of it, then mere mortals didn't stand much of a chance.

She rubbed her eyes and focused on a point in the distance. If you took yourself away from something, it often looked different when you came back to it. It had worked with the CCTV footage, so it might work with Amie's drawings.

After a minute, she reopened the image she'd been looking at and zoomed in on it as far as she could, then back out again. With fresh eyes, she saw a theme emerge. Among the cartoon spiders, dashes and crosses, there was a pattern of parallel lines turning corners and forking right and left, leading from one small square to another. Scattered over the lines were tiny box shapes, and, along the edges, cloud shapes that could easily have been sheep or the tops of trees. Above the clouds sat a cluster of sharper angles, triangles and trapeziums, framed by a square of jagged sticks. And in the top corner, approached by two short lines, narrower than the rest, there was another square, with a number partially scribbled out, surrounded by other numbers. Suddenly the number vanished. It was like one of those optical illusions you could only see if you blurred your eyes, then the next minute it was just doodle chaos. The number looked like 41, but she couldn't be sure.

She blinked and refocused, trying to piece together what the pattern might represent.

Still nothing of any substance. She let her mind wander for a minute and considered her options. She had no authority to do anything official. She could just turn round and go home, distract herself by cleaning out more cupboards, taking clothes to the charity shop and doing the shopping. She could sign the divorce papers and get on with her life.

Or she could follow her gut. The scribbles meant nothing to her, but they must have meant something to Amie. She pulled out her notebook and copied one of them from memory. It was a good test of her recall abilities and it might just help her make the link. She drew sets of parallel lines going in different directions. Quadrilateral shapes of different sizes. What was it all about? What did they represent?

Then she seized and held the idea that was germinating in her mind and came to a decision.

She wasn't going to go home just yet. She couldn't. She had to find Amie.

And, to do it, she was going to use the map that Amie had drawn.

CHAPTER 29

Ronnie pulled out of Pine Walk and turned on to the main road. Amie's map was looking less and less like a map since her decision to follow it. There were so many possible ways to interpret the drawing, and all she had was trial and error to go by. If the parallel lines were roads and the squareish shapes were buildings, it wasn't by any means an accurate representation of the local area, but there was a possibility it might begin to work, once she found herself in the right place. She drove on in search of landmarks, and found herself approaching a roundabout, where she went straight ahead, then pulled over into a church car park to look at the picture again. Suddenly it began to make sense.

What she'd first seen as a black spider with splayed legs, she now realised must be the roundabout she had just passed. The church was symbolised by the cross that she'd originally seen as a plus sign, part of a mysterious mathematical equation. If that was the roundabout, then she wasn't far from the only discernible number on the page: 41. A house number?

The route wasn't clear enough from there onwards, and, having explored the third, fourth and fifth turnings after the roundabout without success, she parked the car and retraced her steps. It was then, coming from the other direction, that she suddenly saw it in front of her, as if put in place at the last moment by a celestial hand. A hairpin bend, barely visible to traffic, and a playground. Swings and slides: triangles and trapeziums. This was the road.

It ran parallel to the new dual carriageway, and its poor state of repair told a story of a community chased away by change. The houses that lined the potholed tarmac were in the process of being demolished. Just four remained to be knocked down. Ronnie stared at the scene in dismay. If there had ever been a No. 41, then it was long gone.

It had been a long shot, so she shouldn't be disappointed with the scribbles turning out to be a dead end. Perhaps the pictures represented a memory, a place that no longer existed. She was there too late to see the house and whoever lived there.

Thankfully she hadn't shared her idea with anyone, and could easily just go back home, slip back into her suspended normality and wait for things to calm down. Perhaps there was no need for her to get involved. The team was on the case and maybe she didn't need to be. Perhaps they should all just trust Amie to come back when she was ready.

The word *trust* grated slightly. Did she trust Amie? She certainly felt a good deal of sympathy for her. Who wouldn't feel sorry for a girl who'd been abused by an adult at fifteen, then watched her family fall apart just as the assailant was back on the streets? Her father was absent physically and her mother mentally. There wasn't much good in her life right now. Amie Slade had a right to a break. Imagining that Daniel Foster could have been meeting her secretly in a derelict house might be taking things beyond the realms of possibility.

Ronnie walked along the pavement, taking in the extent of the disrepair, which seemed to increase with each building she passed. The fourth house stood slightly back from the rest, as if trying to retreat from the wrecking ball. Windows like hollow eyes, some half bandaged with plywood, stared forward over the rubble opposite. What remained of the roof sloped at an odd angle and, where the tiles had fallen off and the timbers had rotted, a torn blue tarpaulin half covered the exposed attic. It was end-of-the-line, in more ways than one. Time to go home.

It was exactly at that moment, where she held her hands up in defeat, that Ronnie noticed something about the door of the house.

Looking back, she would remember that moment when the number 41 had sprung out at her from nowhere. One second it was a 4, the next 41.

It was uncanny. As she took it in, a wave of sickness rose inside her.

Number 4 was clear. But number 1 wasn't a number at all, it was a vertical slash on the woodwork next to the 4. The wood had cracked enough to produce a shadow that you could only see from a certain angle.

Stepping back to look at the whole building, she questioned her own sanity. Was she inventing reasons for this to be the place? It was a wreck, clearly hadn't been occupied for decades.

A crow rose from the timber frame, squawking loudly, flapping wings against leaves, and others followed. Ronnie watched the first one land on the bare branch of a dead tree, and then on the front step, where the faded blue door, half hanging off its hinges, was banging in the wind.

'Can I help you?'

A site worker stood a few metres away, in a yellow helmet and hi-vis jacket.

'Police.' She flashed her badge. 'Investigating an incident.'

'In there?' He pointed to the house and made a face. 'You sure? That place has been empty for years. We're redeveloping the site now, finally, but it's taken bloody ages for them to make their minds up. What kind of incident?'

'Missing person.'

'Well, I'd watch out. The building's not safe. I'll be over here if you need me, just sealing off the construction site.'

Ronnie made her way over the rubble. The half-open door put up no resistance, just swung back helplessly behind her as she stepped into the darkened room. No electricity, of course. She fumbled around where cracks of light broke into what might have once been the sitting room and wrenched off a plank, dropping it as her hands took its weight. She'd expected it to be nailed on rather than balanced against the broken glass. It just missed her feet, but her left hand smarted with pain as the splintered wood grazed her palm. Sunlight streamed in through the rectangular gap it left. Taking a breath for the first time, she retched as the smell of rotting flesh hit her like a slap in the face.

The cat had been dead a few days at least, and was partly obscured by the hum of flies that hovered in and around the makeshift crate. Picking up the plank that had barred the window, she poked away the lid, and a swarm of insects rose up into her face. She staggered backwards, pulling her scarf up over her nose and holding it there, while she rummaged for her phone with her free hand and shone the torch around the rest of the scene. The floor was mostly rubble. A single plank was balanced across two large breeze blocks, forming a bench, a dirty silk pashmina half covering its length. Facing it, on the opposite wall, she could make out a chalk square, like the outline of a television, and placed exactly where a television might have been when the house had been inhabited. Inside the square, a single word, scrawled in the desperate hand of a prisoner calling for help. *Riptide.*

Below the chalk square, some clumps of mud stood in a carefully constructed pyramid with a flattened top, altar-like, bearing an offering that resembled a large pencil case or purse, sitting on half of an old brick. It reminded her of an installation – the sort of thing you'd expect to see at the local art college exhibition. Pulling a glove on, she opened the clasp and took it over to the light to see better. Inside was a plastic yellow box and a coiled length of cable, something that might have been lying around in the garage. Entangled with the cable was a thick swathe of blonde hair, and nestling in the hair was something she would have

239

missed were it not for the shaft of light that cut through the room to where she stood – a small white button.

'Amie?' Her voice was quieter than she'd expected.

There was no reply.

'Amie!' Louder now, but no reply, just falling dust, as if the sudden sound had disturbed what remained of the building. 'Amie, are you in here?'

There was more silence. Ronnie pulled her scarf back up and headed back to the door, where she breathed in long, greedy breaths of fresh air.

The phone rang. It was Lydia again. 'DS Delmar, where are you?' Her voice was irate.

'Ma'am . . .'

'Overton said you took over from him at the house.'

'I did, but—'

Lydia didn't let her finish. 'DS Delmar, you were told you were off duty until further notice. Did I not make myself clear?'

'Look, ma'am, I can explain everything. But you need to see this. I think Amie's been here.' She gave her location.

'And what makes you think that?'

'Something she drew, clues I've been following. It's a long story, but I think there's a connection.'

There was a pause as the DI spoke on another line, then she was back, her tone suddenly urgent. 'You're literally a hundred metres away from an incident that's just come in.'

'Another incident? What happened?'

'An abandoned toddler in an Audi parked on the dual carriageway, child locks on the doors, couldn't get out. A passer-by heard him banging on the window.'

Ronnie's heart began beating faster, as if the world was closing in. 'Is he OK? Whose car is it?'

'It belongs to a friend of the Slades, but no one's seen her since last night. Strangely, we had a call on Saturday night from the same woman. Some hooligan threw a stone at her toddler's bedroom window. The kid was quite badly cut by broken glass. She was very shaken by it.'

'Do you think there's a connection with Amie's disappearance?' It was so instinctive to get involved, even though she knew she wasn't. Lydia would remind her of that, no doubt.

'It's too much of a coincidence, all this happening around one family.'

'Yes, ma'am, I couldn't agree more.'

She waited for the order to leave the scene, but it never came. There was a pause as Lydia spoke offline again, then she was back. 'Munro's on his way over to you from the Slades' house now. Oh, and DS Delmar . . .'

'Yes, ma'am.'

'There has been a development, as it happens. We examined the evidence and we have no reason to believe you did anything to bring the force into disrepute. So I'm pleased to tell you that the case against you has been dropped.'

Ronnie was lost for words.

'This does not excuse your turning up to the scene of an investigation today without due authority, because as far as you were concerned, the rules were still in place about where you were permitted to be, but on this occasion I will overlook your misjudgement. You may continue this investigation as usual in your capacity of detective sergeant.'

Ronnie was still speechless when Lydia had finished. It was an extraordinary turn of events, as if a divine hand had reached down and set her back on her feet again.

'DS Delmar? Are you still there?'

'Yes, yes, I'm here,' Ronnie came back to earth as Munro came into view. 'Thank you, ma'am. That is such good news.'

She ended the call, and Munro caught her eye as he approached the house. 'Well, DS Delmar, we must stop meeting like this.' He grinned, confusing Ronnie even more.

'Turns out they've withdrawn the case against me so I'm back on the job,' she replied, giving him a long, hard look. 'How's the little boy doing?'

'They're just giving him the once-over in the ambulance. No evidence of any shock or trauma, seems to have been asleep all night.'

'That's good news.'

'And even more good news about the complaint being thrown out. Well done, sarge.'

Ronnie's eyes rested on him until he looked away. But the explanation could wait.

'So, what's in here, then?' He indicated the house behind them.

'Don't ask how I worked it out, but I thought she might be here. We're going to have to go back in, take a proper look. From what I've seen, it looks as if Amie may have been hiding out in there.'

'The guy over there says it's not safe. Wants us in hard hats.'

'No time for that. Come and take a look.'

But Munro was already marching across to the site office in search of the appropriate clothing. Wondering if she had imagined the whole thing, Ronnie pulled on the shoe covers she always carried in her bag and stepped back inside. But it was all real enough. Too real. The smell hit her all over again after being out in the fresh air. She shone her phone torch at the festering animal corpse, then at the scrawl in the chalk square, then down to the array of grim exhibits against the wall. At the far end, she could just make out the stairs leading up to the first floor. She stepped over the bench and made her way into the dark recesses of the room.

'Amie?' As she called up the stairs, a flurry of brick dust fell into her face, as if her voice had disturbed what was left of the fragile structure of the building. 'Amie, are you there?' This time there was more of it, a cascade of crumbling brickwork tumbling down the staircase to her feet.

She backed towards the door, holding her scarf over her face against not just the smell but now the dust, which was making her cough. As she went, she took pictures on her phone of everything she could see, including a cluster of footprints in the sawdust, zooming in as close as she could. Then she retraced her own footprints backwards so as not to disturb the evidence any more than she had.

She only found the second staircase when she almost fell down it.

Once you saw it, you couldn't imagine how you'd missed it, but the cracks of light from the boarded-up window had drawn her attention left, towards the fireplace. To the right, crumbling stone steps led down to the cellar.

She heard Munro's footsteps crunching up the path as she shone her torch downwards. The stairs were narrow and uneven, a couple missing, others broken and cracked. No banister. She scanned her torch from right to left, slowly, and caught her breath in shock.

First she saw the foot, twisted at a painful angle. A leather boot, half off, reflecting the torchlight. The rest of the body was splayed out at the foot of the steps, a blonde head turned away, motionless.

'Baz!' Ronnie's voice echoed louder than she expected. She was edging down the steps, crouching at the side of the spreadeagled body, feeling for a pulse on the woman's neck. 'Baz!'

Another beam of light fell on the crumpled figure. 'Jesus Christ. Is that her?'

'It's not Amie. Call an ambulance.'

Munro was already on the phone. 'Any ID on her?'

Ronnie pulled a wallet out of the woman's handbag and shone her torch on it. No credit cards but a driving licence, a photo of a little boy, another picture of a couple taken in a photo booth. She recognised the man's captivating blue eyes. Suddenly things began to fall into place.

She called up to Munro, 'Driving licence says she's Celia Burrows, 24 Riverside Place.'

'Burrows? That's the owner of the car. And the house we were at on Saturday after the break-in . . .' He broke off as the paramedic asked after the state of the patient.

Ronnie shouted up to him, 'She's unconscious but she's breathing. I don't know how much time she has. They need to *hurry*.'

The blare of sirens was approaching as she made her way up the stairwell to daylight. Munro held out his hand. 'Careful, sarge, this place could collapse any moment.' Ronnie took it, but made sure she let go as soon as she was outside.

They looked on as Celia Burrows was carried into the ambulance on a stretcher. Munro closed the ambulance doors.

'That little boy is going to need his mum to pull through,' Ronnie breathed, her eyes still fixed on the retreating ambulance.

'Thanks to you, sarge, she's got a decent chance of that.'

She looked at the time on her phone. 'Have we heard from the school? It's ten-thirty already.'

'Overton was on that. I'll chase it up.' He pulled out his phone and started tapping a message.

'Actually, don't. I'll phone them myself, since I'm back on duty.'

The phone was answered within two rings. After a brief chat, Ronnie hung up again. 'You're not gonna believe this.'

'What?'

'Amie's at school.'

'She's what?'

'Wasn't even late arriving.'

'What? They called us out for nothing?'

Ronnie thought about it. 'Thank God they did – because we'd never have gone looking for this place if they hadn't. Celia Burrows would probably have died if we'd found her any later.'

'So what now?'

'Get a team down here.' She indicated the house with a tilt of her head. 'We need everything we can get. Footprints, for a start. There are plenty of them, some of them much smaller than mine. I'm no expert, but they look recent.'

'What are you thinking, sarge?'

'I'm thinking she was here.'

'Amie?'

Ronnie nodded, eyes closed against the realisation of it all.

'And she wasn't alone.'

CHAPTER 30

When Amie heard the doorbell, she took her time. Maeve was sleeping off another migraine upstairs. Dad had taken Andrew to his precious university. So whoever it was at the door could wait.

DS Delmar, hand raised to ring a second time as Amie appeared, did a double-take. 'You're home . . .'

'I'm home.' She smiled her politest smile.

'Where were you? You know your parents called the police?'

'I know. It was a misunderstanding. I was here all night. I left early for school this morning.'

DS Delmar gave her a searching look. 'Can I come in?'

Amie stepped aside to let Delmar pass.

Maeve was already coming downstairs, one hand on her forehead and rolling her eyes. 'DS Delmar – Ronnie, I'm so sorry to have wasted your time. It seems we were at cross purposes. She says she was here all night after all. I assumed, when I saw her empty room and made-up bed . . . I thought she'd been taken, gone out and not come home. I feel terrible, having called you and your colleagues out like this. I was panicking. I realise that now. It was just after Andrew's accident. It shook me up so much.' Her voice was fluttery, like an irregular heartbeat.

Delmar smiled a half-smile at Amie. 'I'm relieved you're back. We were very concerned about you.' She seemed to be speaking on autopilot, as if her head was thinking something her lips weren't saying.

'I'm sorry if I worried everyone.' Amie did her best to sound sorry. 'Andrew shouldn't have taken Dad's bike.' She scanned the hallway, plucked a jacket off the banister and bent to pick up a pair of Nike trainers with the backs of the heels trodden down. She was like an extension of Maeve in her orderliness. 'I'll just take these upstairs.'

Delmar reached out an arm to stop her, which made her recoil in shock.

'Amie, when you've done that, do you think we could have a chat?'

'What about?'

'There's been an incident, and we need to talk to you about where you were last night. Both of you.' She looked back at Maeve for confirmation, but Maeve only widened her eyes and blinked rapidly.

Amie took her time upstairs, waited for her heart to slow down before coming back down. When she got back to the kitchen, Maeve had made Delmar a cup of tea. She patted the seat next to her and Amie sat, cautiously. 'What's happened?'

'There's been an accident. I can't give you the details, but I do need to know where you were last night.'

'I was at home, as I said.' She looked at Maeve, who tried to smile some sort of encouragement. 'It's not my fault nobody notices if I'm here or not.'

Delmar inhaled deeply and spoke on the outbreath, as if to calm her impatience. 'A lot of people were worried about you, Amie.'

'Why? There was no reason to be.' She tried to give a hard look back in return.

'Think of it as concern. You're not in trouble. I just need you to tell me where you spent last night.'

She was looking so intently, Amie wondered whether she could see right inside her brain. She wondered whether it was looking up and to the right or to the left that meant you were lying – or was it down and to the right? Where should she look so they'd know she was telling the truth?

'I was here. I keep telling you.'

'It's my fault,' Maeve interrupted. 'As I said, I shouldn't have panicked. Can we put this behind us now?'

But Delmar had a look on her face that said she didn't believe either of them. She looked hard at Amie, who just looked straight back at her.

'Why would I lie about it?' Amie felt her voice crack.

'There are dangerous people out there, Amie. You of all people know that, after what you went through.'

Delmar seemed to think that bringing up the past would help, but it just made bile rise in Amie's throat and the blood pump in her ears. 'You mean Daniel Foster.'

There was a pause, then, 'We just need to protect you from him, and people like him.'

There was no point telling her it was too late for that.

'I wasn't with him, if that's what you're trying to suggest.'

Delmar's expression didn't change. She twisted her pen between her fingers and put her chin in her hand, as if it might encourage Amie to say something different.

'Have there been any more attempts at contacting you that we don't know about? Anything online? Facebook . . .' She drifted off, as if trying to think of other online ways of talking to people.

'Nothing.'

'Are you sure? Nothing at all?'

'Of course I'm sure. Why wouldn't I tell you? I said I'd tell you.'

'All sorts of reasons. Protecting him. Shame. Denial.'

'I'm not ashamed.' Amie laughed, a sudden raucous laugh that came from nowhere and sliced through the air.

DS Delmar didn't seem to be so sure. 'Can I have your phone, Amie?'

Amie frowned. 'Why?

'Just routine. As I said, there's been an incident that we aren't able to discuss, and checking phone evidence is important.'

'It's upstairs.'

Delmar seemed unsure about letting her go upstairs again, but eventually nodded her agreement and even seemed surprised at how quickly she returned.

'This is the password.' She scribbled some numbers on Ronnie's pad. 'Will you give it back to me when you've finished?'

'Of course.' Delmar slid the phone into a plastic bag, then gave Amie an earnest look. 'I know you're back home now, but what matters is that you had everyone worried. You need – we *all* need to make sure we communicate. To protect you from danger. So we need your honesty above all else.'

'In case he comes looking for me?'

'Has he come looking for you, Amie?'

Amie shook her head. Because DS Delmar wouldn't understand. She lived in the land of happy families. Normal people. Another world away.

'OK.' Delmar was frowning now, calculating something in her head. 'There's just one more question I have for you, Amie.' She was putting her notebook back in her bag, pulling her scarf around her neck, so Amie expected something harmless, like *Where did you get that lovely bracelet?* but it came from left field and took her by surprise. 'What size shoes do you take?'

Then, when Amie answered, she asked her to come down to the station to be questioned under caution.

'Can she go without me?' Maeve looked up, hollow-eyed and helpless. 'I don't think I can face it.'

'I'm fine on my own,' said Amie, avoiding eye contact with anyone.

'I can ask Susie Marshall to be the appropriate adult,' suggested Ronnie.

Maeve shrank back into the corner. She was the child here. 'Do whatever you want.'

CHAPTER 31

Baz shook his head in disbelief when Ronnie relayed the events on her return to the station.

'I should have followed up with the school earlier.'

'What the hell was Overton doing all morning? Surely that was his first port of call?'

'An unfortunate case of telephone tag, apparently, but, as you said, we'd never . . . *you'd* never have found Celia Burrows.'

'How's our victim doing?'

'The hospital said they'd phone when she was able to talk. But that's a while off, apparently. Stuart's on his way back from Oxford to be with her. It's all out in the open now, their affair.'

Ronnie shook her head. 'What a mess. What's his alibi?'

'In the pub, seen by a few people, then says he went home to bed, woke up in the morning and couldn't get through to Celia. Then he gets the summons from Maeve.'

Ronnie pictured Stuart's face as he told her about his *personal emergency*. It was beginning to make sense now.

'Don't get me started on Maeve. What's she doing, changing her story?'

'The migraines, apparently. "Messing with her memory". It could have just been a panic reaction, seeing the empty room and calling the police. It was as if the thing she'd been dreading had finally happened. It's like she just assumed, *That's it. Foster's come back for her.*'

'Did they look through Amie's phone?'

'No point. Wiped clean.'

Ronnie put her head in her hands, remembering Amie voluntarily handing it over.

'Anything else from forensics on the prints?' She was mentally ticking things off in her head now.

'I don't know how useful this is, but . . .' He tapped in the code on his tablet. Ronnie bit her pen in dread. 'All the officers at the scene were wearing protective footwear, so we know it's no one from here.'

Ronnie bit down harder to distract her from the shock of what she was about to hear.

'There are two sets of footprints, lots of size fives as you know, which are a good match for Amie, and they should be able to confirm that any moment. But also, there's a fresh set of size tens, could easily have been left in the last twenty-four hours.'

He passed her his tablet and she stared at the photo on the screen, partly in disbelief, partly as an excuse to look away, so Munro wouldn't see the horror on her face.

'Stuart's alibi doesn't clear him for the whole night, does it? There's motivation for him to remove Celia from the picture. She's ruined his family life. Maeve might have a canny divorce lawyer trying to take him to the cleaners.'

'I like your thinking, sarge, but wrong size shoes.'

Ronnie put her head in her hands. She didn't like where the evidence was leading them, but not to follow it up was worse than knowing the truth. 'Get someone round to Foster's place. We need to identify the footprints before we interview Amie. We need leverage here.'

'We might have to manage without.' Munro looked sheepish. 'I sent uniform over there straight away, sarge.'

'And?'

'He's not there. Foster's missing.'

Ronnie sank into her chair and spun one way, then the other.

'Lydia knows?'

'She's on the warpath.'

Overton appeared around the partition. Ronnie resisted the urge to have a go at him for the school fiasco.

'We're ready for the interview when you are, sarge.'

'DC Munro, can you start the proceedings? I'll be right down.' She had a call to make. If the day's events had taught her one thing, it was to keep her own family together.

It hardly rang before it was picked up. 'Mum, where are you? I thought you weren't working this week.' Tilly's voice was almost admonishing, which warmed Ronnie's heart.

'Change of plan. I'm back on the job, but I might be here late tonight. Can you forage for something in the freezer for dinner?'

'Yeah, we can do that. Oven chips and ice cream?'

Ronnie smiled. 'Yes, if you can find something to go with it. But stay indoors.'

'What?'

'Don't go out, and don't answer the door.'

'Why? What's happened? Mum, you can't just say that.'

'You know I can't tell you, Tilly. But I will when I can. It's not that you're in danger – I just feel I have to repeat the instructions when I'm not there so that I feel I've done my duty.' She wasn't making much sense, but Tilly seemed happy with it.

She was about to go down to the interview room when a message flashed up on her screen.

Got this photo from Celia Burrows' phone.

This was a game-changer.

CHAPTER 32

The interview room was a cold grey box with no windows, just a square of pale light in the door. Beyond it, heads moved, muffled voices brought reminders of freedom and outside.

The room was bare apart from something on the opposite wall – one of those fire regulations notices in a wooden frame, that nobody read but were supposed to save your life, assuming it was worth saving. Who'd have time to read it in a fire anyway? You'd be racing out of the door, not hanging around making sure you had obeyed all the instructions about walking in single file on the left, no talking . . .

Opposite Amie sat DC Munro, then there was an empty chair between him and the solicitor, who had told her to say *no comment* to everything. Then there was Susie as the appropriate adult. Amie wondered what an inappropriate adult would look like. Probably just like Maeve.

Then DS Delmar burst into the room, slightly out of breath. She and Munro exchanged serious looks and then she looked at Susie for slightly longer, the way women did because they have more to communicate than you can get across in a glance.

DS Delmar took the empty chair, wrote something on her pad and passed it to Munro, who shut his eyes tightly for a second and shook his head. Delmar nodded at Munro, who started the tape and said what time it was and who was there.

Questions were fired at her and Amie sat in silence, waiting for the end of each one before saying *no comment*. Munro seemed to get more and more frustrated, but they couldn't get to her. Nobody could force her to do anything. Susie had helped her understand that.

Then it was Delmar leaning forward, doing the same hand-clasping as Munro, closing in on her, waiting to deliver a killer blow. She braced herself and fixed her expression blank, hard.

'Tell us where you were last night, Amie.'

'No comment.'

'You told us that you spent the night at home, but what you don't know is that we have proof that you weren't at home.' Her voice was quieter, as if that might encourage Amie to say something other than *no comment*.

'We have your shoe prints at a crime scene.' She passed her a photo of a house that looked as if it was falling down, and another photo of a shoe print in the dust. You had to focus hard to see it. 'It's time to tell us the truth, Amie.'

Amie looked up at her, wide-eyed, but didn't respond.

'There were some other, bigger footprints – a man's shoes.' Another photo was passed across to her side of the table. Susie and the solicitor peered at them and Amie steeled herself for what was coming.

'So we think these prints belong to someone who was with you at the house.'

'No comment.'

'Who was with you at the house last night, Amie?'

She didn't have time to answer before Delmar repeated the question, in a much crosser voice. 'Who were you with last night, Amie?'

'No comment.' Her voice was breaking.

'Was it Daniel Foster?'

'No!' Suddenly she found her voice but it was alien and beastly.

The solicitor was looking at her with incomprehension. The *no comment* spell had been broken.

Munro scraped his plastic chair backwards and Amie knew that meant LISTEN, just like Maeve clattering too loudly in the kitchen saying *take notice of me*, like the fire bell at school, slicing through time with its deafening demand for action, the silent line-up, the trooping out to the playground. Time to stand up and be counted.

'Right, so, now you're talking to us, there's something we need to discuss, Amie.'

He leant forward, then slapped a folder down on the table, causing a pile of loose papers to scatter and settle in the breeze. The solicitor put his hand on his notebook, to stop it flying off in the hurricane.

It seemed like an eternity before Munro spoke. Blood thudded in her ears. She stared at a spot on the floor.

'What happened to Celia Burrows?'

Amie went cold inside. She looked at Susie for support, then across to the others.

'Someone tried to murder Celia last night. Pushed her down the stairs to the cellar in the house we just showed you.'

Amie's heart pounded. She couldn't speak even if she'd wanted to.

'Do you know who it was, who did that?'

Amie shook her head, and someone said something for the tape, before Munro went on.

'The thing is, I think you know who did it, because you were there, in that house, where the accident happened. We know this not just because we have your shoe prints at the scene. There's something else.'

Amie held her breath, trying to freeze time, so nothing could happen.

'Just before she was attacked, at around ten-thirty p.m. last night, Celia Burrows took this photo . . .' He slid an iPhone across to Amie. 'Which, as you will see, is an orange bike, which I think belongs to you. Is that correct?'

He carried on now, no pauses, no interruptions. They were on the motorway of the interrogation, going at a hundred miles an hour, with no hard shoulder.

'Celia must have seen your bike lying on the ground outside that house last night and taken a picture.'

Amie flinched as if she'd been whipped in the face.

'She would have been worried about you, out late at night; maybe she was worried you had been abducted, possibly by the man who attacked you once before.'

'It's not my fault you let him out.' It came out in a rush. The solicitor blinked and frowned, but it was too late.

'We didn't just *let him out*, Amie,' DS Delmar interrupted, her exasperated look reminding her of Mum. Amie went all hot inside as her words exploded on to the table between them. 'It's not as simple as that. He's served his time; he has a criminal record and he isn't allowed to go near you. But Celia might have thought that you were in danger; she might have thought, Amie is in there with *him*.' She slowed down her words to make more of them, and Amie stiffened, trying not to let fear escape. 'Was she right? Were you in the house with Daniel Foster?'

Delmar held her gaze and she couldn't reply.

'Amie, you have been the victim of a serious assault. You can understand what Celia's concerns might have been. She would have parked the car and gone to the house to investigate.'

Amie put her head in her hands, wanting it to be over.

'From her injuries, all we can assume is that as she entered the house she was hit on the back of the head with something sharp, and pushed down the stairs into the cellar. That's where she was found, bleeding and left for dead.'

'Why are you telling me all this?' Amie asked, her voice choked and tiny.

'Because the timing of Celia's photo, as well as the prints from your shoes, clearly places you at the scene. Now tell us why you were there, and who with.'

Her voice shook with fear and panic. 'My bike was never there. I never went there. Mum said not to. She said you never knew . . .'

'And she was right to say that, Amie, but you *did* go there. Did someone take you there or make you go there? Someone you were scared of, someone who wasn't a friend at all, someone who was hurting you? Did he panic when the intruder threatened his secret? Was it him that sent her crashing down the stairs, where she almost bled to death?'

Now she was showing her a photo of Celia, bloodied and lifeless in the dark.

She saw spots before her eyes. Susie's hand was on her arm again.

Munro raised his eyebrows as Delmar continued. 'And we have something else to ask you about.'

'What?' She tried not to blink. Blinking would mean something to them, for sure, like looking up to the left or right.

Delmar reached for more photographs, labelled with letters and numbers in the corners, and laid them out on the table in front of her. Amie recoiled.

'We found things in the house; we think you kept things there that must have meant something to you.'

Amie clasped and unclasped her hands, focusing on the repetition of the action, because it would distract her from the words being said.

'Two months ago, you cut six inches off someone's hair in the classroom, and now that hair . . .' she tapped her finger on the picture of it '. . . is displayed at a crime scene.

Don't you think that gives us good reason to think you were there?'

Amie focused on her hands and tried to control her breathing. This would pass. It would pass.

Delmar's eyes pierced hers. 'There were other things at the house, Amie. We are looking into it and we *will* find out where they came from, and, if they are linked to you, you might as well tell us now.'

The solicitor cleared his throat and wrote something down. Munro, Delmar and Susie were all looking at her now, as Delmar continued.

'We found this in Celia Burrows' bag.' She pushed something across the table and said something about an exhibit for the benefit of the tape. It was a plastic bag, like a freezer bag, and inside there was a small photograph, the kind you'd get taken for a passport or if you were messing around with your friends. Celia and Dad, heads together, laughing at the camera.

She felt sick, her head began to spin, and her heart shattered into a thousand pieces.

What Delmar said next floated over her like a wave. The kind of wave that pulls back before a tsunami.

'Did you know about your father's and Celia's relationship?'

Amie turned away in horror. Suddenly the room felt too hot. She ran to the door and beat her fists on it, oblivious to the pain in her knuckles. Her breath came in bursts and gasps as she gulped for air. She slid down the wall to the floor, crouched like a cornered animal, dug her nails into her thighs.

Her vision clouded and blurred. She didn't want to see or hear anything, so she screamed to drown out everything else. Then Susie was there too and she lashed out at her, hitting her in the chest, on her arms, kicking out with her legs, shaking her head wildly, convulsing in terror at what was happening inside her head. She seized a pen that was lying on the table and started stabbing her arms and legs with it. She wanted to feel the pain, wanted to drown out the other pain of hearing that things weren't what she thought they were. Then everyone was on their feet, and two more uniformed officers burst into the room, taking her arms, holding her from behind, telling her to *calm down, breathe, calm down . . .*

The tape was stopped, chairs scraped back, the door swung open, shoes clicked hollowly in the corridor. Amie was held on both sides as they took her out of the room and into the next one down the corridor. Someone brought some water and the door swung shut, leaving her and Susie embraced by grey walls and stained carpet. How many innocent people had sat here before, waiting for their fate to be determined by people who knew nothing?

'How are you feeling now? Any better?' Susie's voice was quiet. Amie could hardly hear her.

There was a knock at the door and a uniformed officer brought in a medical kit. Susie nodded him away, saying she'd take care of it.

'It was a panic attack. And you could have hurt yourself badly.' She was looking at Amie's arms, punctured with red dots of blood. 'This will probably put a stop to the questioning.'

'I wasn't there. It's not my bike,' she offered, lamely.

'It's not just the bike, it's the footprints.'

'They don't have a weapon. I've seen films. I've read books. Police plant evidence if they want to charge someone.'

Susie pulled her chair round to face Amie, leant forward with her elbows on her knees, arms folded, eyes on hers, forcing her to engage.

'You can tell me the truth, Amie. I do understand everything you're going through. It's been a rough time for you. A *really rough time*.' She repeated the last three words deliberately slowly, letting Amie know she was with her, that she got it. 'If there was someone else involved, now is the time to say. But I should warn you: they may want you to be assessed by a doctor, a psychiatrist probably, to see if you are really fit for any kind of judicial process.'

Amie nodded slowly, staring at the plastic cup, whirling the water one way, then the other, concentrating on not spilling it.

CHAPTER 33

Munro held the incident room door open for Ronnie to pass. And he was the one holding the files. Double chivalry today, but it went nowhere towards fixing the dilemma they were in.

'What do you reckon, sarge?'

'We have so much on her, but she's still resisting. What's she hiding?'

'I can only imagine it must be a pretty dark secret.'

'I want to know who she was with, and what she was doing with *this*.' She scrolled down her phone to a picture of the brake cable.

'Someone would have had a nasty accident with that missing from their bike,' offered Munro.

'Bike accident . . .' Ronnie put her head in her hands. 'We're idiots.'

'I'd like to say *speak for yourself*, sarge, but—'

'The bike Andrew was riding – it must have crashed because of the cable being disconnected.' She couldn't tell if Munro had put the pieces together. 'Can you go back there and have a look? Assuming Andrew hasn't taken the bike with him to Oxford.'

'I'll get over there now, sarge. By the way, how did you know for certain that the hair was cut from that girl? You can't get DNA from hair unless it has the follicle attached.'

'That's right – and I didn't know for certain.' Ronnie made a face. 'It was worth the risk, though. She won't have known that. And she didn't deny it.'

Baz shook his head. 'You had me fooled.'

'No news on Foster, I presume?'

'Nothing, sarge. Hasn't been seen for two days.'

'Damn. We need forensic evidence of his presence in the house, or it's a dead end.'

Baz leant on the desk and looked right and left in search of answers. 'He was careful. They're generic trainer soles, but there's a decent chance.'

'Could be anyone. Get Overton back to the scene to check the site workers. Any of them could have been in there before Celia was attacked, or even after.'

'They would have called it in, surely.'

Ronnie shook her head. 'Not necessarily, if they didn't look down the stairs, or if they went in before the attack happened. And the house could easily be a homeless person's winter shelter.'

Baz nodded. 'OK, fair enough. How about the other set of prints? I presume that wasn't a lucky guess as well.'

'Hang on, we have news.' Ronnie checked her phone and Baz leant over to read. 'So yes, a lucky guess. But we were 99.9 per cent sure they were her shoes.'

'So, she was there.' He let out a sigh and sank into the chair opposite Ronnie.

'But who with? We can't pin it on Foster unless he shows up.'

'We'll have to ask someone in Oxford to have another chat with Andrew. Overton can do the site workers, and I'll take a look at the bike.'

'Thanks. And now, we've just got to work out the relevance of the other trophies. There's no real link with Amie.'

'Yet. And if it's somewhere they *both* hung out together . . .'

'You don't think . . .' Ronnie zoomed in on the scrunch of blonde hair. 'You don't think she cut the girl's hair for *him*, do you?'

Until now, she hadn't contemplated the idea that Amie might be working as an agent for Foster, but there had been countless assaults on children committed by mothers at the behest of a psychopathic partner. It wasn't out of the question that Amie might do that for approval, or something equally incomprehensible. But she'd told Susie it wasn't her that cut the hair at all. A double cover-up? The idea needed more thought. For now, they had to act on what they had.

'Who knows, sarge – apart from the hair, and possibly the brake cable, the rest could be a red herring, a collection of bits and pieces picked up off the street.'

'And no weapon?'

'Nothing near the scene with the sort of sharp edge we're looking for.'

Ronnie slapped the table in frustration. 'So we can't charge her with anything, and we can't put Foster at the scene. We have no weapon, the evidence is circumstantial, and she's unstable.'

'Unstable is an understatement. Oh, I've called Samuels, by the way,' Baz said, getting up to go. 'The DI said only he would do. He's on his way down here now.'

Anyone who had seen the state of the house would agree there was plenty of reason to question Amie's state of mind, and her behaviour during the interview gave them even more cause for concern. The wounds on her arms and legs from the pen were superficial, but there were others, Susie said – bruises and cuts right up to her shoulders and down to her ankles.

Craig Samuels, the psychiatrist Susie had trained with, was coming to finalise the arrangements. Released without charge, Amie would be sent to Ferndale psychiatric hospital pending an assessment of her mental state. The investigation would continue.

Ronnie sat at her desk and spun her chair round to look outside. So much progress, and yet none at all. There was nothing but a collection of mementos and an anonymous second set of footprints to go on. Her mind wandered to Elisa, the influential friend that Susie thought was leading Amie astray. The better-than-nothing friend. The discoveries at the derelict house had temporarily removed the need to find out more about her, but now she was certainly worth tracking down.

She sent a text to Louisa giving her the latest updates and asking if she might be free for a quick chat. Then she sent another one to Susie, who had seen a photo of Elisa and might remember where it had been posted. It was a blind alley in all probability, but just for the sake of covering bases, Susie might consider bending the rules a tiny bit just one more time . . .

The next thing on her list was Maeve Slade, like a piece of jigsaw puzzle you desperately wanted to fit into the gap but it didn't quite go. Her words, *do whatever you want*, still echoed in Ronnie's head. This was a woman who had given up but who couldn't tell anyone why. Her prickly anger had been subdued into resignation; her need for control had dissipated to the point of passivity. She had clearly been terrified of going with Amie to the interview. She seemed to have become afraid of life itself. Or perhaps she was just sick and tired of police turning up at her door, and sick of facing it all alone. Her husband had left, and her daughter had at the very least witnessed the attack on her father's lover. Things couldn't get much worse for Maeve. She had every reason to kill Celia, and she and Andrew only had each other as half-baked alibis. But, without evidence, both of those avenues were closed off.

Her phone buzzed. It was Eddie, asking when she'd be home. She typed a quick reply. *In an hour. Why?* As a teenager, the only reason she'd ever asked that was to find out how long she had to clear something up, or get rid of her party guests. She'd be more than an hour, for sure, but it was always wiser to err on the side of early.

CHAPTER 34

'Would you have a few minutes, DS Delmar?' Lydia's stern tone wrenched Ronnie from her thoughts.

'Of course, ma'am.'

She jumped up and followed the DI into her office. The blinds were drawn against the darkness, which crept in earlier and earlier these days. Ronnie took a seat opposite her boss. Presumably this wasn't for a telling-off, but she'd never known Lydia want a chat for any other reason. She was a woman who made the most of her authority wherever possible.

'Firstly, now the allegations against you have been found to be without merit, I need to offer you my congratulations on your work on the Slade case, DS Delmar.' Lydia bestowed a smile upon her junior detective, examining her for a reaction.

'Thank you, ma'am.' Ronnie sat up. She hadn't expected actual praise. She'd forgotten how gratifying it could be to be on the receiving end of a compliment.

'And now we have her footprints confirmed at the scene, as well as photographic evidence of her . . . unique . . . bicycle, I look forward to the psych report on the girl so we can push for a charge. She is clearly *compos mentis* enough to be charged as an accessory to attempted murder, or worse . . .'

'Worse?' Ronnie ignored the assumption that Amie was mentally stable.

'Well, our victim is hovering between life and death. So accessory to murder remains a possibility.' Lydia peered over her glasses, back in schoolmistress mode.

'We have the second set of footprints . . .' Ronnie began.

Lydia interrupted before she could go any further. 'Which there is no accounting for. We can't put Foster at the scene until he turns up, and we certainly don't have the funds to examine the shoe racks of the entire neighbourhood looking for a match to what is, I am told, a common trainer brand.'

Ronnie held her breath, then let it out slowly as Lydia continued.

'Don't waste time on it, DS Delmar. Foster will turn up, and with his prints identified we will solve the case. He's our man.' She paused for effect. 'All our resources will be going towards tracking him down. We'll need you and Munro contacting everyone he's ever been in touch with, and by the sound of things, he has plenty of friends who might help him out.'

'Yes, ma'am.'

'And let's just get the girl out of Ferndale with a clean bill of health, with no questions over her ability to go on the stand. I assume I can rely on you to make that clear to the powers that be?'

Ronnie raised her eyebrows. Thankfully, Lydia didn't seem to need an answer, but waited to make sure her message had got through before she continued.

'So all investigations are to be channelled solely into finding our suspect. Is that clear?'

Ronnie murmured, 'Yes, ma'am,' without conviction, but Lydia didn't seem to need it. She had some good news she couldn't wait to impart. A smile was breaking out on her face.

'As for the allegation that was made against you, DS Delmar, we can only assume it was fabricated by someone who was disappointed that he hadn't been the recipient of your full attention during the evening.'

She was speaking in riddles again. Ronnie waited to see if there would be any further clarification. So far, it felt as if she was striking a deal – *I'll get you reinstated if you get the Slade case sorted once and for all.*

'It does seem that you may have been rather the worse for wear when you left the bar, but what bothered me more was finding out *how* you left.'

It was an unnecessarily slow revealing of the facts. Even having pardoned her, Lydia was trying to claw back some mud to throw at her again.

'How I left? What do you mean, how I left?' Ronnie was losing patience but willing herself to stay calm. This would be over soon, and the main point was that she had her job back. She just had to get through the next few minutes.

'You left with a man. We don't know who, and we can't trace the source of the complaint, but we think they are the same person. We think he may have tried to persuade you to go home with him, and made the complaint after you refused.'

How could Lydia possibly know what had happened to her when she left the bar? The CCTV from Hemingway's hadn't shown her leaving, with or without a man in tow. But it *had* shown her that DC Baz Munro was no more than a few metres away from her. None of this made sense.

'How do you know all this? I have no memory of it at all.'

Lydia ignored her question. 'I know you don't remember. You were, as I said, extremely unwell, barely able to walk, and it is not too far-fetched a conclusion to draw that this man spiked your drink in order to get you to leave with him.'

'Rohypnol?'

'Possibly, or even just alcohol. It's more common than you think. Not everyone can get their hands on date-rape drugs.'

'I was so sick the next day.'

'I can imagine. Anyway, you're tougher than you think, DS Delmar. Even in that state, you managed to fight him off, get yourself into a cab and go home.'

Ronnie took a moment to absorb it all. It was worth another try at her original question. 'And you know this because . . .'

Lydia's smile said *This is why I am a rank above you* . . . 'We have a witness who saw the whole thing. The

273

important thing is that you're off the hook, and I owe you an apology.'

Ronnie nodded, tried to process what she had just learnt. It took a few seconds to fall into place. Somebody who knew that the allegation had been made had come forward to refute it – somebody whose status permitted them access to the details of the case and who could be trusted to confirm that the alleged incident hadn't happened.

That witness could only be one person, and she had misunderstood him profoundly.

'Thank you, ma'am. And I think I owe someone else thanks, too.'

The twins were in the kitchen when she got home, and there was a smell of something delicious.

'Surprise!' Tilly turned from the stove where she was stirring something and Eddie rushed forward to take her jacket.

Bemused, Ronnie wriggled out of her sleeves and accepted a gin and tonic. 'What have I done to deserve this? You didn't say you were cooking dinner?'

'You've been at work all day.' Eddie hoisted himself on to the worktop and grinned at her. 'And we thought we'd give you a treat.'

Tilly pushed him off. 'Get the plates out.'

The table was laid for three, napkins folded, knives and forks the right way round for a change. It was one of those days that things turned around. Serena would say it was the universe taking care of her in some kind of natural justice process. She didn't have a problem with that. The universe was most welcome.

'So, am I allowed to ask the dreaded question?' Ronnie brought a forkful to her mouth and waited.

'*How was school today?*' came the chorus.

'Go on, give me a bit of news.'

Tilly spoke first. 'Lara's invited me on holiday with her family next summer. Can I go?'

Lara and Tilly had met on the first day of secondary school. They had plenty in common, with top predicted grades, divorced parents and a passion for Broadway musicals. Lara had invited Tilly to see *Hamilton* in London when it opened, and since that day Tilly had been hooked.

'Don't tell me: not New York?'

'No, it's Greece, I think. *Please* can I go?'

Ronnie looked at Eddie and back at Tilly. 'Only if we can come and stay next door. I need a holiday too!'

'Can I bring a friend?' asked Eddie, jumping on the bandwagon. 'Maybe a couple?'

Tilly dropped her fork on the plate. 'What? No, you can't. Oh, my God, Eddie. Why do you have to spoil everything?'

'Now look, you two,' Ronnie held out a hand left and right on the table, 'we will all go on holiday next summer, but let's spend some time thinking about it. I'm not ruling anything out at this stage.'

There was a disgruntled mumble from Tilly and a grin from Eddie. But Ronnie's last words echoed in her head. *Not ruling anything out.* It wasn't a bad mantra for a detective. She should keep it in mind.

In bed that night, she opened her phone laptop and read her messages. The last one was from Louisa Emsworth.

Thanks for the heads-up. The staff here have been told on a need-to-know basis. All confidential, of course. I feel terrible for not realising what an awful state she was in. I emailed the magazine to see if Amie ever submitted anything, but I haven't heard back yet. Will give you a call at the weekend. LE

Louisa was the kind of witness that was thin on the ground these days – intelligent, perceptive, with a curious mind and a real desire to do good. But, with the interview having come to virtually nothing, they were at a standstill, for the moment.

Craig Samuels had undertaken to produce some sort of verdict on Amie's state of mind, but that would take weeks, and what it would lead to was anyone's guess. At least Amie had accepted the idea of going into hospital. Perhaps home life was that bad – and Amie recognised that she was going somewhere she would be properly cared for, listened to, even cured.

A text pinged on to her home screen and she felt her shoulders release all the pent-up tension they had been holding. It was Susie, offering to go along to ease the handover. She had been such a support to Amie, impartial yet kind, professional yet gentle. Ronnie was in awe of whoever had combined all those characteristics and mixed them up into a delicious cocktail of human being. *You're an absolute star*, she replied. *Yes, please.*

CHAPTER 35

Amie was collected from home in the morning by Susie Marshall and a police officer in uniform who looked nervous, as if he were the one going into the asylum. Maeve had tears in her eyes when she said goodbye. It didn't seem like such a bad plan, going to stay somewhere else for a while, but Amie tried to look sad so Maeve wouldn't think she was happy to go.

'No laptop,' the police officer said, relieving her of one of the two things that made her feel normal. They still had her phone and seemed to have no intention of returning it now. 'They have computers where we're going, don't worry, there will be plenty to keep you busy.'

They let her send one last message on email. A last goodbye to Elisa, who had promised on the phone the night before that she'd write, she'd visit, and she'd be there for Amie come what may. They were good words, but they were just words. They couldn't take away the fear that was creeping in and taking her over.

Ferndale was only twenty minutes away by car. Then they seemed to drive for miles down a long drive with barriers and gatekeepers to something that looked like

278

an office block in a park, and she was told that this would be her home for a while and to unpack her stuff and put it away. It was like being kidnapped, but there was no point in calling the police because they *were* the police.

Amie had never imagined it would be like it was, clinical and echoey and cold. She hadn't thought about the medical side of things, either. But when they weren't in therapy or lessons, there was a constant stream of nurses delivering small white pills in miniature plastic beakers, two every day after lunch, and the occasional extra one now and again if they felt she was getting agitated or just unco-operative.

No visitors for the first two weeks, so no Elisa, but she couldn't help imagining what Elisa would think about the pills. She'd be disappointed in her for letting them take control of her body like that. She'd encourage her to stand up for herself, to take responsibility, not just go along with things that weren't her choice.

So Amie started hiding the pills inside a box in her underwear drawer. It was easy to do – make a big show of putting them in her mouth, pretending to swig some water, doing a big fake swallow saying how disgusting they were, and then going over to get something or other from the chest of drawers. The pills had to sit in her mouth for a minute sometimes and left a horrible taste, but it was worth it, as she began to feel less dopey, more like she remembered herself to be. It was much more interesting lying in bed listening to the nurses chatting and telling each other their secrets than having all those muddled-up dreams you had when you took the pills.

It was only then that it dawned on her that two weeks had passed and Elisa hadn't been in touch. And with no access to social media there was only one way to contact her. Putting pen to paper felt old-fashioned and desperate, like a marooned sailor putting a message in a bottle, but if this was the only way to get her back, then this was how it had to be.

Dear Elisa,

It's week 3 of my incarceration.

They say they have released me pending further investigations, but this feels like the opposite of being released. They have locks on the outside of my room, but they say it's for my own safety. I'm not sure how safe I would be if there was a fire out there and everyone was dead and I couldn't get out. That doesn't sound safe to me, but Craig says that doesn't sound likely either. I don't think he's going to change the rules just for me.

They have visiting times, but only for an hour a day, and that's probably been decided by the visitors. It's not the sort of place you'd want to visit, like a stately home or a museum or a special garden. There are just long corridors where you can hear echoes of people howling and then the voice of a nurse trying to calm them down, or calling for a doctor, which means there's going to be more noise as they force down the medication. Some people might want to come here just to stare at people and then go home and feel lucky.

What I wonder most is, why is everyone here? What have they done that means they can't live in the real world any more? But no one tells you that – it's confidential.

Craig is the psychiatrist. He's supposed to be writing a report on me for the police, but he won't talk about that. He asks all about you, and he's trying to trip me up, but I won't be tripped up. He's trying to find out how my mind works, but I won't show him. I won't tell him anything. I tell him it's confidential. But he keeps push-ing me into a corner, trying to trap me, moving closer. It makes me feel stifled, like I can't breathe, and I just want to escape.

My fellow inmates are mostly teenagers with dark pasts and secrets that mean they can't go back to their real lives. I tell them I'm not like them and they laugh. They say we're all the same in here. There's a girl called Alex who won't eat and nobody can make her. She comes to drama therapy, where we have to sit in chairs and play the role of our own mother or father, and she just sits and stares into the distance. When I'm in the mother seat, I do Mum's looks, staring emptily, like a corpse, and the others say it's too scary to watch. But that's what I had to watch, all the time. I think Mum would prefer Alex as a daughter, not wanting to eat, being so thin she could dress her up in fancy clothes and show her off to everyone. Looks like we were born into the wrong families.

Then there's Stefan. He talks to himself all the time, as if he's actually two people. He tells himself off, puts on voices. It's like watching a film and he's playing all the parts. I wonder if it's catching, what he's got. Maybe that's why they lock us up – so it doesn't spread.

I am grateful for one thing, though. Daniel Foster can't find me here, and I don't have a phone, so he can't message me. The hospital is like a fortress, so there's no way for him to get in. I guess what I'm trying to say is that I'm safe. Even if I'm locked up.

Write to me, or call the switchboard and they can put you through to my room. And I'm sorry, by the way, for whenever I got things wrong. Please come and visit me, even for a few minutes. I need to see you. Don't abandon me now.

Amie x

It was Friday afternoon, when she felt almost back to her normal self, that she got a phone call from Elisa. The phone that travelled around her floor on a table on wheels was in her room because Stuart had just rung to say he couldn't make it to see her that day but Maeve would be coming. Then the phone rang again, and, since the nurses hadn't come to take it away yet, she answered it.

'Amie?'

It was like hearing the voice of someone you thought was dead. Amie was shocked just as much as she was delighted. Her voice shook as she struggled to find words.

'Elisa? Oh, my God, I can't believe it's you!'

'I can't be long,' Elisa whispered, 'just wanted to say I'm not writing to you or coming to see you because Mum says to wait till you're out before being proper friends again.

She thinks it will interfere with the treatment or something. So I might have to hang up suddenly.'

'Oh, OK,' said Amie, relieved. Any reason was good enough for her. She was suddenly better again.

'We'll see each other when you're back.'

'Assuming they ever let me out of here. What am I going to do?' Amie's voice rose in a slight panic, as she registered how little time they might have to talk, how the call might be cut off at any moment.

'You'll find a way through. I know you will.'

'I hope so,' said Amie. How could she be so sure? she thought. 'Celia saw my bike,' she said. 'They've got my footprints, but they don't know who the other set belong to. I won't tell them.' Her heart skipped a beat, remembering the night, the fear and the secrecy of it all.

'Amie?' Elisa muffled the phone and said something like, 'Just a second more,' and then, 'Are you going to tell them the truth?'

Her voice was suddenly serious and Amie shivered.

'You're going to have to think of something, Amie, to put them off.'

'Well, Mum had every reason to kill Celia. Dad was leaving to be with her best friend. They had a *child* together.'

'If she knew that. Does Andrew have an alibi?'

Amie hesitated. Did he? What had he told the police? 'Andrew? No. I don't know . . . He probably said he was home, but Mum would have been out of it on her migraine pills and wouldn't be able to back him up.'

'He was bad to you, Amie. So was your mum. You don't need to protect either of them.'

Seconds ticked by like hours.

'I don't want to go to prison,' Amie whispered.

'And you won't end up there.'

Amie said nothing. It wasn't up to Elisa, and Elisa knew that.

There was an intake of breath, voices muffled by a hand over the receiver, then nothing. She heard the phone click and the empty tone that followed. She said, 'Elisa?' her voice rising in panic. 'Elisa, I didn't tell them anything. Please come back.' Pointless, desperate words to a dead line.

As she hung up, placing the phone carefully back on the trolley, she had a sense of someone standing outside the door. You developed that gut feeling after a while in an institution, that someone was out there, listening.

She slipped out of bed and, as her bare feet touched the cold floor, the mattress springs creaked, and suddenly there was a *click click click* of footsteps down the corridor. Someone called out something that sounded like, 'Mrs Slade,' but it could have been, *What have you mislaid?* or *This way!* She couldn't be sure. If it was Mum, she would have come in to see her, not run away.

She jumped up and ran to the door, but the nurse was there before her, holding her wrists, shouting at her to calm down. She cried out, 'Mummy!', her voice high-pitched in panic, and, once she'd said it, it just wouldn't stop. 'Mummy! Mummy!' She was screaming, wrenching her arms from the nurse, who was calling for help now.

She kicked and tried to headbutt her, her throat hurting with shouting, 'Mummy! Come back! Please come back!' Breathless, gasping, hyperventilating, her throat raw, her head spinning. More nurses dragging her back to her room. An injection and then total darkness.

Two days later, DS Delmar arrived and told Amie her mother was dead.

CHAPTER 36

She didn't just say it like that, with no introduction. It was much worse. They all trooped into Amie's room – DS Delmar, Susie, Craig, the tall red-haired nurse called Rachel, all trying to hide the awkwardness and looking at each other like conspirators, waiting far too long before they actually said why they were there.

'We have some news, Amie, some bad news,' began DS Delmar, perching on the edge of the bed, then looking as if she wished she hadn't. She glanced at Craig for support.

Then there was a pause, while Amie waited to find out what the news was, and the others all waited for one of them to say something. Amie wondered why they hadn't decided who was going to do the talking before they came in. It made it worse, just waiting.

'There is no easy way to tell you this, Amie, and I hate to be the one to have to say it . . .' DS Delmar was speaking again now, and the others were looking down, glancing at Amie, then her, then looking down again. 'Your mother passed away on Friday night.'

The words were just words, words you could read in any book or hear someone say in any stupid film, but their effect at that moment was to send Amie's world crashing in on itself – like a road collision so violent and unexpected that you just lost consciousness, blacked out, and then woke up in hospital. But she was already in hospital, and the blackout didn't happen. Instead, a new, cold horror enveloped her, filling her stomach and seeping through her body to the back of her eyes.

'How?' she managed to whisper. 'Why?'

'Sometimes, things get too much for people.' Susie waited a second. Her eyes were saying, *I've got you, I'm holding you,* but Amie felt herself slipping away. Nobody had her. 'You know she had been unhappy for a very long time, and when people find themselves unhappy all the time, they sometimes feel they can't bear life any more, and they do something to end it, so that they can be at peace, escape their sadness, stop all the hurting.'

Amie stared at her, prayed for the blackout, but she knew there was no waking up from this nightmare.

'It was me, wasn't it? I made her unhappy.'

'No.' Susie took Amie's hand and held it in both of hers. 'It's not your fault, Amie. There's nothing you could have done about it. Nothing at all.'

Amie took all her pills that night, every single one she'd stashed away in the drawer, swallowing them one after the other, refilling the plastic cup with water to make sure they went right down and into her blood and took her away from there.

She woke up, bleary and sick, with a tube in her arm, her throat sore from the pump they had used on her stomach, and Craig and Dad and red-haired Rachel all standing over her looking sad again. She drifted back to sleep, back into the fog. Maybe she could recapture the oblivion, like a dream you could go back to when it wasn't quite over . . .

There were conversations she had no part in, and that put her at a disadvantage again: locked in, locked up, looked in on from time to time. It was enough to make anyone go mad. They made her take her medication, checked inside her mouth afterwards and left her no space to do anything unobserved. Craig came to see her every day, waiting for her to say something, but she just talked about other things. She knew he'd wait. Sometimes he talked to her in a less obvious way, asking her to say the first thing that came into her head when he said certain words, then he used a tapping thing on her head while he asked her questions about her earliest memories. He said the rhythm of the tapping took the stress out of it, made it easier to say, but it wasn't doing anything for either of them. It was all static, she was just hanging there in time, waiting for something to break through and smash up her fragile world.

CHAPTER 37

Craig and Rachel came with her to the funeral. They stood glued to her side like bodyguards, maybe afraid she'd turn on the congregation with a loaded gun, more murders, more suicide. She imagined Elisa there and it calmed her.

Celia Burrows was still in intensive care, but she probably wouldn't have come anyway, with her being part of the reason Mum was dead. The congregation was made up of whole crowds of people Amie didn't know. Dad whispered that they were from her work, from her bridge club, university friends. Amie was shocked to see all the other people Maeve Slade mattered to, who would have known her in so many different ways, seen different sides of her.

There was a hymn that went 'Nearer and nearer draws the time, the time that will surely be, when the Earth shall be filled with the glory of God . . .' *Mum's favourite,* Dad had said. Amie didn't know she had one. Maybe she didn't know her as well as she thought.

The last time Amie had been in a church before then was Christmas, two years earlier. Maeve used to take her and Andrew to midnight mass until they were old enough to refuse to go, and the atmosphere always made Amie feel uneasy. Nativity overshadowed by death. The end of one man's story sitting alongside the beginning. Even when they were supposed to be celebrating his birth, Jesus was up there on the cross, gruesomely injured and bleeding, gazing down with pity and forgiveness that she didn't want, didn't need.

She couldn't look at him, even now. One side of her wanted to be a part of it, this family where you were accepted for everything that you were, but when she tried to connect, another voice said *you don't belong*. So she stayed there on the outside looking in. And as for God, well, he seemed like a pretty unreliable father.

The coffin stood in the aisle at the front. Amie forced herself to look at it and to remember who was inside. The two priests took turns to chant sections of the Eucharistic prayer. They were asking God to keep her safe, with all the saints. They called her *your servant Maeve Louise*, but on the order of service it just said *your servant N.*

At the crematorium, Dad spoke a few words, but his voice was choked and distant, his face drawn. Nobody could hear him and he didn't seem to care. Amie couldn't look at the coffin as it passed behind the curtains. She kept her eyes tightly shut until it was time to leave. There was a muttering and rustle of raincoats as the congregation turned to go, the smell of the rain on wool, the heavy grey sky. In her mouth was the bitter taste of misery. Outside, engines started and cars pulled away, as more black-clad families arrived for the next incineration.

They went in a cab back to the house; Andrew, home from university with longer hair than ever, chewing gum, staring out of his window, Dad in the front murmuring things to the driver. Nurse Rachel was next to Amie in the back seat, probably just in case she tried to escape. There was a feast laid out in the dining room. Mary Morrison was there, putting the finishing touches to it all. Amie's face must have lit up, because she said, 'Amie, how lovely to see a smile on your face!'

There was a second when they must have both been thinking about their farewell party, when Amie broke the bowl, when everything started going wrong in her head. Here they were again, this time at the table in the Slade house. No *clink clink* of pink fizz and Hawaiian shirts, just sober murmuring and blackness.

'I am so sorry about your poor mum.' Her face was all love and sympathy. 'I can't imagine how it must feel for you, poor love.'

Amie looked down. 'Thank you.'

'I've got something for you – just a minute.' She bustled out of the room, leaving Amie with Colin, who didn't say much, probably because he only knew jokes. The other guests were mingling politely, not wanting to be seen having too much fun, too many sausage rolls or glasses of sherry. The clinking of forks on plates could be heard above the muted chatting. Nobody wanted to be heard in case they said the wrong thing.

'I found these when we were going through her things with your dad.'

It was Mary again, standing with a pile of scrapbooks and photo albums in her plump arms.

'I thought you might like to sit down and have a look through them, you know, before you go back.'

Go back. Of course they found it difficult to say the words *Go back to the institution for the psychologically unstable.* Amie couldn't blame them for that. She didn't want to spell it out either. She didn't mind if they didn't talk about it.

Rachel nodded her consent and Amie took the scrapbooks and sat on the sofa in the living room. She hadn't been there for so long, but nothing had changed. The afternoon sunlight was struggling to get past the conifers, leaving the room in dusky shadow, but the last rays pointed accusingly at the piano that was fast gathering dust. She got up to close the lid, before opening the first scrapbook.

Andrew – 4 years old, read the inscription above the photos and drawings. Andrew sitting on Dad's lap, Andrew dressed up as a cowboy, Andrew's drawing of some sort of war, millions of stick soldiers and some scattered giant guns pointing this way and that.

Amie aged 8 – the next album showed Amie in her Brownie uniform, then on the next page in her ballet outfit with her hair all scraped back in a bun, a big smile for the camera.

On other pages, drawings of little cottages with roses around the front door, rabbits and puppies copied from birthday cards, little limericks written for birthdays. *There was a nice neighbour called Mary* . . . Amie had done a poem for everyone in the family, everyone they knew. But she had no memory of it at all. Everything she had done as a child had been eclipsed, rubbed out by what had happened after.

She imagined Maeve keeping hold of those memories, sticking the drawings and photos into the albums, writing their ages so they'd be able to look back and laugh at the funny little people they once were. Or rather, the way *she* saw them and wanted to keep them, not necessarily the way they actually were.

Andrew came in and she shut the album. 'So have they decided if you can stand trial yet?'

She looked at him coldly.

'It was just a question. No need to give me the look.'

That just made her want to give him even more of a look. 'So easy for you, isn't it, Andrew? Always leaving me to pick up the pieces, take the blame.' Amie felt her anger beating on the door, desperate to be released.

'What are you trying to say?'

Amie paused for a second, to see if she could detect someone listening outside the door. Then she said, in a lower voice, 'Did the police ever ask you where *you* were the night Celia was . . . attacked?'

'I think their suspicions lay firmly elsewhere.' He raised his eyebrows at her. 'They came and asked me questions at Oxford, after they found her. I told them I was at home all night. Didn't come out of my room – lucky to be alive after my bike accident, remember?'

He was back on the attack again, so Amie retreated and changed the subject.

'I want to know what happened to Mum,' she said, in a small voice. 'Can you tell me that at least?'

'They said I shouldn't give you any details. You know. It might be *too much*.' Andrew shifted in his seat. His eyes darted left and right, making Amie nervous, but she persisted.

'I need to know, Andrew. Just tell me.'

He didn't put up much of a fight in the end. He had come home for the weekend, and they had spent Friday morning going round estate agents. They had a buyer for the house, which kind of put the pressure on finding a new place for Mum. It was Saturday morning that he found her, lying in a bloody bathtub. He had grabbed her, shaken her, felt for a pulse and dialled 999. The police and ambulance were there in minutes, but hours too late.

Amie listened, stared in disbelief as the scene unfolded in her imagination.

'You were supposed to be looking after her.' Her voice cracked. They just came out as words, but behind them was a roaring-inferno fury, tearing across the room to swallow him alive.

He looked away, leaning forwards, elbows on knees. 'It wasn't *my* fault, Amie.'

'Where were you then?' She glared at him now, her face ablaze with anger. 'Skulking in your room? Listening to music? Blocking everything out?'

'That's really unfair.'

'If only I'd been here, she might still be alive. I wouldn't have just let her die.'

'What?' Andrew sneered.

'You literally sabotaged the whole family. You never made an effort. You just came downstairs at mealtimes and blocked yourself out the rest of the time. You didn't help, you just made things worse. And then you're the last one to see her before she commits suicide. What are we supposed to think?'

He was momentarily silent. Then he spoke, as if it was something he'd forgotten to say that had just popped into his head, or as if she'd said the magic words that opened up a secret door to the next paragraph. He faced her, spoke blankly and without pausing, like Alexa.

'Actually, that Friday afternoon, she said she was going to see *you*. She went to the hospital, but couldn't go through with it for some reason. Not sure why. Just thought you should know that *that* was the last thing she did.'

Amie turned her gaze to the garden where the last leaves were falling fast. A squirrel was scampering across the grass, stopping and starting, looking this way and that, then shooting up a tree into invisibility. She wanted to be that squirrel. She wanted to not know anything at all. But then she wanted to know everything, blow everything apart, the only way she knew how to be, in chaos and alone. The finger was pointing at her, like a searchlight, so she spun it around and pointed it back at him.

'So where *were* you, then, when Mum died? You still haven't said.' She was still staring at where the squirrel had been. She didn't want to look at her brother.

'Out with a friend.'

'How convenient.'

'Are you seriously suggesting I killed Mum?' He dragged his words out, his face moving towards hers like a thundercloud.

'I don't know what you're capable of, Andrew, do I?'

He was struggling to stay calm. Perhaps if he hit her, now, with all the people in the next room, he'd get arrested, and be seen for who he really was.

Then he spoke, just loud enough for her to hear. 'At least I *have* friends.'

Amie spat her reply straight back at him. 'You know nothing about me.'

He got up to leave. 'When the police came after I found Mum, guess what I told them.' He gave her a wry smile, then added, 'It was you that killed our mother. *Schizo.*' And the door slammed shut behind him.

Nurse Rachel was keen to get back to Ferndale, but Amie said she needed the bathroom, so she let her go upstairs.

Everything in her bedroom was as she had left it. On her desk next to a pile of school textbooks her pencil case sat zipped up, redundant. The teachers at Ferndale gave you everything in the lessons and took it away again, maybe in case you tried to stab someone with a pencil, or pick the locks with a ruler.

In her desk drawer she found what she was looking for, exquisitely untouched, keeping her past safe and holding the key to her future. She slipped it under her jumper and shut herself in the bathroom. Behind the locked door, she opened up the laptop for one last time, reset the settings and concentrated hard as the keys clicked softly under her fingers. How she had missed this. Words were like magic spells that made your thoughts get into other people's heads, made them think what you wanted them to think, painted a picture they had no choice but to believe. Immersed for a while in words, she forgot everything.

Then Rachel was knocking on the door asking if she was OK. All she needed to do was slip the laptop back into the drawer as she went past her room and the job was done.

One last look over her shoulder and she let herself be ushered out of the door and down the stairs. She didn't say goodbye. It wouldn't be long now.

CHAPTER 38

'Amie Slade is a *fascinating* case,' Dr Craig Samuels said, as he strode ahead of Ronnie down the corridors of the hospital. 'My office is just here.' He swung the door open for her and she stepped into his room, where books and papers littered the desk and most other surfaces, including the windowsill and most of the carpet.

'Sorry about the mess.' He was suddenly a naughty child caught with an untidy bedroom. 'Not much wriggle room, nowhere to put anything, but it is what it is . . .' He propped a bag of golf clubs against the wall, whereupon it promptly fell down again. '*They're* a waste of space. Can't remember when I last even played.'

'Well, you're living up to the image we all have of a mad professor, at least.' Ronnie stepped over an open lever arch folder and settled into a low armchair as Craig shut the door and carved out a path through the debris. 'So, what can you tell us?' she asked him, taking out her notebook.

'Not much, if I'm perfectly honest, at this point. She's keeping her cards close to her chest, she's breaking records in terms of her lack of response to therapy, and yet she is being what you might call a *very good girl*, taking her meds – properly, under supervision now; not making a fuss about the rules. She has moments of lucidity, where you wonder what on earth she's doing here, then the next minute her mind flips into chaos and we're starting over.'

'What kind of chaos are we talking about?'

'She makes sense, and then she doesn't; she expresses normal emotional reactions to things we discuss, then none at all.'

Ronnie made notes as Craig continued, with an expression of deep concern.

'There is evidence of self-harm, cuts on her arms, she was covered in bruises on her arms and legs when she arrived, but then she completely denies doing it and won't give any other explanation either.'

'What's your instinct?' Ronnie shifted to the front of the chair as she grappled for answers that she could make sense of. 'Any link between how she presents and what she's been through? I'm thinking about the sexual assault in her last school as a starting point. I mean, how much can an experience like that influence you, change your personality? It must have been a major trauma, and she's never had any therapy, so is there a chance it could all just snowball internally like a kind of cancer?'

Craig was nodding enthusiastically already, which gave her a sense of relief. 'The onset of this kind of mental illness can absolutely be linked to trauma or loss,' he said. 'It could come from a latent genetic predisposition triggered by the key event. Recovery depends on the person, the support they get – not necessarily professional support, but family, community, friends – but, even with all of that, the event itself can have monumental consequences for ongoing mental health.'

He dropped his pen on the desk and rubbed his eyes for a moment, as if he'd reached a full stop and was starting a new chapter.

'Then the other issue is, *did* it change her personality, or has she always been like this? We didn't know her before. Where do we go to find that out?'

'I see. So the whole causation issue is debatable in itself.' Ronnie still wasn't going to get the black and white certainty she needed.

There was a brisk tap on the door and a face appeared, pale and smiling beneath a shock of red hair.

Craig half stood. 'Ah, Rachel, good timing. I have DS Delmar here. We're discussing the Slade case. Do you have anything more for us?'

Rachel held out her hand in greeting to Ronnie, who grasped at the chance for another, more satisfying answer to the question on her mind.

'What's your take on it all, Rachel?'

'Actually, it's been interesting working with Amie. She is one of a kind, that's for sure. I'm not sure she's a criminal. I know it's a cliché, but I just don't think she's got it in her. She has been bullied at school, and at home by her brother, neglected by her parents, and that's all on top of a sexual assault that has left her paranoid and terrified.'

Ronnie felt momentarily vindicated, but Craig just tapped his pen on the desk and nodded slowly. He spoke up as soon as Rachel paused for breath.

'Look, Rachel, please don't take this the wrong way. I absolutely agree with you. To all appearances, this girl couldn't hurt a fly. But we know that the greatest murderers – if I can use those words together – have all appeared harmless on the surface to *someone*. It is in the make-up of the psychopath to deceive and deliver a completely opposing message.'

Rachel tried to interrupt, but he held his hand out. 'One second – I know what you're going to say. Amie's mind has been messed with by a sexual assault, a trauma that she has never really talked about. She comes from a family that brushes things under the carpet, anyone can see that. She's lonely, and even more so since her parents split up. On the surface, it's a tragic story of a girl who has been wronged at every turn. You're right: she's been bullied, ignored, neglected, for sure. But in so many cases where we question the ability of a patient to commit a particular act, we need to acknowledge that there is very much more to it than appearances, and none of the witnesses' testimonies can be relied on outside a courtroom. I have to take all angles of approach, look for every loophole, consider every alternative story to the one I'm being told.'

Ronnie began to understand and remembered her conversation with Susie about this man's legendary passion for his work.

Craig wound up with a final sentence accompanied by a gentle thumping of the table, if there could be such a thing.

'There are people out there looking for a way out, and I don't want to let them abuse the mental health defence for a crime, because it gives our *genuine* patients with *genuine* conditions a bad name.'

Rachel raised her eyebrows. Lydia would be delighted with this, Ronnie thought.

Craig's face softened. 'Sorry, Rachel, rant over.'

Rachel looked unruffled. Her smile said she had heard the story a few times before. 'No, that's fine,' she said. 'I mean, you make a good point, as always, and I absolutely agree with you that we need to defend our science and our practice, apart from anything else, but it's a fine balance we need to strike – to ensure we don't have blood on our hands, I mean.'

Craig looked pleased to have been understood. 'I know exactly what you mean, and you're right. I am constantly aware of the need to find that balance.'

Ronnie smiled in agreement. Balance was something she had spent her life searching for.

'Sorry not to be more clear-cut,' he said, turning back to Ronnie. 'I'm sure you were looking for a bit more than a philosophical debate.' He sat back in his chair. 'Is there anything specific I can try to answer?'

Ronnie pondered for a second, then remembered the question that had been on her mind, unresolved. 'There was something I was wondering – perhaps you can help. Is there anyone she talks about – a school friend, someone who has an influence over her?'

'Ah, now would that be Elisa?' He beamed as he said the name.

'So you've heard of her, then. What do you know?'

'She talks about her as her best friend, but it seems it hasn't all been plain sailing. She's got her into trouble a few times, but then she's the first person, probably the only person, she turns to when things get tough.'

'She writes to her,' chipped in Rachel, 'but I think she must have moved house. The letters come back undelivered.'

'So they're effectively out of touch,' mused Ronnie, pen poised. 'What address is Amie using for this Elisa?'

Rachel made a face. 'I don't know offhand. I'll try to find out for you.'

'Thank you. Talking of writing, there was something Amie was doing at school, which we're looking into as a possible source of information. Some sort of competition. Her teacher – Louisa Emsworth – is trying to find out whether she entered and what she wrote about. Might shed a light on her state of mind if nothing else.'

Craig and Rachel raised their eyebrows in harmony. 'Go on . . .'

'Apparently Amie's a talented writer and Louisa thought she could do with a challenge and a distraction from what was going on in her life. The subject she had to write about was "confession", which is a bit heavy, I thought, but interesting, in the circumstances.'

Craig tapped his pen on the table. 'I think it's a brilliant title for young people to get their teeth into, and it would be an interesting read, for sure, if you get your hands on it at some point.' He stood up, signalling the end of the meeting. 'And now, if that's all, I need to get on with some rather boring paperwork . . .'

'Actually, that's not quite all,' said Ronnie, hopefully. 'Do you have just a couple more minutes?'

'Of course.' Craig sat back down, and Rachel released the door handle.

'Following Maeve's death, I've been going over the interviews with the rest of the family, hoping it might give us an indication of what was going on for her, and whether there was any link with Celia's attack.'

Craig nodded vigorously. 'Go on.'

'The father is in a bad way, but it's the brother I'm interested in. He thinks Amie blames him for their mother's death.'

'Yes, I agree with that. She certainly thinks it was his neglect that allowed it to happen,' said Rachel.

Ronnie paused to articulate her thoughts.

'I think there's something else going on with those two. Something neither of them is telling us. The way Andrew talks, just the body language, the things he repeats, leaves out, struggles with, all make it look as if he's nervous and angry about something.'

Rachel nodded. 'Yes, but that could just be because his sister's blaming him for his mother's suicide while he's grieving over his own loss of a parent. It's a cocktail of negative emotion that needs to find a way out.'

'Are you wondering if he was involved?' Craig asked Ronnie.

'In Maeve's death? Well, he has no motive. But he did mention, when the officers first attended the scene, that he thought it was Maeve's visit to Ferndale that drove her over the edge. It sounded like lashing out with blame, so I didn't think anything of it, but now I'm wondering if there was something in it . . .'

Craig looked slightly taken aback. 'I wasn't aware of a visit taking place. Rachel, can we look at the visitor records?'

'Yes, of course. If she came it will be logged on the system, and I can get the camera footage as well.'

Craig pulled his laptop towards him. 'Can you bring it up – I think we can access it on here, can't we?'

Rachel stepped unsteadily over the books and files and opened the laptop, taking no more than a few seconds to bring up the CCTV footage of the top-floor corridor. The image was blurry and pixelated, but Ronnie could just about make out a small, neat figure making her way down towards Amie's room, then stopping outside. Her hands went to her face and she looked one way and the other, then upwards towards the camera – or to God? The next minute she was out of the picture.

'She didn't go in,' observed Rachel.

Ronnie bit the pen. 'She didn't go in, and then she went home and took her own life.'

Craig nodded and held her gaze. 'Looks like that was the order of events, yes.'

Rachel looked back at the screen, replayed the footage and folded her arms. 'So, what do you think is going on there?'

Ronnie looked at her. 'Maeve could have heard something.'

Craig shut the laptop. 'Or maybe there's no connection at all. She just changed her mind about visiting, lost her courage. I mean, we know their relationship was strained. They didn't have anything bordering on a mother-daughter bond.'

'What do you think, Rachel?' asked Ronnie.

'It's possible you're right.' She looked over at Craig, apologetically. 'I mean, we know she was managing to hide her anxiety meds, because she took them all at once, the day she was told about her mother. So Amie wouldn't have been herself on the day Maeve visited.'

'You mean, she *would* have been herself, as in her unmedicated, normal self,' Ronnie pointed out.

'Yes.' Rachel looked flustered for a moment. 'I see what you mean. She was back to her old ways, I suppose.'

'Whatever those old ways are.' It was beginning to make sense, and Ronnie's mind was racing from one presumption to another. 'So we're back to the question of diagnosis.'

She looked at Craig for a response, and Craig pondered for a moment. He had the gravitas that allowed seconds, possibly even minutes, of pondering before anyone would interrupt. Eventually he looked up at Ronnie, clasped his hands and picked his words carefully.

'Underneath all the physical manifestations that can often be a complete distraction, I think we are dealing with something unique. In a lot of cases, especially sociopathy and psychopathy, the investigations are very complex and lengthy, and we don't get a black and white answer.'

'You're saying she's a psychopath?' Ronnie put her pen down. This wasn't the kind of conversation that translated into note form.

'I'm not saying anything conclusive. I'll have a full report for you next week,' he added, drawing a line under it.

'How is the investigation going, in general?' asked Rachel.

'Oh, it's still ongoing,' said Ronnie. 'We need a decision on Amie's mental capacity, and it's all hands on deck in the search for our main suspect, Daniel Foster.'

'And the victim?'

'Celia is out of the coma, thankfully, but remembers nothing at all.'

Craig sat back in his chair, hands clasped behind his head. 'So, you need Amie to be fit for questioning.'

Ronnie was imagining Lydia, peering over her glasses, waiting for her to confirm to Craig what they wanted from him. She settled for a compromise. 'Are you optimistic that we can get to that point?'

'I am hopeful. If I had to call it, I would be inclined to let her take the stand, with the appropriate medication in place, of course. Give me a few more days before I have a definite answer.'

Ronnie stood up, extending her hand. 'Thanks so much for your time, Craig. I'll get back to you. Rachel, lovely to meet you properly, and thanks for all the updates.'

Craig shook her hand warmly. 'My pleasure entirely. Please don't hesitate to call, or email, or whatever it is you do these days . . .'

CHAPTER 39

Back home at the flat, Ronnie poured herself a gin and tonic and stood on the miniature excuse for a balcony that looked over the park and to more bland modern estates beyond. The sky was clear and still. A man was walking a slow Labrador around the perimeter. That was the kind of routine that secretly terrified her. At least her job kept her brain alive and her heart engaged, and she was always learning something new.

Today it was the fact that *at the end of the day, we know nothing about each other*. Maeve had been a mystery from the outset. Her obsessive tidiness and pursed lips disguised a whole other story that never came to light, and her death was a tragedy that it pained Ronnie to think about. Had she let her down, failed to spot the signs that she was treading a fine line between living and dying? She had been impatient with her on the day of Amie's disappearance. Her transition from OCD to sickly child had been dramatic to say the least. Then there was Stuart, whose good looks were a distraction from his almost sociopathic moral weakness. He hadn't shed a tear at the news of his wife's death and had barely visited Amie at Ferndale.

Amie seemed to have inherited traits of both parents. Panic attacks and emotional detachment. Her reality was something far removed from what the rest of the world saw.

And as for Baz Munro – he wasn't after her job or filing anonymous complaints, but going out of his way to get her out of trouble. He'd been working day and night with the uniform team looking for Foster. It was bad luck that the few leads that had come up hadn't led to anything.

Louisa was another one she might have misjudged. She had thought of her, and described her to Craig, as Amie's greatest ally, seeing every behavioural aberration as the natural consequence of neglect and abuse. But maybe her thinking wasn't as clear-cut as that. Ronnie decided to call her and see if there was any progress with the magazine.

She answered within a couple of rings.

'I've been meaning to call you, but you know how things are . . . I managed to get hold of the magazine, asked them if they'd had anything sent in by Amie at all, and the answer was no.'

'So she never submitted anything?'

'It seems that way. I didn't have any other entrants from the class, so I rather took my eye off the ball as far as see-ing who won. I still can't quite believe what's been going on since we last saw her in school. It's been a nightmare, keeping the girls from gossiping about it.'

'I can imagine. But we don't want to jeopardise any trial in the future.'

There was a pause as both women contemplated the prospect of Amie standing before a judge and jury. Ronnie felt a shudder pass through her. That was the last thing she wanted to happen. Louisa echoed her thoughts.

'Let's hope it doesn't come to that, for her.' Then she brightened up. 'How's she doing, anyway? Do you think they're making progress?'

'She's in good hands. They're trying to tackle so many issues – self-harm, frequent panic attacks – and we're still waiting for a verdict on her mental capacity. The strange thing is, she's always denied being at the scene of the crime at all, despite the overwhelming evidence.'

Louisa frowned. 'Sounds like she's got a secret she's guarding with her life. I wonder if there's anyone else she might open up to. I mean, I'd give it a go, but I'm thinking more like someone her age. It's tough for teenagers when the only help they're offered is from the generation they're trying to break away from.'

Ronnie thought about her own teenagers. They weren't bad on the communication front, but who knew what was really going on in their lives? What she could see might just be the tip of the iceberg. Louisa had a good point, and it reminded Ronnie of the reason she had wanted to speak to her in the first place.

'I've been meaning to ask you about another student, a friend of Amie's at Merrymount that we'd like to talk to about her.'

'Oh yes? In my form group?'

'A girl called Elisa. I don't have the surname.'

There was a pause. 'Not in my form, but she could be with her in Maths or English. I don't know the whole year group, I'm afraid. I'll ask the other teachers.'

'OK, Amie's been writing her letters which are getting sent back undelivered. The address is unoccupied, it seems, so perhaps they've moved away anyway.' Finding Elisa could wait. Foster took priority, as Lydia had made very clear.

'I wonder if she's made friends in the hospital that she talks to,' Louisa added. 'Maybe you need to bug her room and record her conversations . . .'

It was a nice idea, but not one that fell within the realms of acceptable police practice, and Ronnie wasn't going to go down that path again any time soon. 'Sadly, if I go around obtaining evidence by underhand means, it's not going to look good in court.'

'Maybe someone else could do it for you . . .'

Ronnie laughed. 'Kind of you to offer, but I'm not sure we'd get much. There are other avenues to explore still. We're not out of options just yet.'

Next morning, she was woken by a phone call from Munro. His tone was urgent, almost panicky, something she hadn't heard in him before.

'Sarge? Sorry to bother you so early.'

'What time is it?' She fished for her phone on the long cable by her bed. 'Blimey, Baz, it's five-thirty. What's happened?'

'Do you want the good news or the bad news?'

Ronnie sat up in bed. 'Good, please. What is it?'

'Foster's back.'

'What? Where was he?'

'Staying with a friend up in Liverpool.'

'Liverpool? Who's been up there? Was there a tip-off or something?'

'Handed himself in. Reported into the station a few hours ago. The friend he was hiding out with says he arrived in a terrible state, seemed completely traumatised and couldn't be persuaded to get help. Kept saying he couldn't cope any more, that his life was ruined. Hid in his room and wouldn't come out. The friend had no idea he was wanted by the police.'

'When did he arrive there? Does that give him an alibi for the Monday night?'

'He got there on the Tuesday, so no, but . . .'

Ronnie's heart began to beat faster. 'So have they checked his shoes? Are they his footprints in the house?'

Baz paused a second too long for her comfort. 'That's the bad news.'

Ronnie groaned. 'Go on.'

'He's a size twelve. They're not his footprints.'

Her heart sank. '*What?*'

'We're back to square one, sarge.'

'OK. Give me half an hour. We need to go over our thinking on this. We must have missed something.'

Ronnie went straight into work the second she got off the phone with Munro, still reeling from the shock of the news. Foster was in the clear – in trouble for going AWOL, but in the clear nonetheless. That meant backtracking on all of their presumptions and revisiting the evidence.

Their first port of call was 16 Pine Walk.

'Bloody Lydia. If she'd been less obsessed with money, and more obsessed with finding out the truth, we'd have been here weeks ago.' Ronnie switched off the engine and stared at the house.

'Before the whole scene was contaminated by the funeral party, and God knows who else,' Munro added. He was as disappointed in the boss as she was, and Ronnie had to suppress a smile at the idea. Someone else noticing the DI's imperfections was always gratifying.

The Slades' house was as she remembered it, except for the For Sale sign at the edge of the drive. Stuart opened the door before they knocked. His face looked drawn and distant. He barely acknowledged the warrant. 'Knock yourselves out. Not sure what you expect to find in here now.'

Inside, the few signs of family life and any detritus from the wake had been removed. Work surfaces were clear, coat hooks empty, curtains drawn against the winter.

Upstairs, all the doors were closed, throwing the landing into darkness. Ronnie opened Amie's bedroom door. The yellow curtains were half drawn, letting the morning sun in through the gap. On the wall above the neatly made bed was the framed print of Van Gogh's *Sunflowers*. Nothing else. She thought about Tilly's bedroom, the walls plastered in photo collages and the floor festooned with discarded clothing. Cushions everywhere, and nowhere to sit down. This was the opposite. Apart from the bed, the only other furniture in the room was a wardrobe and an empty desk. In the desk drawer, under a pile of paper, notebooks and plastic folders, lay a small black laptop. It was as good a place to start as any.

'Get this over to the tech team.' Ronnie slid the laptop into a bag. 'Take it apart. Their lives are all online these days. We know there's nothing on the phone, so this is all we have left.'

Back at the station the next day, she sat down at her desk and stared at her screen. It was beyond comprehension. Her mind refused to compute what she was reading.

Baz stood behind her, stroking his chin.

'Well, they've certainly done their job here. Last thing in the world I expected.'

'He doesn't have an alibi, does he?'

'Not a reliable one,' said Baz. 'Not anyone that's still alive, at any rate.'

They shared a moment of understanding that gave Ronnie an overwhelming sense of relief. She and her DC were a team again.

'That girl has been through it, that's for sure. Deserves a break perhaps.' She was thinking aloud, as if to try to convince her heart of what her head had decided was true.

'Well, the next step will be to go and deliver that break in person.'

If there had been any doubt in her heart about the outcome of their house search, it was put to rest by the look on Amie's face when they entered her hospital room. She was a rabbit in the headlights, a frightened little girl about to have her secret torn open and shouted out to the world. You wouldn't want to be her right now, and you wouldn't want to have gone through what she had been through.

CHAPTER 40

After Maeve's funeral, the doctors and nurses had been kind. They'd treated Amie like something precious that kept breaking and had now been glued together, just managing to look the way it used to from afar, but on close inspection cracked, useless. The pills had damaged her liver and kidneys, and nurses were forever popping in, testing her blood, and blood pressure, to make sure everything was functioning. They knew she didn't care, so they sent people who did. Susie came to visit once, and then one day, when she could sit up again in bed and read, and was feeling almost normal, DS Delmar and DC Munro came back.

Amie had been expecting them, but not this soon. They must have worked fast.

'Hi, Amie.' DC Munro must have a special way of talking to mental health patients. He looked her straight in the eye, spoke slightly slowly as if she were deaf. 'How are you doing?'

Amie nodded and blinked back the genuine tears which were pricking at her eyelids. She hadn't even practised for this, and yet here they were, on demand. Don't cry, don't cry, she said to herself. Not yet.

'We wanted to come and see you for a chat. Would that be OK?'

'Of course, yes.' It felt serious. It felt like the real deal.

'Do you mind if Craig joins us? So he knows what's going on and that no one's asking too much of you.'

Amie said it was fine, and Munro looked around the room before bringing his gaze back to her.

'You see, Amie, there have been some developments in the investigation.'

'What sort of developments?' She made an effort to look concerned.

'As you know,' he continued, his voice gathering pace now, 'at the same time as you've been undergoing treatment here, we have been continuing to investigate Celia Burrows' accident.'

Amie nodded.

'It has taken a few weeks, collating all the evidence, because we were waiting to identify the second set of prints, and what with recent events . . .'

He was talking about Mum's death, but he didn't want to say. Amie nodded. She didn't want him to think up more new ways of saying *death* without actually saying *death*.

'And also because of your illness, and the current state of our only other witness, who isn't out of the woods yet, we have had to go through things very thoroughly, and repeatedly, leaving no stone unturned . . .' The police officers exchanged glances before Munro continued. 'To make sure we have the full story about what happened.'

She held her breath. It was Delmar who came out with it.

'We have eliminated Daniel Foster from our enquiries.'

They were waiting for her to react, but Amie just looked at them blankly.

'And you obviously weren't keen to tell us, or anyone else . . .' she glanced at Craig and then back at Amie, 'who it was that was with you on the night in question.'

Amie stayed still, giving nothing away, because she still wasn't sure they had found it. Then, with every word that followed, she let out the breath she was holding, until her lungs were empty.

'So we looked at everything again. And that's when we found the document on your laptop.'

After every sentence, Delmar paused and looked at her again, slightly inclining her head as if in need of confirmation but then continuing anyway, slowing down as she got to the point.

'When you were first brought in for questioning, we spoke to your teacher to find out more about you, and she told us you had written a piece for a short story competition.'

She shifted slightly in her chair, glanced up at Craig and then back at Amie.

'It's good to get things down on paper. Therapeutic. I can understand why you did it.'

You will never, ever understand, Amie thought.

'We found the story you wrote.'

Good, she thought. Carry on. Tell me everything. Don't leave anything out. Tell me how wrong you've been about me, how mistaken they were in putting me here.

'It's your story all about that night at the house where Celia nearly died.'

Amie nodded. Well done.

'We read what you wrote. It explains everything – why you've been protecting the perpetrator of the assault all this time.'

There was a moment where Amie imagined what Craig was thinking. How could she have kept this from him, with all those pills and therapy sessions, all the gentleness and confidentiality?

And it was Craig who asked the obvious question.

'Protecting who?' He should have said *whom*. 'Not Foster?'

Delmar shook her head.

'No. It wasn't Foster.'

Craig looked relieved, then confused.

Then Delmar said it.

'Andrew.'

There was a shocked pause. Amie kept her poker face, while Delmar continued.

'We obviously didn't just take Amie's word for it. As well as Amie's, there were footprints at the scene, which we now know belong to Andrew. We found his trainers, and the residue on the soles was a match for the crime scene.'

'What about the weapon?' asked Craig. 'I thought that at the moment there was nothing to link the crime to either of them.'

Munro spoke up. This must have been his doing. 'We have the weapon as well. Found it in a box at the bottom of a drawer full of old computer games.'

He had everyone's attention now.

'A piece of glass, with his fingerprints on it, and Celia Burrows' blood.'

Craig let out a sigh of something like relief. It was as if someone had just done his job for him. He looked from Delmar to Munro to Amie, but nobody met his gaze.

'Why didn't you tell us this at the time, Amie?' asked Delmar.

Amie was silent.

'Were you afraid of what he might do to you? Did he hurt you?'

She nodded, slowly, then dared to say a few words, just a few, because it was safe now.

'He said I shouldn't, because he was over eighteen. He'd go to prison. And he wouldn't be able to stay up at Oxford with a criminal record.'

'How did he end up there, in that house with you that night?' Delmar wasn't done asking questions yet.

'He followed me. Wanted to see where I went.'

'And then what? Why did he attack Celia Burrows?'

Amie just looked at them as if they were the ones who needed locking up. 'Because he wanted her dead.'

'Did he tell you that?' Craig frowned at Delmar, but she wasn't going to be stopped. 'Amie?'

Amie put her head in her hands. 'After I found out about Dad and Celia, Dad's other family that he was leaving us for, Andrew went to her house and threw a brick at Alfie's window. He wanted to show Dad he wouldn't be replaced that easily.'

Delmar and Munro were alert now, looking at each other, frowning.

'He told you he did it?' Delmar was looking right at her, testing her.

'He didn't need to.'

'What do you mean?'

'He made me go with him. He took a broken brick from the building site next door, gave me the other half. Made me promise to throw it at the same time as he did. But I didn't. I ran home when I heard the window smash and Alfie screaming.'

There was a shocked pause while they took it all in. 'Why didn't you tell us before, Amie?' Munro was angry. Delmar gave him a look.

'I was scared. He scared me.' The tears were back, and now her hands were shaking too. 'He hurt me.'

Munro nodded at Delmar and left the room. As the door swung shut, Delmar's face relaxed, as if the horror film had just come to an end.

'You've helped us a lot, Amie, thank you.'

'What's going to happen now?'

'Andrew will be questioned in relation to the attack. With what we have, and what you've just told us, it's very likely he will be arrested and charged, and in due course, when Dr Samuels deems it appropriate, you will be discharged and allowed to go home.'

CHAPTER 41

Munro threw the file on Ronnie's desk in an outburst of frustration.

'I still don't get it. If he did this, why did Amie not say something before?' He was pacing up and down like a caged lion again.

'Baz, you heard what she said. This is a complicated family. I don't think we can expect normal behaviour from any of them.' She shuddered, remembering Stuart appearing behind her in the doorway the morning after Amie's disappearance, Maeve's glassy-eyed absent look, and the chilling altar of trophies at the crime scene. 'And if Andrew's capable of the assault, I can believe he's capable of convincing her to take the flak for him. Craig said she was covered in bruises and cuts when she arrived at Ferndale. She was obviously terrified. Who knows what he threatened her with?'

Baz took it all in and nodded. 'But why not get rid of the weapon?'

'Panic? If you don't know how to get rid of something safely, you might hang on to it, at least for a little while. Every cop show has a weapon showing up at the scene of

322

the crime that leads them to the offender. In the heat of the moment, that will have been his reaction. Where is he now?'

'Downstairs in the interview room. Denying everything. Furious. Saying she's a liar. Among other things. *A manipulative evil bitch*, I think were his words.'

'You've arrested him? No charge yet?'

'Lydia is happy to go ahead. She's talking to the CPS. The pieces of the puzzle fit, at last.'

Ronnie was remembering how determined Lydia had been to pin the blame on Amie. It hadn't taken her long to focus on a new suspect and release her original prey from her jaws.

Craig and Rachel had been dumbstruck in their own ways.

'This comes as a real shock,' Craig had said at the debrief in his office. He was standing behind his chair, holding on to it as if he might otherwise collapse with the unexpectedness of things. 'Well, I suppose I should say congratulations.' He'd held out his hand to each of them in turn. 'You've done a great job, DS Delmar. And if there's anything else I can help with in the future . . .'

Ronnie had seen something in his eyes that said he wasn't convinced. Or was it just that the new evidence had removed him as the linchpin in the case? His opinion on Amie's state of mind had become irrelevant overnight, and his services were no longer required.

'Thanks for everything, Craig.' She'd held his hand with both of hers. 'I'm sure we'll meet again, but in the meantime take care of yourself. Oh, and try to get out on that golf course one day soon.'

'I shall do both of those things. And Amie will be discharged according to official protocol, of course. In cases like this, we ensure that our patients have ongoing medical supervision at whatever level is deemed appropriate. It's not over for her.'

Ronnie had nodded in appreciation. It was never over.

'He's right, sarge,' Baz had said as they left. 'You're a good boss, and a good copper.'

Ronnie had looked at him quizzically.

'I mean, you should never have been suspended. Good thing you were disobedient enough to carry on while you were off.'

They had never spoken about that night, Ronnie realised.

'I know you got the Hemingway's footage. We went in just after you'd left.'

She stiffened, remembering seeing Lydia's car pulling up. 'And?'

'I know you saw me on the film, sarge. I wasn't hard to spot.'

'You saw me leave, didn't you, with . . .'

'The bloke in the Burberry, yes. Followed you out. Didn't like the way he was holding you up, and ushering you out. He was in a hurry, that's for sure.'

'I don't remember any of it.' Ronnie shuddered at the thought of her brain being dismantled by the intervention of a stranger. 'I thought it was you, to start with, making the complaint about me.'

'I know. You'd be a hopeless spy, sarge. I could tell you'd seen the footage, and I guessed you just presumed I'd gone behind your back, probably thought I wanted your job. Your face, the next time you saw me, was full of disappointment. I'll never forget it.'

'And you were the one who put Lydia right. I have never actually thanked you.' She cringed inside, wishing hard that she'd done the honourable thing at the time.

'Nothing to thank me for, sarge – just setting the record straight.'

'So what were you doing there? Apart from bodyguarding me?'

Baz looked at her quizzically. 'I go there quite often on a Saturday night, as it happens.'

'Oh?' Ronnie waited for more, but all he gave her was the beginnings of a smile. It was none of her business, and she knew it, but she felt a desperate craving for the truth, to fill in the gaps and tie things up properly, the way she had never been able to do when her father died.

Baz watched her discomfort for a second, seeming to enjoy her battle with herself, before he told her what she wanted to hear. 'My girlfriend, Amber, works there.'

Ronnie did a double-take.

'You've met her, of course.'

There was nothing wrong with Baz having a girlfriend. It wasn't that. Or was it? Ronnie composed her face into a smile that said she was nothing but pleased.

'Of course. Sorry, it really was none of my business.'

Baz laughed. 'No worries. Now you know, anyway. I have a life outside these four walls . . .'

'So what happened? To me, I mean. What did you see?' Ronnie was feeling impatient again. Baz was holding all the cards, and she didn't feel completely comfortable with that, especially after the humiliation of her suspension.

'I followed you outside. He got a bit over-friendly and you weren't having any of it. You put up a good fight, though.'

'A fight?'

'More pushing away than actual fighting, or I'd have intervened, obviously. I didn't need to do anything, but I'm glad I was there.'

'So am I!' Ronnie shook her head. 'Thank you, Baz. I really appreciate you stepping in to stand up for me.'

'No worries. I'm sure you'd do the same for me.'

She could have sworn he winked as he strolled away.

CHAPTER 42

A month after her release, Amie was sitting in the conservatory of their new home, watching the last of the leaves blow and skitter round the garden. The sky was leaden, the temperature too warm for winter, too cold for autumn. It was as if nature was holding its breath between seasons, long after it should have moved on. The scene calmed her, reminded her of the cycles of the universe. Everything came and went, lived and died and lived again. Dad might have been right about just going with the flow. There was no other choice, when it came down to it.

She picked up a pen and hesitated as it hovered above the page. Writing by hand was a habit from Ferndale that she hadn't shaken off.

14 December
Dear Elisa,

It's been a while. I thought that given everything that has gone on, it would be better to make a go of it on my own, rather than keep pestering you. If you've moved on, you've moved on, and I need to accept it.

They say I'm free now, but I'm not really. Doctors and psychiatrists still rule my life, constantly reminding me that I may not be guilty of a crime, but I am suffering from an illness that 'can cause pain and damage to myself and others if not treated'. I don't think they have any idea what's good for me, but I go along with it most of the time just because it's easier not to fight it.

At least I'm not in that prison of a hospital any more. They sold the house in Pine Walk and I'm living with Dad, Celia and Alfie just outside Millhurst, down a few winding lanes, so nobody comes nosing around. It's a house that's been adapted for wheelchairs and has ramps and lifts for Celia because she can't do anything at all for herself now. I don't know why Dad doesn't just put her in a home, but he probably feels guilty, since he's the cause of all this, after all.

I can leave the house when I like, as long as I'm not babysitting Alfie; I can use the computer, even go online, and I don't get locked in at night. So, comparatively, it's a life of luxury. I know I should make the most of it.

They said I can do the school year again somewhere new, next September, or I can get a job, an apprenticeship maybe, but Dad says there's no rush. He's probably worried who's going to babysit if I'm out at work somewhere.

Dad went to see Andrew this morning as usual. So I still don't get to see him on a Saturday even now, and Andrew still does, which is kind of ironic when you think about it. The detention centre, or whatever they call it to make it sound less awful, is an hour's drive away, so that's a whole morning, sometimes longer, that I have to be here with HER. The carers are here most of the time, probably because secretly nobody trusts me, but I can show them I am worthy of trust, over time.

When Dad comes back from seeing Andrew, or whatever else he does all day, because he's never here, his face looks older, and he takes himself off into the garage, pretending there's something he needs to be getting on with, but I listened at the door once and heard him crying like a baby. He's probably regretting everything he did, wishing he hadn't gone with the flow after all.

I wonder what Celia would do if she had any awareness that he was visiting Andrew – or maybe she doesn't even know who put her in that wheelchair. It would be funny to tell her, watch her face when she finds out.

And then there's Alfie. He still remembers that night he spent on his own in the car, and it's useful being able to scare him, to make him do what I want. I say 'tidy up your toys or the baddies will come and take your mummy again' or 'that man will come and break your window again' and he tidies up like his life depends on it, and I take the credit. Dad's usually busy, so he doesn't know any better. If he sees me staring at Alfie, he says, 'Be nice to your brother,' and it makes me sick. I don't want him as a brother. I don't want any brothers.

The carers are bathing Celia upstairs. Alfie is watching TV. I'm supposed to be cooking his fish fingers. And green beans, which he hates, but that doesn't matter. He can learn to like them like I did. He can eat his dinner in the lounge.

He's not really supposed to, but Dad doesn't know and probably doesn't care. I make the rules now and I don't want him in here with me, getting in the way.

I think about Mum sometimes. As the drugs drag my brain into sleep every night, I can hear the click click click of her heels in the corridor as she hurries away from my hospital room, just as I'm putting down the phone to you. I still don't know what it was that sent her over the edge that night, but I suppose I didn't leave her much to carry on living for.

There's a photo of her by my bed that Mary gave me at the funeral. It was taken at their leaving party. She's standing in the garden with a glass of pink wine in her hand, half looking at the camera, half not, as if she's not sure if someone is photographing her or reading a text message. The expression on her face is anxious but pretending not to be – her eyes give her away, haunted by something she doesn't dare talk about in case it comes true. There's a shoulder in the picture – I think it's Colin's. Dad is standing behind them, his back to Mum, deep in conversation with someone just outside the frame. When I look at it, I'm suddenly back there, seeing them through the window, a family about to be undone, the people that made me, about to disentangle and say, 'Let's press back-space and start again.'

We got a Christmas card from the Morrisons. It was full of news about what their boys had been doing – finishing university, getting jobs, living their lives while their parents sat back and watched. Mum never got a chance to do that.

I still miss you, Elisa. You were my soul sister, my missing half. I didn't always agree with you, and sometimes I hated you, but I always needed you, and without you I'm just a shadow of what I should be. Please come back.

Amie x

CHAPTER 43

Ronnie was leafing through a medical journal when the call came in. Medicine, especially psychological disorders, had become of peculiar interest to her since the Slade case. She still pondered the outcome, as she had the intervening stages.

It was the switching of focus that had wrong-footed her. Amie as victim of assault, Amie as traumatised schoolgirl spending time in a derelict mausoleum, Amie as suspect in an attempted murder, then as the victim of duress and coercion, forced by physical violence into taking the fall for her brother because the consequences were more serious for him. At each point, the evidence had seemed conclusive, and then, moments later, the stitches had come undone and the opposite was true.

Susie Marshall was equally baffled, and had told Ronnie on more than one occasion how guilty she felt about Amie's incarceration at Ferndale. 'If there was any connection between her being sectioned and her mother's death, that's too horrific to contemplate.'

Ronnie did her best to draw a line under it. 'Oh, Suze, you of all people know that blaming yourself is a fool's game. Nobody saw this coming, and she only revealed what she wanted us to see. Everything we did was by the book . . .'

A shadow crossed her face for a second. Self-justification always implied uncertainty. Still, she might have pressurised Susie into sharing confidential material, but the photos she'd sent had been crucial to saving Celia Burrows' life.

The latest psychiatry journal she was reading contained a number of articles on personality disorders, most of which seemed to overlap and interweave to the point that it was impossible to distinguish between them. Even for the experts, it must be hard to see where illness stopped and personality began.

She put it down, just as the phone rang.

'DS Delmar? Sorry, Ronnie. It's Louisa Emsworth.'

'Of course, Louisa. How are you? How can I help?' Ronnie felt a twinge of something like guilt. Was there something left over she hadn't done? After a case was closed, if anyone associated with it came knocking on the door, she felt the panic of a surgeon who had accidentally left a swab inside the chest cavity.

'Can I come in and see you about something, in an hour or so?'

'Of course – what is it?'

'I don't have time to explain right now – I'm driving and I need to get off the phone to hear the app tell me the route. Don't worry, I'm on hands-free, before you go hunting me down. But I might have something new on Amie Slade.'

'What kind of something? You're being very mysterious.'

'I don't actually have it yet, but bear with me and I think I will do very soon.'

'Are you sure you can't tell me more?'

'No, you'll see why. Best if you're out of the loop on this one. You know, evidence rules and all that. I'll be in touch a bit later.'

Ronnie hesitated. 'OK. I'm here most of the day, barring emergencies. You're not going round to see her, are you?'

The signal cut out, and Ronnie felt her stomach turn over with discomfort. There was nothing wrong with a teacher visiting her pupil at home, was there? It didn't feel right somehow.

It was getting late when she noticed the time. She checked her phone against the office clock to be sure. There were no missed calls. Louisa had said an hour.

Ronnie forced her mind back to the scene in the derelict house and wondered for the hundredth time how a teenager could lead a double life like that, imprisoning herself in the wreckage of an abandoned building with only the relics of her past for company. The feeling of intense discomfort returned, the shocking smell of the rotting animal corpse, the sacrificial altar holding the lock of hair cut from the head of her classmate at school. Even if Amie had been wronged and was safe now, what was her state of mind, and where had the madness gone, if indeed it had gone? Was the medication and clinical supervision she was undergoing enough to keep this kind of behaviour in abeyance?

The Slade case was a perfectly documented story that didn't fit. But perfectly documented was enough for the law, and Andrew's upcoming trial was in all probability a formality.

Ronnie just couldn't hold the whole thing in her head at once. It was too much to be going on in one family.

She tried Louisa's phone again, then had a flash of an idea and flicked through her phone contacts. She should call Craig Samuels. At their final goodbye, when Amie was released, he had seemed taken aback by the suddenness of things, as if he didn't believe it was over. She pressed voice call before she could change her mind, and he answered straight away with a voice full of avuncular jollity. 'Ronnie, I was just thinking about you.'

'Oh, really?' He had had a knack of disconcerting her, second-guessing her next move.

'I'm always running over things in my head – never really let go of the Slade case, I suppose. And I know the trial is imminent, so you were on my mind.'

'Well, that's exactly why I'm calling. There may be a development. Can you get down to CID, soonish?'

'Is there new evidence?'

'Possibly. Don't worry if you're busy. It's a bit of a long shot and I don't want to waste your time.'

Within what seemed like minutes, the phone on the desk buzzed. 'It's Dr Samuels for you.'

He strode in and put his hands on his hips, taking in the scene. Ronnie was reminded of her visit to his office, and thought hers must seem like an obsessive-compulsive paradise in comparison.

'It's been a while.'

'Only a month, would you believe? Seems like an age.'

He moved the pile of medical journals to set it down on the desk. If he noticed the journals he didn't react, which sent an unwelcome wave of disappointment through her.

'So, how can I help you?' he asked. 'What's the new development?'

'What was your feeling about the way things ended with the Slade case? Did we get it right? Could we have done more?'

'We all run on limited resources. The whole medical profession is the same. I don't see what more you could have done, personally. And doing *more* isn't always a good thing, of course.'

'And if you ask the DI, I already get way too involved in everything that uniform could deal with, I don't delegate enough.'

'Ah, delegation is all about trust. The minute you hand it all over, it can go wrong and you'll be to blame.'

'And I'm struggling with that right now. Louisa Emsworth called to say she had something more on the Slade case, needed to sort something out and then would come straight here, but she hasn't turned up . . .'

'And you think something will go wrong?' He finished off her sentence neatly.

'Lydia would probably be delighted that someone else was doing the donkey work for us, but there's something about it that bothers me.'

'Is it that you're not keen on letting someone else walk into the firing line?'

'I'm not sure I'm that selfless. It's probably more about not getting the blame if they mess up. Although there's the alternative: getting the credit for things that go right. That's always a bonus.'

'That's honest of you.'

It wasn't the kind of thing she would normally admit, but confessing to a psychiatrist was so much easier, because they could probably already see inside your head.

'But whatever she's on to, Ronnie, you've done your job here. More than done your job. So what time are we expecting her?'

'About an hour ago.' Ronnie glanced at the time again, then went to the window, as if she might find Louisa outside, waving from the café across the road.

She flicked through her contacts and clicked on Louisa's name. The call went to voicemail.

'I have to say, I don't feel entirely surprised that she still feels there's more to find out,' he said. 'Amie was a fascinating patient. There may be many aspects to her that we aren't aware of, and may never be. What's your hunch, DS Delmar?'

'Irrelevant, I suppose. A hunch doesn't stand a chance against hard evidence.'

'So, what's your theory, then, if you were allowed such a thing in court?'

'Well, you remember at the time we thought Maeve's suicide might be related to something she saw or heard when she went to visit Amie at Ferndale. She signed in, went up to Amie's room, but when she arrived, before even going in, she turned and went back. Did you ever find out what Amie was doing in the room at the time?'

'Only that there had been a phone call, an authorised call, and the phone was still in her room when Maeve turned up. It's a phone we move between rooms for calls to and from family, usually supervised.'

'So, it may have been that she overheard a phone conversation.'

'The authorised call had ended a while before, there's no outgoing line without a code, and she wouldn't have known that code.'

'Did another call come in?'

'Not possible. It would have had to go through switchboard.'

'So whatever it was that Maeve overheard, according to Andrew he told Amie that it may have driven her mother over the edge that night.' Ronnie cast her mind back to their interviews with a surly, unco-operative Andrew, then to her conversations with Maeve, whose mind had remained a mystery until the end. *I may have made a mistake.* She had never found out what the mistake was, or if it was even relevant.

'Go on.' Craig folded his arms and Ronnie brought herself back to her thought process.

'But she can't take on the responsibility of causing Maeve's death, can she?'

'I don't imagine she wants that, no.'

'So she might want to shift the blame, once and for all.'

Craig raised his eyebrows, encouraging her to continue.

'It's a thought that's been in the back of my mind, itching to get out. I don't want it to be true, believe me. Every bone in my body wants that girl to be OK, exonerated and safe again. Every instinct in my body says this is all wrong. But someone once said to me that sometimes trusting your gut isn't enough . . .'

The words came out without filter, and she heard herself imply the unthinkable.

Craig understood. He took a breath and held it, letting it out slowly before he spoke.

'You think she framed him?'

'Is she capable?'

'Everyone's potentially capable of anything. While Amie was with us at Ferndale, we kept transcripts of her therapy sessions. She talked about the events leading up to the assault by Daniel Foster, the aftermath of that. As part of the background, it was important that we had an insight into the major traumas in her life. A major part of the defence case if it came to court would have been that that these traumas had caused her significant harm, which impeded her ability to distinguish right from wrong.'

Ronnie scribbled some notes on a pad. However little influence this could have over the trial, it was worth hearing, because this man was a brilliant observer of people. Her curiosity was piqued.

'Anyway, when I read the transcripts afterwards, long afterwards in fact, after she was sent home, it just didn't sit well with me. She talked about things as being necessarily consequential, one thing leading to another in an inevitable series of events.'

'What did it make you think?'

'You and I discussed briefly the issue of psychopathy, if I remember rightly. You were shocked that I was using the word, I think, which I understand. It is overused by the masses, and tends to create a feeling of disbelief, just because it's a word that is bandied around so much. But so much of Amie's behaviour, if we could fill in the gaps, could easily fit the definition.'

Ronnie's heart missed a beat as she took in what he was saying. 'So you think my theory is possible too, then?'

'Absolutely. But, when you came up with evidence against Andrew that was irrefutable, the whole thing was put to bed once and for all. No more scope for gut feelings, or hunches, or theories, whatever you like to call them.'

Ronnie pulled a file out of the back of the cabinet. 'Trophy-collection is a sign of psychopathy,' she said, slapping it down on the desk. 'I know that much.'

She turned the pages, then spun it round to face Craig and sat back in her chair. He looked at each photograph in turn, as if consigning it to memory, or feeding it into a computer that might spit out the answer any minute.

'All these trophies, and all of them "won" off other people, presumably.'

Ronnie frowned. It was a line of enquiry they had been prevented from pursuing when Lydia tightened the purse strings.

'What I have never understood,' she began uncertainly, 'is why collect trophies in the first place? Why not keep the secret safe rather than line up your winnings for all to see?'

'Because the truth needs a way out?' Craig suggested. 'There is a theory that the human mind needs to share any burden of guilt. Emotion needs an outlet.'

'I suppose that makes sense.' Ronnie thought about her own feelings of guilt. At times, they seemed to have complete control over her every action, as if her whole life were a penance.

'So what did you find out?'

She came back to earth, wondering how long he'd been looking at her expectantly. This was not the time to dwell on the past.

'With the way things worked out, they were just like a sideshow to the main event. We don't know where most of them came from. If there's no crime, there's no investigation.'

'No *reported* crime.'

'Exactly. A handful of random objects isn't going to justify opening a new case. It's not an escape room.'

Craig was frowning and tapping the picture of the pencil case. 'The hair, we know, was cut off in the classroom.'

'That's right.' Ronnie remembered jumping the gun by bringing it up at Amie's interview when the lab results couldn't possibly have been conclusive.

'Now this case here . . .' he pointed to the photo of the yellow zipped box that had never been identified, 'looks like an EpiPen holder.'

Ronnie looked at it more closely. Of course. She jolted backwards with the memory of the second incident at school, which they had taken as just another example of teenage girls going through a difficult phase.

'That's it. I remember now. An EpiPen belonging to one girl was found in another girl's rucksack. But if this was the case for it, then . . .' Ronnie thought back to the story Louisa had told.

'Was Amie involved in that, do you think?' Craig asked, a grim expression on his face.

Ronnie thought it through. Amie could have kept the case after disposing of its contents in the other girl's bag. And if the other girl was the one whose hair she had cut . . . The thought landed in her mind like a stray firework, spitting and hissing its message. You missed something there, Ronnie Delmar . . .

'And this brake cable. What's the story there?' Craig asked.

Suddenly Ronnie was on a speeding treadmill she had to race to keep up with. At least this one she had been halfway towards solving. 'Andrew – earlier on the night of the attack. He'd fallen off his bike. It could have been because Amie tampered with the brakes. We never checked it out because we had to suspend investigation on all these objects until Foster reappeared.'

She put her head in her hands, leant forward and closed her eyes to concentrate. At the first interview with Amie, she had hardly noticed when she said the words. *Andrew shouldn't have taken Dad's bike.*

'She did it. But it was her father's bike she tampered with. She meant it to be Stuart.'

'A punishment for leaving?'

'It's all about revenge. She did all this.' Ronnie felt sick. It felt as though her worst nightmares were coming true. She had missed things. She had got it wrong. There was a whole scenario of evidence she hadn't pursued and investigated. Lydia might have given the orders, but she could have at least tried harder to persuade her.

What made it even worse was that it was her conviction, her gut instinct, that had made her so determined to protect Amie. She had been some sort of reflection of Serena and it had been Ronnie's chance to make things right. But that wasn't how life worked.

Craig saw the distress in her eyes and pulled out his phone. 'Hang on – before you talk yourself into a corner, remember that there was plenty of evidence of her being hurt by someone else. Remember those bruises on her arms? It all fits with the allegations she made against her brother, forcing her to keep quiet. They weren't self-inflicted.'

Ronnie stood up and went to the window, thinking as she spoke. *No stone unturned*, she heard Baz echoing her words. She turned back and leant over her chair, resting her chin on the leather headrest, and looked at Craig. Gut instinct wasn't enough. She needed to be braver now.

'They *could* have been self-inflicted. If you're trying to make it look like someone else did it, you think about that stuff – you work out which way they'd be facing, the angle they'd be coming from.'

'But we know he was there, with her. You matched his footprints and the residue on the trainers. And you heard it from Amie that he took her with him to Celia's house that Saturday night, when he found out about Stuart's double life.'

What Ronnie was thinking, she couldn't articulate. She forced her mind back to the afternoon when she'd found Amie back home after being presumed missing. She had been in a hurry to clear up, taking a jacket and a pair of trainers upstairs.

'What if Amie put on her brother's shoes that night? As well as her own . . .' The words came out in a whisper.

Craig's eyes narrowed. 'What about Celia's blood and Andrew's fingerprints on the weapon?'

'They weren't good prints. Could have been from a long time before. They last years,' said Ronnie.

'So I've heard, but couldn't the reason the prints were bad also be that he would have done his best to remove them? Your average murderer has probably seen enough movies to know to wipe the weapon clean.'

'It wasn't clean, though. If you're cleaning it, you clean it.' It was true that most assailants made a better effort than Andrew had. Ronnie's heart was pounding now. 'I don't buy it, never did, about protecting Andrew, whatever pressure he was putting on her to stay silent. He had no motive to follow her there, whatever he thinks about his father's affair and his new little brother.'

'Some sort of sibling rivalry? Trying to set her up for something?'

'They didn't even get on well enough to have that going on. Both loners, didn't want anything to do with each other, as far as I can gather.' She paused, feeling the frustration build as she hit brick wall after brick wall. 'I just feel that we never found out what she was like, who she really was. We never got close to her.'

'I don't think anyone did, except the friend she talked about. The one who used to persuade her to act out of character. Did you ever talk to her?'

'Elisa? She never turned out to be a suspect or a witness, so no. Apparently not in Amie's tutor group but possibly in another class. I never heard back from Louisa on that. Another piece of the puzzle that never found its place.' Ronnie flicked through the file, then stopped when she got to the images from Foster's phone of his Instagram contacts. 'Hang on a minute.' She picked up her phone and swiped down her messages. 'Amie showed Susie Marshall a photo of Elisa and she sent it to me a while back, but I never paid much attention to it. It didn't seem hugely relevant, but now I'm having second thoughts.'

Craig pored over the file. 'Looks like one of those social network things. She looks very young.' He was pointing to the pale-eyed pouting girl in bed they had extracted from Foster's gallery of friends.

Ronnie was staring at her phone screen, then back at the file. 'It's her. They're the same.'

'Who?'

'It's Elisa. On Foster's phone, along with Amie and others, if there are others . . .' She trailed off.

Craig frowned. 'I don't understand what you're getting at.'

Ronnie had to concentrate to keep the train of thought now. 'This account – this girl in the photo requested to follow Foster on the day of the assault, and he followed her back, along with Amie and several others. Young girls, all underage, all underdressed, as you can see there in the file.' She looked up at Craig, then back down at the photo on her phone. 'But look at this.' The phone screen was small, but zooming in made up for that. 'The background is the same.'

'The same on the two pictures of Elisa?'

'No, it's the same on all of them.' She handed the phone to Craig. 'Look at the wall. There's the corner of a picture visible in both the Elisa photo and the Amie photo. Looks like a framed painting of something.'

'So, they took them together, in the same room?'

'What about this one?' Another of Daniel Foster's followers was photographed with the same backdrop; if you looked carefully enough, the detail of the frame could be just about made out. 'I think Amie created these accounts, and maybe others too.'

'How on earth do you do that on this . . . Instagram thing?'

'I imagine it's easy to fake a photo, to replace your face or Photoshop it to look completely different, and just as easy to forget to blank out things in the background. There's a frame like this above Amie's bed. *Sunflowers*. I remember from our first search of the house.'

'Could be a coincidence,' Craig offered, lamely.

'Or it might be the needle in the haystack we've been searching for. And it would explain the letters coming back undelivered, the fact that Louisa never mentioned her as a friend in the class when I asked about that stuff. I'm sure I mentioned her name, but Louisa never picked up on it.' Ronnie was thinking aloud now, her mind racing. 'Why didn't I notice that?'

Craig leant back and cast his eyes around the room. 'Well, if it's a fantasy friend, then we have a much more serious case on our hands than I thought.'

'I can't believe we missed it.'

'Could have, might have, we don't know for sure yet.'

'Let's think back to the trophies. We never worked out where this came from.' She was tapping the photo of the brick, which would have easily passed for rubble if it hadn't been deliberately placed with the other objects on the makeshift altar.

'Looks as if it could do some damage.'

Ronnie thought back to Amie's account of the break-in at Celia's house and groaned inwardly. With every discovery came more disappointment as her preconceptions were torn apart. 'She said Andrew gave her the other half of the brick when they smashed Celia's window.'

Craig was still looking at the trophy photos. There was one left they had never discussed. 'What about this shirt button?'

'We never even got a theory together on that.'

'A red herring?'

'I suppose it could be, unless . . .' Ronnie broke off.

Craig looked closer. 'What?'

Ronnie's pulse quickened. '*Torn* off a shirt. Look at the threads. It hasn't just fallen off.'

'You're thinking Andrew?'

'No . . . not any more.' Ronnie slammed the file shut with a bang that made Craig sit back in shock. 'Foster,' she said, her face rigid with determination.

'But that wasn't her doing. He wasn't a conquest of any sort.' Then, catching Ronnie's expression, his face went white. 'Unless, surely not – you don't think . . .'

But Ronnie was already typing a text to Louisa Emsworth.

Get out of there now.
You could be in danger.
Get away from Amie.

CHAPTER 44

The minutes that passed seemed like hours.

Outside, rain began to fall. Inside, Ronnie's phone pinged.

'Is that her?'

'It's her. She's sharing her location on WhatsApp.'

'And?'

'Oh, my God, she *did* go there.'

'To see Amie? Alone?' Craig looked alarmed.

Then there was a second ping, announcing a recorded message, twelve minutes long. Ronnie pressed *play* and Craig moved closer to listen.

CHAPTER 45

Amie had her independence and, as long as she took her medication, everyone just let her get on with it. There was a giant Tupperware box in the cupboard next to the fridge full of all the meds for her 'condition', plus the steroids she had been taking since the overdose; and there were sleeping pills for all of them in the house except Alfie. It was ironic that he was the only one who could sleep at night. Amie crumbled her pills into her mug in the morning so that when she used it at night for her tea it was all ready and she didn't need to think. It gave her just enough time to clean her teeth and get into bed and then she was out like a light.

The rest of the pills, she took when she felt like it. Life was so much duller when she was medicated. The world was greyer and bleaker. She needed a break from that from time to time and, as nobody seemed to notice, those times got more frequent.

Then, one day, out of the blue, she had a visitor.

Normally she wouldn't answer the door or the phone if she wasn't sure who it was, but it just happened that she was putting out the rubbish when a car pulled into the drive. It had rained in the night and water dripped on to her shoes as she lifted the lid of the bin. Just then, as the car crunched to a purposeful halt, showers gave way to a burst of sunshine between clouds. Perhaps this new arrival would bring good news.

Amie was down the side passage of the house, out of sight but with a good view of the driver, who climbed out slowly, putting her glasses up on her head as she looked up and took it all in. There was a ramp leading up to the front door with big white railings on each side, which people sometimes saw and then looked down or away as if they were embarrassed. She was just looking away like that when she saw Amie with the bin bag in one hand, her other hand already raised in greeting.

'Amie!'

It took Amie another second to recognise her. 'Miss Emsworth. This is a surprise. How did you find me?'

'You're still on the school records, as is your change of address.' Pulling her handbag on to her shoulder, she slammed the car door behind her. Or maybe she just closed it. It felt decisive. There was a *clip clop* of heels as she made her way over the glistening tarmac. 'I wanted to see how you were doing, have a chat about your plans. May I come in?'

'Sure,' Amie said, opening the front door for her guest.

She saw her visitor notice how tidy it was, not a thing out of place. This was how Amie liked it, tidying up the classroom at break, tidying up Jess Fleetwood's hair. Amie always made sure everything was as it should be, nothing getting out of control. No mess. Mum taught her that.

'So how have you been?' Miss Emsworth asked.

Amie relaxed momentarily. A social call perhaps. 'I've been OK. Thank you. It's been tough, though, especially for Celia.'

The teacher nodded. 'I can imagine. But what a lovely house this is.'

'It's a bit remote, but we like it like that.'

'Nice to be away from the hustle and bustle.'

She meant prying eyes, and she'd be right. Dad didn't want people feeling sorry for him, didn't want the pointing and whispering, and in a small town, word could spread fast, whatever the police said about keeping you out of the limelight and your name out of the press.

'It wasn't easy to find, I must admit.'

'There's a shortcut that the apps don't seem to know about. When you go down the lane, it's left and left again and you're back on the main road.'

But the teacher didn't seem to be planning on leaving, not just yet.

'And a new start for you. That's just what you need.'

'Yes. A new start. That's just what I need.' She turned away, so the teacher didn't see her smile.

Amie let her follow her to the kitchen, where everything was clean, ordered, not a thing out of place. White tiles gleamed, granite surfaces sparkled. What a good house-keeper she was. Responsible. Essential to the running of the home. Amie watched her take it all in, then filled the kettle up with water from the hot tap. It took less time to boil that way, and she didn't like that awkward bit where you were sitting there listening to the boiling noise and couldn't hear each other talk.

'Tea or coffee?' she enquired automatically, turning back from the tap and setting the kettle on its base.

'Black coffee would be lovely, thanks, Amie.' It was the smile that had always made Amie feel at ease. 'No sugar.'

Amie smiled back and for a second they were back in the classroom, sitting either side of her desk by the open window, the breeze lifting and rustling the papers in front of them as she pointed out this and that about Amie's writing, suggested new ideas, expressed delight and pride in what she'd done.

The teacher pulled out a chair from the table and sat down. Amie opened the cupboard that housed the coffee and tea and took out the jar of decaf. No caffeine allowed in this house. From the next cupboard she took two mugs, one shouting *Keep Calm and Carry On*. It was good advice.

Amie sat down at the table. Her chair scraped on the tiles and she made a mental note to buy more of the stick-on felt blobs. They kept coming off. She should stock up.

The teacher's smile had disappeared, and Amie realised she had gone from relaxed to tense in seconds without even noticing. Stress inhabited her like a squatter. It had rights. Every time she threw it out, it came straight back, taking over her body with the arrogance of a school bully. She breathed deeply and tried again to expel it from her limbs and organs where it had taken hold, but she couldn't quite get there.

This wasn't just a social call. There was something else.

And then the sun went in again.

'Anyway . . .' Amie's daydream was shattered by a bulldozer of reality. 'Let's get to the real reason I'm here.'

No, let's not. Let's stay here pretending it's just this, just hello, Amie thought.

'I found something interesting I thought I should bring to show you.'

It seemed the wrong time to get up and make the coffee, so Amie let her carry on.

'It's this.' She pulled something out of her bag. A magazine. 'I always wondered who won the writing competition you entered.'

Amie shook her head, feeling heat rise up from the pit of her stomach. She flailed about for a response. 'What does that matter?'

'To be honest, I thought you had a good chance. You're a fabulous storyteller. You have a real way with words. Enviable. I wish other students wrote as well as you.'

The teacher was taunting her now, a cat taking a swipe at the mouse, letting it run, just a little way . . .

'So I got in touch with them to find out. Because I was curious to see who on earth had beaten my top student.'

'And?'

'I asked if they'd had anything from you, and they hadn't.'

The tension in Amie's shoulders eased slightly. But it was like coming up for air in a riptide, because the teacher had more to say.

'But that was the wrong question. What I should have asked was *who won?*'

Amie just looked straight at her, giving nothing away, willing the heat to cool, her heartbeat to slow.

'And there was a winner. But no contact details for the writer of the winning entry.'

'Oh. How strange.'

'But they published it anyway to see if the writer would come forward.'

There was a new look on her face. This was a side to her Amie didn't know.

'They sent me a copy of the magazine with the winning entry. I had to read it, of course.'

'Of course.' Amie nodded again. Her plan hadn't quite come together yet. She was stalling. She did her best to look puzzled as her mind raced ahead, pushing against every door to see if it would open, let her through . . .

'I recognised the story from the press. It was about the assault on a child by a caretaker in a school. It was a very familiar story, in fact. The perpetrator served eight months in prison for it.'

Amie sat completely still, willing herself invisible while she worked out the answer to what was coming.

'At the time, the media had never revealed the name of the girl, for confidentiality reasons, but the author of the story did give her name. No other details, just her name.'

'What name?'

'Elisa Mead.'

'Oh.' They stared at each other before Amie asked, 'So, sorry, what are you saying exactly?'

'I looked at the name, and it seemed to ring a bell, but I wasn't sure why. It was as if I recognised it from somewhere. Then I remembered the detective asking me if she was in your class, which she wasn't, but at the time I presumed she was in your Maths or English class.'

Amie's voice tightened. 'Miss Emsworth – do I call you that still? I don't understand what you're trying to say.'

The kettle pinged as the boiling point was reached, plunging them back into silence.

'I think you know very well what I'm trying to say, don't you?'

'What do you mean?' Amie's stomach tightened in anticipation of the blow.

'Elisa Mead is *you*. It's an anagram of your name.'

Amie scrabbled for a foothold as the landslide pulled the ground from under her feet and fingers. There was silence. She looked the teacher in the eyes, hard and steady.

'How clever of you.'

'How clever of *you*, Amie. But only unless, and until, anyone found out about who Elisa really was. Then you'd be in a bit of trouble, wouldn't you?' She half smiled before going on. 'Because if Elisa is the alter ego you invented, then this confession here implicates you in destroying the life of an innocent person.'

She was pointing at the magazine. On the cover, a bunch of glossy teenagers grinned up at them.

'I just assumed that you'd never sent anything in. I assumed, as we all did, that the confession story they found on your laptop about Andrew was the one you were writing for the competition but hadn't submitted.'

She fixed Amie with the gaze of her once trusting eyes, now full of disappointment.

'But you did send a story in. This story.'

She shook the magazine open and slid it across the table. 'Well? Tell me I'm wrong.'

'Let me make that coffee.' Amie stood up. Calm returned, but like a butterfly settling on a leaf, as temporary as the moment.

Absently, she took two more mugs out of the cupboard and spooned coffee into both. The water was still steaming. She poured it over the coffee granules and brought the mugs to the table, placing them side by side like sentries, the first line of infantry to be defeated before the real damage could be done.

'I doubt anyone else would have made the connection, and, even if they had, they might have assumed it was a vindictive retelling of a story about an abused child.' Miss Emsworth picked up her mug, then put it down again. 'And nothing would have come of it.'

She nursed the mug in her hands, elbows on the table – a friendly pose, two women confiding their secrets at a coffee morning, divulging suspicions about a husband's affair, the eating disorders of their teenage daughters.

'Was it easier to confess in someone else's name? Was that it?'

Amie stared through the rising steam, hands in her lap, thinking nothing at all, and everything, at the same time. Steam wafted hotly upwards.

'You're not denying it, then?'

She spoke, and everything changed. 'No.'

This was how it felt when she didn't take the medication. Alive, ready for anything. Even without her gladiator sandals.

The teacher's face went white. In some fantasy scenario, she must have hoped for a denial and a happy ending, just as Amie had hoped for understanding, because it was about time someone understood.

'You have no idea what it feels like to be about to watch everything collapse around you,' she said. 'Dad was going to leave us. Leave me. Mum was never going to survive. Andrew was going away. He didn't care about anyone. No one gave a damn about me.' Her fists were clenched, glued to the table.

'I see that you must have felt like that, but to do *this*.' The teacher pointed at the open pages in front of them, which Amie refused to look down at. The volcano was about to emit its last gush of toxic vomit and she was just a building in its path, immobile, a sitting duck. They were priest and parishioner, saint and sinner.

'And the thing is, Amie, if this story by "Elisa Mead" was your confession, and if everything you've written here is true, I'm not sure you should be trusted any more.'

Amie stared into the steam. 'Perhaps you're right.' The grey wave of truth rose between them, ready to smash everything in its path. *Surfers know how to deal with waves. Enjoy the danger. Get into the right position and ride it.* She steeled herself and smiled. They had turned a corner now and there was no going back.

The teacher's eyes widened in shock. Surely this couldn't be Amie, her mouse-like student who preferred sharpening pencils to hanging out with the college boys next door. Or perhaps it was admiration. Amie deserved admiration, surely, for getting this far.

The teacher took a deep breath. Rummaging in her handbag, she pulled out a hanky and blew her nose quietly, checking her phone as she did so. Amie couldn't tell if she was crying or she had a cold.

She put the phone and the tissues on the table. Bag, mugs, magazine, phone, tissues. It was getting messy. Amie felt an overwhelming urge to tidy it all up, to close the magazine and put it in the rack, to put the handbag on the floor, to say, *No phones at the table*, which was what adults always said to children. But then she thought better of it.

'What do you mean, "perhaps I'm right"? That you shouldn't be trusted?'

'What do you want to know?'

'I want to know everything.' But Miss Emsworth's voice was shaking. She wouldn't be saying that if she knew what kind of everything it was.

'Andrew had been getting in the way from the beginning: he never did what Mum wanted, made her sad and angry and difficult to live with, and then Dad went and found someone else. Andrew was supposed to look after Mum, but he didn't and she died. And then he had the audacity to blame me for it, so I punished him. It's what happens.'

'It isn't, Amie, not in normal life. Not if people are honest and kind.'

'No one was honest and kind to me.'

The teacher stared back at Amie in disbelief. Then it was too tempting to feed her the facts, in dribs and drabs to keep her on the edge of her seat.

'I had that piece of glass for a long time. It was from something that broke, a glass bowl I dropped at a party at the neighbours', years ago. I crashed into a closed window, thinking it was open. The boys laughed at me, humiliated me. Andrew picked up the broken glass and I kept a piece of it, just in case. You know . . .'

'I'm not sure I do.' Her voice was quiet, lips trembling.

They sat in silence while the room darkened. Rain was forecast. She should shut the window in the bathroom when this was over.

The teacher took a sip of coffee. Amie relaxed, just a little.

'So what did you do?'

And then Amie told her everything. For the first time, someone was listening to her side of the story. Better than confessing on paper in another name. This was real.

'It was dark, the windows were boarded up and I wasn't aware of anyone outside until a torch shone through the gap in the window. I panicked for a minute that it might be Daniel Foster. He definitely wasn't going to let me get away with putting him in prison for eight months. Or Andrew. He would have jumped at any chance to make fun of me. Could easily have followed me there. I was getting less and less careful about that. Then she pushed the door open, all delicate and so innocent and brave.'

Miss Emsworth seemed to shudder then, which gave Amie the energy to hurl the rest of the story at her, in a deluge.

'I held up the piece of glass and rammed it so hard into the back of her neck that it sent a shaft of pain down my arms, my shoulders, made my head spin. She went bumping down the stairs to the cellar, screaming, thumping, and then everything went quiet. I went to look to see if she was alive, but I couldn't bring myself to touch her.'

'After that, everything had to be meticulous. I crept into the house after midnight and left for school early to give myself time to work out what to do. I didn't realise they'd come for me so soon. I had to run upstairs and hide the shoes and the glass when that detective came knocking on the door. Thank God Andrew had left by then. I suppose I was lucky.'

She gave the teacher a questioning look then to see if she was enjoying it. She had asked, after all.

'At Mum's funeral, when Andrew said it was my fault that she died, that was the last straw. How dare he suggest that? So I did the rest, filled in the gaps. It only took me a few minutes to rewrite the "confession" story, putting Andrew at the scene, Andrew the jealous, angry brother who beat me up to shut me up, and him with his fancy university degree to do. And it could easily have been him throwing a brick at Alfie's window. And the police accepted my version of events without question. It was flawless.'

Amie watched the teacher listen, saw the horror on her face as the truth was laid bare, and felt a shiver of excitement as she continued.

'When I had to leave the house, leave my room, leave my whole childhood behind for the last time, I left the story on the laptop. I wrote it in the same document as the original confession I'd already sent off. I changed the date settings on the laptop first, so it didn't show that it had been modified later.'

'Do you have any idea what Andrew will have been through in police custody?'

'You get your own room, a TV, you can learn stuff, work. It's a holiday camp compared to where I was locked up.'

'Amie . . .' The teacher scraped her chair back from the table. They stood for a moment in silence. The teacher shut her eyes and opened them again, as if everything might vanish and the world would be fairyland again.

'What are you going to do?' Amie asked blankly.

Miss Emsworth stood with one hand on the back of the chair next to her, staring out at the colourless garden where the bare branches of the laburnum stood starkly against the pale grey sky.

'I haven't decided,' she said eventually.

She was lying. She had definitely decided.

'They won't believe you.'

'Oh, they will.'

She should go. Instead, she was fiddling with her phone again.

For a brief moment, Amie wanted to be what the teacher wanted her to be – the repentant sinner. An unfamiliar prick of genuine shame touched her soul and she stared at the floor, wishing for nothing and wishing for everything, but most of all wishing for another chance at it all, a chance to start again, rub it all out, find another way, another life.

But she had to hold on just a little longer.

Between them lay the typed paragraphs, written in someone else's name. The headline read, *APPEAL FOR THE AUTHOR OF WINNING COMPETITION ENTRY*. It had arrived without an address, email or phone number, and therefore the prize-winner couldn't be notified or rewarded. Below the shaded box, the story was written in full. The truth Amie couldn't put her own name to. The excerpt was enough.

There are moments where life reaches a fork in the road, and things could go either way. Sometimes you end up down the wrong branch of the fork, where it's impossible to turn back. I wanted him, his arms tight around me, making me complete, his lips on mine. Perhaps he was imagining that too. Maybe he was thinking about what might happen next, if we couldn't stop things in their tracks. We could both imagine how that would feel, the slow release of the tension that had held us captive; bending back the iron bars that caged us. Free to touch, hold, kiss, explore each other, and no one to see us or stop us.

'I want to kiss you.'

The next few seconds passed like hours, painful, agonising hours, as he looked at me with a mixture of pity and shock. He was pulling away.

I was horrified by what I'd said, but instead of retreating, I flung my arms around him and sank my face into his neck, my lips on to his lips to stifle his words, my hands under his T-shirt, feeling inside his jeans. He froze and told me to stop. Then I went down on my knees to do that thing to him that all men want. Only he didn't. And there was nobody there to see my shame, no one to share that humiliation.

So I panicked and made it my story. I told them he'd assaulted me, tried to force me to do things that I can't even write here. Once I started lying, I couldn't stop. The police were kind, as if they heard this sort of thing every day, wanted me to tell them everything.

And afterwards, there was nothing more to prove, because everybody believes a child.

I lied because Dad was going to leave us forever. The text I saw when I pulled his phone out from under the seat said: 'I can't stop thinking about how much I want you . . .' and I needed him to know I needed him more. I used the same words to fake a message from the man to me, while he was doing the paperwork reporting my accident in the corridor. Didn't take me long to make a trail of communication between us. It was context, background, the stuff you're supposed to include in an essay to make things more real. It made him look guilty.

I did it to remind Dad that he needed to stay, to protect me, and he did stay, for a while. Then the spell I put on him wore off. He left, and I was lost.

Mum knows. I thought she had just pulled up in the car, but when I got there, she had her head in her hands, as if she'd seen everything. She's been different with me since then, sadder, less angry, kind of hopeless. I don't know why she didn't say something at the time, or in the months afterwards, but I think she wanted Dad to stay too. She let me do what I did and let an innocent man go to prison. It was a mistake, I know she knows that now, but she can't turn back. If she ever does say something, tell the truth about what she saw, she would be in the wrong as well. It's what they call mutually assured destruction.

'I read it all.'

Amie looked up. She'd almost forgotten the teacher was there. 'Yes, I realise you must have.' Amie leant on the table now, staring the teacher in the eye. 'I had to do it,' she tilted her head to one side. 'Don't you see?'

'No, I don't. I really don't see that you had to do any of this.'

'Well, that's what you think.'

'But then, why confess?' The teacher's hand was shaking, Amie was sure of it, as she pointed at the magazine on the table. 'Why even do this? Why not go to the grave with your dirty secret?'

'Risks are exciting, aren't they? I mean, you came here . . .'

Miss Emsworth blinked and looked around the kitchen for inspiration. She'd be wanting to leave now, having learnt more than she'd bargained for.

'Now you don't have Elisa any more, what happens to you?'

'This.' Amie stood up, spread her arms, made the teacher look at her. 'There's no balance any more. Everything can tip over one way or the other at any point.'

'But Elisa didn't give you balance. She destabilised you.'

Amie's eyes narrowed. 'You think I was stable before-hand?'

Just then, the teacher's phone buzzed. It must have been a message, because she glanced at it and the next minute she was putting everything back into her bag and preparing to leave. She seemed in a hurry now, glancing at her phone again and doing something else on it. The oldest trick in the book, Amie thought.

She headed for the door and Amie held it open for her.

'Goodbye, Amie.'

Amie watched her totter down the drive, climb into her car and drive off to do whatever she felt was right, turn her in or let her be, but it didn't matter either way.

She hadn't finished her coffee. That was a shame, really. Amie didn't want to have to go out in the rain.

CHAPTER 46

She watched as Miss Emsworth slammed the car door shut just as the rain began to fall hard. In the wing mirror, she must have seen Amie go back inside, then she swung left out of the drive and out of sight.

She probably hadn't expected the second confession. She had probably just wanted to look Amie in the eye, hear her confess to framing Daniel Foster before deciding whether to go to the police. Perhaps at some level she hoped there might be another explanation. But Amie wasn't in the business of making people's wishes come true. Nobody had ever taken any notice of hers.

Left and left again was what Amie had said. So that was the way she would have gone. The lane was narrow and her vision would be obstructed by high hedges, waving wayward brambles. Puddles would already be forming up ahead. A fog was descending, so visibility would be bad.

Amie heard the car jolt into second gear, taking the turn at a higher speed than was ideal. The water would be deeper on the bend, but the car would just hold the road. She must have reached the place where thick hedgerows gave way to a tree-lined lane. The sound of the engine began to fade.

Amie needed to act quickly. Her heart was thumping in excitement and dread. This was the biggest risk of all.

Her bike was where it always was, chained up at the side of the house like a trusty horse, ready to take her away at a moment's notice. The shortcut through the orchard was muddy but passable. She'd miss out on the blind bends and narrow lanes that Miss Emsworth would be navigating in the pouring rain. She'd be there at just about the same time.

When the teacher saw the flash of orange and the face in the windscreen, it would have been too late to stop. The car swung sideways, wheels losing grip of the wet tarmac. There was a squeal of brakes, the slow crunch of metal, then silence. She wouldn't have seen the ditch, let alone realised how deep it was.

Standing a few yards from the wreckage, Amie threw down her bike and took in the scene. The front passenger side of the Fiat was crushed against the gnarled trunk of an oak. She might have been aiming for a gap in the trees, but that would have been impossible at that angle. The rear half of the car was sticking out of the ditch, both back wheels off the ground.

There was a chance she was still alive. Amie pulled her sleeve over her hand. The door was surprisingly easy to open. There was a nasty cut on the teacher's forehead, and blood dripping down her left cheek. Then, out of the depths of the passenger footwell, Amie heard her own voice speaking to her, a tiny sound behind the hammering of the rain on metal and glass. She had been right about the recording, then. She should have been a detective.

I punished him. It's what happens.

She had to reach across the teacher's body to find it. No movement, no sign of breathing, but she couldn't be sure. It was lucky she hadn't bothered fastening her seatbelt. It was luckier still she hadn't actually hit Amie. Maybe she had been killed by her own kindness.

Taking the teacher's hand from the steering wheel, Amie pressed her forefinger on the home button and the phone lit up in recognition. She placed the hand back on the wheel and, straightening up, let the door fall gently shut. The next few seconds were crucial. Her forehead was wet. Perspiration and rain, a tropical sweat.

Voice Memos.

Delete

Delete recording?

Yes.

Then there was the accident to explain. Using your phone, not wearing a seatbelt, were good solid reasons to crash. Scanning through the contacts, she clicked on *Mum*, then on the mobile number that appeared below. Only two rings before the call was answered.

'Hello? Louisa? Hello?'

She threw the phone back into the car, shut the door and walked back up the road through the puddles to pick up the bicycle. Once she was home and dry, she'd be home and dry, literally. The thought made her chuckle. It was the perfect ending, almost an anticlimax. She hadn't been sure the plan would even work, but everything had fallen into place like clockwork. Elisa would have been proud of her. Perhaps she was still working her magic from afar.

The sound of a car engine interrupted her thoughts. She grabbed the handlebars and quickly looked for a gap in the hedge where she could take cover.

CHAPTER 47

Ronnie saw the bike first as she rounded the bend, then through the rain-spattered windscreen she locked eyes with Amie, who looked back at the wreckage of the Fiat, then at Ronnie, as if formulating a reason for being there, for witnessing the crash, the way your brain fits an alarm clock into your dream to make sense of it all. She threw the bike down, dropping to her knees in the wet, leaning over the frame like the last piece of floating wreckage of a ship.

'Stay there! Don't move.' Ronnie's voice was more commanding than usual.

Amie stayed motionless except for the occasional shudder, which could have been tears, or laughter.

Ronnie radioed the station to confirm her location and call an ambulance, then she climbed out of her car, eyes still fixed on Amie, and made her way to the crumpled Punto. Pulling open the driver's door, she leant in to feel for a pulse on Louisa's neck and listened for breathing sounds. She checked her watch, then stepped away and let the door swing shut. They wouldn't be long now. In the distance, she heard the siren, then, on her radio, confirmation that they were two minutes away.

'It's over, Amie.' She crouched down next to her by the bike, reaching out a hand. 'Time to come with me.'

Amie was frozen to the spot, hands gripping the saddle, knuckles red with cold.

'You can get up now, Amie.'

If she said anything in reply, the rain and now the sirens would have drowned it out. Ronnie looked up to see two police cars swing into view, followed by an ambulance.

Overton was first on the scene, pulling Amie to her feet, handcuffing her while the paramedics got to work on Louisa.

Munro pulled up behind them. He leapt out and came over to where Ronnie was standing by the open door of Overton's car.

'You OK, sarge?'

'Yes, just about.' Ronnie looked down and saw her hands shaking.

'Craig's still at the station. He gave us the gist. We were en route in no time.'

'Thanks for getting down here so quickly.'

Baz assessed the scene. 'Don't tell me: she came out on the bike and caused the car to swerve and crash.'

'Looks that way. Trouble is, she really shouldn't have bothered.' Ronnie took out her phone and checked the message was still there. She hadn't dreamt it. Amie's confession was intact. 'We've got what we need.'

The paramedics had revived Louisa and were putting her in the ambulance. One of them gave Ronnie the thumbs-up. 'Looks like she'll be fine. We'll keep you posted.'

Amie let herself be led to the car, staring at Ronnie as she was bundled into the back seat. 'Where are you taking me?'

Ronnie leant in, patted her on the arm.

'Oh, I wouldn't worry about that. It's a bit of a holiday camp, I've heard.'

CHAPTER 48

The flat was buzzing with chatter when she got home. Eddie was peering into a steaming oven, which made Ronnie do a double-take, and Tilly was sliding a bowl of something chocolatey into the fridge. Serena was doing her utmost to wipe away the mess they left in their wake. Alice Delmar, seated at the head of the table, clapped her hands together as Ronnie opened the door.

'Veronica! Serena told us the news. No details of course, don't worry,' she added, catching Ronnie's sudden anxious expression. 'But I thought it called for a celebration,'

She stood and held out her arms. Ronnie let herself be embraced and looked around at the hive of activity which brought tears to her eyes. Tilly brought champagne flutes to the table where Serena stood, bottle poised. The first one overflowed, and Tilly raised it to her lips, then put it back down.

'Oh, Mum, don't cry. This is supposed to make you happy!' She wrapped Ronnie in the tightest hug, before pulling away. 'Eddie and I have cooked dinner, almost without an argument. *And* we have a surprise guest for you.'

'Well, not that much of a surprise, to be fair,' said Eddie, just as the doorbell rang.

Ronnie pressed the entry phone buzzer and Susie came in. She was rosy-cheeked and beaming, leather trousers glistening with raindrops. 'Blimey, it's wet out there.' She shook out her umbrella and balanced it upside down by the door.

Ronnie's face lit up. 'Susie!'

'Oh, my God, Ronnie, it sounds like a nightmare. Are you OK?'

'I'm OK, but Louisa's likely to be in hospital for a while. They say she should make a full recovery.'

'That's a relief.' Susie accepted a glass of sparkling wine, glancing around to make sure they weren't being overheard. 'And Amie?'

'Under arrest. She'll be charged eventually. The initial search of the house turned up an almost full cup of black coffee laced with zopiclone.'

'Zopiclone as in the sleeping pill? In Louisa's coffee?'

'Looks like that was the first plan, to make her fall asleep at the wheel. There was a medicine cabinet full of the stuff. Intended for more innocent purposes, I imagine.'

'But Louisa didn't drink it, so plan B?'

Ronnie nodded. 'Got it in one. You can take a woman out of the police force . . .'

'No regrets there on my part.' Susie raised her glass and Ronnie clinked hers against it.

'Thank you, my friend, for taking a risk for me.'

Susie grimaced. 'Ah, yes, I'm still having sleepless nights about that, to be honest.'

'If you hadn't sent me those pictures, I wouldn't have found the house, and we wouldn't be where we are. Celia would have died for sure.'

'The thing is, Ronnie, I don't think anyone else would necessarily have thought that a mass of random doodles was a map to a crime scene. You're the one who saw the wood for the trees.'

At that moment, Susie was summoned by Alice, and Ronnie took Serena aside. Through the window, they could see the man with the slow Labrador leaving the recreation ground through the side gate. For some, it was just the end of another day.

'You know what?' Ronnie said quietly. 'I think I need to thank you.'

'For what exactly? Last time I checked, I was the depressed Valium addict and you were the high-flying super-detective.'

'You know what I mean.'

'I'm not sure I do,' said Serena, 'but go on.'

'It all came down to keeping an open mind.'

'You mean, not assuming that it's men who are always in the wrong?' Serena was wearing her *I told you so* expression.

'More than that. I mean, we don't necessarily always have the time or the resources to find out the truth, but it doesn't mean we can't keep thinking about it, making sure we're on the right track. You're open to things not being what they seem. I feel I've learnt a big lesson. I only saw what I expected to see. The truth was almost too hard to believe.'

'So our dad was right, then?'

'He may well have been, but you're the one who questions my assumptions on a day-to-day basis. I know I don't always like it, but please don't stop doing it.'

Ronnie gave her sister a squeeze and then found herself attached to her poncho tassels. Susie came to the rescue.

'I thought you'd be doing an all-nighter, Ronnie, with all that's been going on,' she said, freeing the sisters from their woolly shackles.

'Baz and Lydia have taken over, told me to go home. They're probably cursing me for opening up a can of worms.'

'You think they'd rather you'd let the brother do the time? Surely not.'

'No, and they're probably very grateful it wasn't me secretly recording conversations with witnesses. That might have given Lydia a heart attack.'

'You didn't send Louisa to do it, did you? Ronnie?' Serena gave her a sideways look, which made her hold her breath for a second. It had been on her mind. She had hoped not on anyone else's. She didn't want to think about what might have happened if things had gone differently.

'Of course not.' She had barely uttered the words when Eddie rescued her.

'Mum, look at this. What do you think?' He thrust the evening's culinary creation between them. 'Ta-*daaaa*! Not bad for a beginner, eh?'

Susie whooped and inhaled theatrically. 'I'm most impressed! Your son has hidden talents, Ron. Invite me over more often.'

Ronnie squeezed Eddie's shoulder. 'Wow! Looks ... what do you call it? Peng?'

'Mum!' Eddie gave her a look of shock and disbelief. 'I told you, you can't say that.'

'That's absolutely fine with me. Come on, I'm starving.'

ACKNOWLEDGEMENTS

Starting at the beginning, where the idea was first conceived, I would like to thank Charlie Haynes: fairy godmother, baker of cakes and surrogate mother to us all on the Urban Writers' residential retreats, and all the writers I met on those retreats who supported me along the way. Thank you Claire Dyer for reading the very first draft and cheering me on. Huge thanks and appreciation must go to my agent Sophie Hicks, who introduced me to the wonderful Malcolm Edwards at Welbeck Publishing Group, where brilliant editor Rosa Schierenberg guided me through the latter stages up to publication. Thanks to Cara Hunter, a true expert in this field, for reading and applauding, and to Matt Rees for the same.

Outside of the publishing world, thanks go to Nick, Adam and Gillian for their tips on police procedure, my brother Richard for his genius writerly input, and to my partner, Will, for all his patience and for re-reading the whole thing every time I changed anything. Thanks to every single one of my friends and family for their support, and especially to my three fabulous children, just for bringing me joy and inspiration everyday.